FALSE MONEY

An Abbot Agency Mystery

Veronica Heley

This first world edition published 2010
in Great Britain and in 2011 in the USA by
SEVERN HOUSE PUBLISHERS LTD of
9–15 High Street, Sutton, Surrey, England, SM1 1DF.
Trade paperback edition first published
in Great Britain and the USA 2011 by
SEVERN HOUSE PUBLISHERS LTD.

British Library Cataloguing in Publication Data

Heley, Veronica.
  False money. – (An Abbot Agency mystery)
  1. Abbot, Bea (Fictitious character)–Fiction. 2. Widows–
  England–London–Fiction. 3. Women private
  investigators–England–London–Fiction. 4. Detective
  and mystery stories.
  I. Title II. Series
  823.9'14-dc22

ISBN-13: 978-0-7278-6985-2   (cased)
ISBN-13: 978-1-84751-305-2   (trade paper)

Except where actual historical events and characters are being
described for the storyline of this novel, all situations in this
publication are fictitious and any resemblance to living persons
is purely coincidental.

All Severn House titles are printed on acid-free paper.

Severn House Publishers support The Forest Stewardship Council [FSC], the
leading international forest certification organisation. All our titles that are
printed on Greenpeace-approved FSC-certified paper carry the FSC logo.

Typeset by Palimpsest Book Production Ltd.,
Falkirk, Stirlingshire, Scotland.
Printed and bound in Great Britain by
MPG Books Ltd., Bodmin, Cornwall.

ONE

Widowed Bea Abbot ran a domestic agency whose watchword was 'discretion'. Every now and then people brought her problems they couldn't or wouldn't take to the police. Occasionally this meant she dealt with murder.

Friday afternoon

Bea walked into her office and found a bouquet of flowers on her desk.

Was it a gift or a bribe?

The flowers wouldn't be from her live-in assistant. Maggie had green fingers and looked after their secluded back garden with energy and style; both of which she had in spades. In the winter Maggie filled the huge planters in the paved court-yard garden with a selection of bulbs, winter pansies and cyclamens. Through the French windows Bea could see a host of miniature daffodils just beginning to show colour.

By this time in March the trees should be budding and the birds should be shouting that spring was on its way. Unfortunately the country had plunged into a cold spell, and the outside temperature indicated midwinter rather than spring.

Maggie did not care for cut flowers, so it wasn't she who had put the bouquet on Bea's desk.

Bea rarely bothered to buy cut flowers either, being content with one or two strategically placed pot plants, which didn't object to central heating.

So, who had brought her flowers?

A name leaped into her mind.

Ah. Of course. She picked the bouquet up to make sure, but there was no card with it. It wasn't an expensive bouquet. It was made up of carnations, chrysanthemums and one rose bundled into a cellophane wrapper, with a sachet of plant food taped to it. It looked as if it had been plucked from a bucket on the way out of a convenience store. Bea could see where an attempt had been made to rip off the price tag.

She weighed the bouquet in her hand, thinking about the one person who was always asking her to do things for him that she didn't want to do . . . and dropped it into the waste-paper basket.

She liked flowers. What she didn't like was bribery and corruption, and she could smell that a mile off.

He'd be lurking in the vicinity, of course.

She threw her suit jacket over the back of her chair and stretched to ease her back. She was tired. She'd been out of the office all morning, even skipping lunch to do some shopping for her daughter-in-law, and this was the first moment she'd had to sit at her desk and boot up her computer. In a minute, her elderly and pensionable but refusing-to-retire personal assistant would knock on the door – which was entirely unnecessary, but the elderly Miss Brook liked to observe the formalities – and enter with the few items from the day's post that she felt her employer should see.

Meanwhile, Bea accessed her emails.

'Boo!'

Of course. He'd concealed himself behind the long curtains framing the French windows.

Bea set her teeth. 'No,' she said. 'Whatever it is you want, the answer is, "No."'

'You don't really mean it.' Chris slid into the chair before her desk. Nineteen years old, he had a narrow head under a mop of chestnut hair, was of medium height and well made. He had startlingly blue eyes and charm enough to get his own way ninety-nine times out of a hundred. He was out-of-this-world clever in some respects but, in Bea's opinion at least, made up for it by being totally lacking in common sense.

As Bea had expected, Miss Brook now tapped on the door and brought in the post. Chris jumped up and reached out to take the stack of letters from her, but fumbled the job and let the papers fall to the floor.

Bea rolled her eyes at Miss Brook, who pinched in her lips and said, 'I don't know how he got in, but Maggie's back from her last job and she's upstairs. No doubt he got round her. How is your grandson today?'

Bea's son Max and his wife had produced a baby boy some months ago and Bea had been called over to help out that morning. 'A trifle fractious, I'm afraid. Don't you bother to pick up those letters, Miss Brook. Chris knocked them down, and Chris can pick them up.'

Which, indeed, he was scrabbling around on the floor to do.

'I should think so, too,' said Miss Brook, who was one of the few people impervious to Chris's charm. 'There's nothing in that pile that can't wait, so if you don't mind, I'll be off now.'

Bea looked at her watch. Of course, Miss Brook always liked to leave early on Friday afternoons.

The elderly lady continued, 'I'll be in tomorrow morning with the new girl, who's shaping up well.'

The 'new girl' would never see sixty again. Bea – in her sixties herself – liked to give older women jobs, believing them to be more stable and better trained in office work than girls fresh out of school. They took less time off work, too.

Bea nodded, and Miss Brook closed the door soundlessly behind her.

Chris dumped a messy pile of papers on her desk and opened his mouth to speak.

'No,' said Bea. 'Whatever it is that you want, the answer is, "No." As I've said many times before, you may not move into the spare room. You may not bring your synthesizer in here to practice, and I am not taking you out in my car to give you a driving lesson.'

'That's not fair. I've passed my test.'

'At the eighteenth attempt?'

'Oh, come on! It was only my fourth try.'

'Is your driving instructor now on tranquillizers?' She held up her hand to stop him. 'Let me continue. I'm delighted – though surprised – to hear that you've managed finally to pass your driving test, but no, you may not borrow my car under any circumstances. What's more, whether you are gainfully employed at the moment or not, you may not waste Maggie's time by chatting to her when she ought to be working. Anyway, aren't you supposed to be out and about, making another art-house film?'

He opened his mouth to reply, but she got there first. 'No! Don't tell me. The film's held up for some reason, your father's fed up with you hanging around the house, and you can't go back to university till next terms starts—'

'I'm not going back to university.'

'But you will, Chris. You will. In due course you'll see the sense of it. Whatever you decide to do in life, a university degree helps. What's more, it teaches you discipline, which is something you lack. At this very moment you should be catching up on all the work you've missed by dropping out. I suspect you haven't opened a book in weeks. So, the answer is, "NO!"'

He grinned. 'You haven't heard what it is I want yet.'

'I don't need to,' she said, returning to her computer and deleting some spam. Why did you always have to check your spam nowadays? To make sure nothing had dived into the wrong slot?

He put on his puppy-dog face. 'I only wanted you to—'

'Cloth ears, have you?'

'My father suggested that—'

She lifted her eyes from her screen. His father was some sort of high-up civil servant, a grey man with influence. She liked CJ, and she rather thought he liked her – not in *that* way, of course. But she trusted him, which is more than she did his likeable but harum-scarum son. 'If your father wants me to do something for him, he can ask me himself.'

'He's busy. Tied up with a court case, being an expert for the prosecution, hanging around for days, you know. Never at home.'

'You've always got an excuse.'

'Honest. He did say I should ask you to help.'

Despite herself, she hesitated. 'To do what?'

'To find my library books.'

'WHAT! Get out of here before I lose my temper completely!' She jabbed at her mouse and lost the email she'd been trying to read.

Chris fished his bouquet out of the bin, went down on one knee and presented the flowers to her elbow. 'Please, pretty please?'

Bea closed her eyes and counted five. She knew she ought to count to ten, or even twenty, but failed to get further than seven. 'Get out of here before I call the police.'

'You wouldn't do that.' His smile was blindingly white, full of confidence.

'The trouble with you, Chris, is that no one said, "No," to you when you were a child. You think you only have to express a wish, and the world will rush to grant it. Now, I have work to do, so if you don't mind—'

'Oliver said that if anyone could find them, you could.'

'What?' Oliver was her much-loved adopted son, who'd propelled the agency into the big time with his computer skills and know-how, and was now in his second term at university. Oliver and Chris had been at school together and, despite being opposites, had remained good friends. If Chris was a little boy made of charm and flashes of genius, Oliver was a steady, hard-working, trustworthy, intelligent young man who could make computers do a fandango.

Bea frowned. 'Oliver suggested you approach me about your lost library books? I don't believe it.'

He hunkered down, folding his legs into a lotus position. 'Oliver knows her, you see. The girl who took my library books home with her. He says she wouldn't go missing without returning the books. I mean, it's the sort of thing I might do . . . Have done, come to think of it. But she's like Oliver. Conscientious. She'd never go off like that without at least telling me where I could find the books.'

'What?'

He leaned forward, confident at last that she would listen. 'Some people look drab and ordinary when you film them, and some light up. The planes of their cheekbones reflect the light, they can act with their eyes, and when they turn their heads they still look elegant. Tomi is—'

'Who?'

'Tomi. Short for Tomilola, which is short for something else. Her parents are Nigerian, doctors, came here when she was two. Her name means "God is enough for me". Cute, isn't it?'

Bea struggled with the impulse to box his ears. 'I am not even going to ask who Tomi is. For the umpteenth time, get out of here!'

'No, no. You're not listening. Tomi is not a professional actress, of course – she works for some magazine or other during the week – but she's the main character in the short film I made last year, which won that special award, remember? The one which my father said if I won the award I could leave uni and concentrate on film-making?'

'He didn't think you'd win.'

'I know that!' He grinned. 'Of course, it was a fluke, and entirely unexpected and all that, but the fact is that the rest of the entrants were all terribly dreary and worthy and making left-wing political propaganda, whereas mine was thoughtful and, well, fun. People like fun. Especially when the going gets rough. And it's gone down a storm on YouTube.' He sobered up, allowing Bea a glimpse of the real Chris, layers below his usual light-heartedness.

Bea's hands dropped from her keyboard. 'So Tomi is someone you've known for quite a while, and you believe she's not the sort to let you down. So what happened?'

His eyes dropped from her, and he picked at a speck of dirt on his jeans. 'She's disappeared. We were having a half of bitter together in the pub up the road one Saturday morning, and I was telling her what I'd like to work on next, and we got arguing about shadows and how they could be distorted. That's what my next film is going to be about: people having the wrong shadows, or no shadow at all, and what that might mean. It's a folklore tale set in modern London. Tomi was enthusiastic about it, hinted she might know someone who could put some money into it, which I'm telling you would be just great. Well, that doesn't matter now.

'The thing is, we went on to the library to take out some books on artists who use shadows in different ways, and there were quite a few, so she helped me carry the books out. I got talking to a friend outside, and she said she needed to catch up with someone on the other side of the road and went over to talk to them, and that was the last I saw of her. I rushed back home because I was going on to a party that night. She wasn't there, but I didn't think anything of it because we know all sorts of people and she might well have been going to someone else's do. Only, next morning I discovered she'd walked off with a couple of my books.

'It was a good party and I didn't surface again till Sunday evening, when I rang her, but she didn't pick up. So on Monday I went round to her place, and her flatmate said she must have slept over with a friend, though she didn't usually. I expected to hear from her. Nothing. On Wednesday I rang her at work, but she'd sent them a text to say she'd taken some holiday time due to her and had gone to France for a week.'

'Just like that?'

'Just like that. So this Monday I tried everyone all over again. They've heard nothing from her at work and are most annoyed and surprised that she's let them down. I tried her flatmate again. She said she'd had a text, too, saying Tomi had decided to go off with a friend who'd offered her a lift in his car touring France, and that she didn't know when she'd be back. Tomi hadn't left any money to pay for her room, and the flatmate was not pleased. She said she'd tried Tomi's mobile phone and left a message, just as I'd done. Tomi hasn't rung her back, either. The flatmate can't afford to keep the flat on by herself so she's cleared Tomi's things out of her room and is going to relet.'

'Flatmate's name?' said Bea, intrigued despite herself.

'I have it here for you, and the address. Flatmate doesn't approve of me. Thinks I'm feckless; can't imagine why.'

Bea took the piece of paper. A foreign name, an address not far off. 'What about the man she went over to talk to, last time you saw her?'

'The thing is, I didn't really see who it was. Someone I know came up to me and we were chatting, you know how it is. Tomi said she was off, and I said, "See you!" or words to that effect, and that was it. It might have been anyone. A friend from her church, perhaps? They disapprove of me, needless to say. Tomi's a committed churchgoer, by the way, and terribly moral, but she doesn't talk about it to me because I get the giggles when religion's mentioned.'

He held up his hand to warn off Bea's protest. 'Of course, that's very naughty of me, and I'll probably straighten out in middle age, but that's the way it is at the moment.'

Bea blinked and tried to recap on what he'd said. 'Going back to the flatmate. Miss . . .' She accessed the piece of paper with the name on. 'Drobny? Is that right? You went round and asked her if you might look for your books, and—'

'She let me in, under supervision. She breathed on me heavily all the time I was going through Tomi's things, which were piled up in the hallway. The books weren't there. At least, I couldn't spot them. Tomi might have left them somewhere else in the flat, but the flatmate didn't like me being there and wouldn't let me look.'

Bea got up and went over to the windows. The late afternoons were getting lighter, but the sun didn't seem to have much warmth in it yet. Twilight was beginning to shroud the paved garden, but the sycamore tree at the end – still leafless – made pretty patterns against the sky. Through the tree she could see the floodlit spire of St Mary's Church.

Tomi was a Christian. Tomi was a hard-working, responsible girl. It wasn't like her to go off on a bender.

Bea checked that the French windows to the garden were locked, tested the security grille, let down the blind, and drew the floor-length curtains. From above her office came the faint sounds of pans clashing together in the kitchen. Maggie loved to cook when she got home. Bea had missed lunch and was looking forward to supper.

Chris hadn't moved. He was waiting for her to pull the rabbit out of the hat for him.

'She has a boyfriend?'

'Someone called Harry. A Hooray Henry.' Chris pulled a face. 'He rubs me up the wrong way. I did ask him. He got a text message from her too, saying she was off to France for a break. He's . . . Well, he was upset, but says now that he wasn't serious about her. Got another girl in tow.'

'Tomi's beautiful?'

He screwed up his face. 'Not strictly. Too long a nose. But stunning. I haven't a single shot of her which makes her look dull. There aren't many girls with faces like that, you know.' He narrowed his eyes. 'You'd probably be the same. Some time, when I need an older woman, I'll see what the camera can do for you.'

'Thank you, but no thank you.' She'd been there, done that, and knew such promises were rarely kept. Bea's first husband, Piers, was a well-known portrait painter. He'd talked about painting her several times, but had never got round to it. 'Back to Tomi. What do you think has happened to her?'

'I tried the police, if that's what you mean. They say she's old enough to look after herself and if she wants to disappear, she can. I've rung round the hospitals – that was my father's suggestion, by the way. Nothing. Her job's in jeopardy, of course. They're furious that she hasn't been in contact.'

'She texted her workplace, her flatmate and her boyfriend, but not you. What happened when you tried her phone?'

'She didn't pick up. A voice said to leave a message. So I did. Three, maybe four times. She hasn't got back to me. I'm worried about her.' He rose to his feet without needing to hold on to the desk or chair.

Oh, to be so young and supple.

'She's not my girlfriend, you understand. I only go for blondes. She's just . . . an itch at the back of my mind.'

'And you want her back, to start making your next film.'

'I can get a dozen girls to stand before the camera and go through the motions. None of them have her presence, or patience. Or real talent. But if she doesn't turn up soon, I might have to start looking around for a substitute.' He gave her a stark look, allowing her to see his concern. 'Dad said you'd find her if anyone could. I asked Oliver. He knows her, and he's worried, too. He'll be back when term ends, won't he? He could help you.'

'Did you look to see if her passport was with her things?'

He flushed. 'I didn't think of it. What a fool I am!'

'I suppose I could see if it's still at her flat. I can't promise anything, but if her passport's gone, then I think you may have to resign yourself to looking for another film star.'

Claire was a natural blonde with feathery curls around a heart-shaped face. She had big, wide-open cornflower blue eyes. Sometimes she wore fake eyelashes with glitter on them, though not when she was working, of course.

She loved her job and was much in demand as a short-term day nanny for families which had struck a difficult patch, such as an unexpected illness. She never stayed at any place after the youngest child was ready to attend nursery.

Despite her small stature she was a tough little person, who earned brownie points by being helpful even outside her regular working day; especially in clearing out medicine cabinets.

Just lately she'd stumbled across a situation so wonderfully promising that she could hardly concentrate on the job in hand.

Steady as she goes! she told herself. No need to hurry.

*You've got nearly ten days to get rid of the rest of them; well,
maybe not all of them. It doesn't pay to be greedy.*

*Her clients thought she was a sweetie-pie and SO good
with baby.*

Her boyfriend said she was the cream in his cocoa.

*She didn't think of what she was doing as murder. It was
looking out for number one, that's all.*

TWO

Bea saw Chris out of the door, checked that everything in the office area was safely locked up for the night, and sat down to email Oliver.

Oliver dear,

We're so much looking forward to having you back with us. Let me know asap when I may collect you at the end of term. Maggie will want to come, unless you've got so much stuff to bring back that there won't be room for her in the car.

I've had your friend Chris round, bothering the life out of me about a girl's disappearance. Her name's Tomi. He says you know her, too? What do you think? Ought he to be worried? He says he asked you about it. Did he? He said at first that he wants me to find her because she's got his library books, but I think he's really worried about not having her for his next film.

He also says he's passed his driving test. Has he, really? I'm amazed.

Let me know about picking you up.

She signed off as 'Bea' and hit the 'send' button.

Oliver was not her son by birth. Of mixed race, he'd been adopted as a baby by a professional couple, but had never fitted in and had been tossed out into the world when an undersized but brainy eighteen year old. Dragged home to Bea by Maggie, and tutored by a man who ate computers for starters, Oliver had blossomed into a well-balanced young man who'd been the mainstay of Bea's agency till – a year late – he went up to Oxford. He'd recently taken Bea's name, discarding the one he'd been given when adopted. Perhaps one day he'd seek out his birth parents; perhaps not. The main thing was that he understood Bea and Maggie loved him and that he could always rely on them, even though Bea was old enough to be his grandmother.

She'd asked him to use her first name, and perhaps some time soon he'd manage it. She shut down her computer and knocked something on to the floor. A DVD, which certainly had not been there before. Had Chris left it there? Ah. Yes. The label said it contained his short film, the one which had so unexpectedly won a prize for an independent production. She dropped it into the waste-paper basket. Then retrieved it with a sigh and put it in the pocket of her trousers.

Should she view it now? No, it was getting late; she was tired and hungry. She rescued the flowers Chris had given her and climbed the stairs to the ground floor of her Georgian house. She checked that the grilles were locked over the windows at the back and front of the big through living room, straightened the portrait of her dear dead husband, which the cleaner always left askew, and drew the floor-length curtains. She found a vase and popped Chris's bouquet into it, placing it on the coffee table in front of the fireplace.

'It's up!' said Maggie, appearing in the doorway, mobile phone to ear. Meaning supper was up, presumably. Maggie disappeared into the kitchen; tall and gangly, her hair black and spiky this week, her outfit consisted of orange and green layers over jeans and was finished off with enormous moon boots. Maggie was scared of men and dressed to frighten them away.

Maggie was not brilliant at office work, but had a talent for project-managing alterations to houses and flats. She got on with everyone from the highest paid architect to the lowliest of plumbers, provided they didn't ask her out for a date.

In the kitchen Bea spotted their long-haired black cat sitting fatly on the work surface, waiting for titbits. Maggie half-heartedly swiped at him. He drew back to avoid her hand, then laid himself down again in exactly the same place. Winston. Another orphan who'd homed in on Bea.

Supper was minted lamb chops, mashed potatoes and fresh green beans, followed by a dish of stewed plums with cream. Bea did it justice, while trying not to be irritated by Maggie chatting away on her mobile throughout. Maggie had a number of friends in their mid to late twenties: all in good jobs, all playing the field, and all far from ready to commit themselves to any permanent relationship.

To Bea's mind, none of them had grown up yet. The one currently on the phone seemed to have got drunk and promised to go out with her brother's best friend, or maybe it was his uncle. Bea couldn't work it out.

Maggie came off the phone only to have it ring again, and this time it was work; the tiler she'd been using. Apparently, he was making excuses about work not being done to standard, or time, or something. Maggie slipped from girlfriend mode into that of employer. With a sharp edge. Who did he think he was kidding? Didn't she know him of old? Had he gone to the races instead of working? She forked food into her mouth while giving the man a hard time, only relenting when he promised to work overtime next day. Without charging her for the extra hours.

Finally Maggie killed the call, and before the phone could ring again, Bea said, 'I know you're going out to meet your friend but, before you disappear, did you know this girl Tomi that Chris is in a flap about?'

'Of course. She's the star of his film. Stunning, in an unusual way. I mean, not one of your anorexic blondes, which is what he usually goes for. Gives one hope he might eventually grow up, if you see what I mean.'

'She's disappeared with his library books. He says. What do you think?'

A shrug. 'It's not like her, but if she's found someone more gorgeous than the self-centred and oh-so-boring Harry, then maybe . . . ? Can one blame her?'

'You've met him?'

'No, but she told me all about him.'

'She's also left her flatmate without paying her rent.'

Maggie sucked her forefinger. 'Mm. Not like her. You don't really mind my going out tonight, do you? I'll get up early tomorrow to finish the estimate for the flat in Earls Court. I've got all the figures in, bar for the new kitchen cupboard doors, but I doubt if we'll get the job because the client thinks in pennies instead of pounds.'

'I trust you for that. Would you have trusted Tomi to pay her share of the rent on time?'

'Yes, of course.' She screwed up her face. 'At least, I

suppose there might have been some circumstance that . . .
Only, I can't think what it might be. Her people went back to
Nigeria, I think. Both doctors, both earning good salaries there.
I seem to remember they wanted her to go back with them,
marry a Nigerian, and so on. But she'd have said if that was
what she was going to do, wouldn't she? Worked out her
notice and all that. At least have told Harry, or left notes for
people. No, you're right. It doesn't make sense.' She looked
at her watch; a man's watch with lots of dials on it. Maggie
was running late. She gave a little scream. 'I must go.'

Once left alone, Bea fished out the telephone number Chris
had left her for Tomi's flatmate and dialled it. 'Miss Drobny?
Have I got the name right? Your number was given me by a
friend of Tomi's, who—'

The phone quacked indignantly. 'I don't want to hear
about—'

'I understand she's gone missing under mysterious circumstances—'

'Hmph. Is a new boyfriend something to be mysterious
about?' Not pleased, and not British, though the accent was
slight.

'Not like her, though.'

A pause. 'Well, I thought that, too.' A middle-European
voice. Polish accent? No. Further south. Bosnian, possibly?
Not all that young. Decisive.

'The thing is,' Bea said, trying to be tactful, 'that people
are worried about her and have brought their troubles to me.
Someone always gets dumped on to sort things out, don't
they? Her friends can't understand her not letting you know
she was going away and not paying her rent.'

'That is true. It is not right.'

'Not at all what you'd have expected from her. I agree. Her
friends have asked me to call you, see if I could help in any
way—'

'Are you going to pay her rent? It is due a week ago. I
cannot afford to keep the room vacant, waiting for her to
return.'

'You've been to an agency to find someone else?'

'I put an advert in the paper.'

'Suppose I ask her friends if they would agree to pay her
rent for a couple of weeks. Would that help? I mean, if she

really has gone off for a holiday, she can repay them when she gets back.'

'Very well. You give me a cheque for a month's rent and I keep her room. I am only this minute back from work and must cook supper. I will expect you in one hour, hour and a half. I am in the basement flat. Understood?'

'I'll be there.' It would be worth paying the rent to have a look at Tomi's belongings. If her passport had gone and the library books were still there – Chris probably hadn't looked for them properly – then she'd gone off with a boyfriend. If her passport was still there, and there was no sign of the library books, then . . . Bea decided to think about that later.

She was putting the dirty dishes from supper into the dishwasher when the phone rang. 'Mother, is that you?'

Who else would it be? It was Max, her self-important Member of Parliament son, who was married to that vacuous blonde, Nicole. The marriage had had its ups and downs, but currently was in an 'up' period. Bea hoped.

Unfortunately, Max's recently produced son and heir was depriving them of sleep and patience. When Bea had suggested that a change of formula might be a good idea, she'd been informed with angry tears that she was completely out of date, had no idea of how to bring up a baby in this day and age, and they would thank her to keep her mouth shut on the subject. Bea was well aware that each generation thought they, and only they, knew the right way to bring up babies, but she found it disturbing that little Pippin did not appear to be putting on weight.

Nicole and Max were completely under the spell of the latest Bringing up Baby guru, who was making a fortune by telling new mothers what to do. In consequence Nicole now lived by the clock, feeding baby when he wanted to sleep, anxiously putting him down to sleep when he wanted to play. And so on. Some babies thrived under this routine. Little Pippin didn't like it. He didn't like the formula that replaced mother's milk, either. Result: one hungry, dissatisfied baby.

Nicole refused to allow Bea even to touch baby because, she said, he needed to bond with his mother, but she found her mother-in-law useful to do all the jobs around the place that baby's routine prevented her from doing herself. Bea had been over there only that morning to do the shopping and clean the flat while Nicole tried to rest between the short times she allowed herself in the baby's routine.

To Bea's suggestion that Nicole should employ a nanny for a couple of months, the girl replied with yet more tears that no, she would never, repeat never, abandon her child to the attentions of a nanny. Besides, Nicole said, it would give entirely the wrong impression to Max's constituents. A privileged background, said Nicole, cut no ice back in the Midlands.

Now Max was joining in the battle. On Nicole's side, of course. 'Mother, I really thought you had more sense than to upset Nicole. What do you know about bringing up babies nowadays? I suppose you thought you were trying to help, but all you've managed to do is make Nicole feel really unwell. She was in tears when I got home, and that set Pippin off and—'

Bea knew what she had to say, and said it. 'I'm so sorry, Max. I do know that what works for one baby doesn't work for another.'

'Right. Well, I suppose you thought you were helping. The thing is, we're missing his toy mouse. Nicole says he had it this morning before you came. Did you tidy it away somewhere?'

Bea hadn't thought Pippin was particularly attached to the mouse, which was blue and red and hardly a thing of beauty and a joy for ever.

'Er, yes. I mean, no. I found it in the pocket of my coat when I got back home. I fell over it this morning when I was carting the shopping back up to the flat and must have popped it into my pocket by mistake.' All that lifting had made her back ache, but Max wouldn't be interested to hear about that. 'I'll drop it back to you tomorrow.'

Bea had advised Nicole to attach all his toys to his recliner so they couldn't get lost, but Nicole believed in total freedom for her son to throw things around . . . which kept her tied to the baby's side. Not a good idea, in Bea's opinion.

'He won't go to sleep without it,' said Max, which might possibly be true. Bea could hear him wailing at that very moment. 'If you bring it over straight away—'

'I've got an appointment. Can't you fetch it?'

'Certainly not. I'm leaving for my constituency within the hour. You know I have a Saturday morning surgery there, and I won't be back till Sunday evening at the earliest. As for Nicole, she's exhausted, thanks to you upsetting her.'

'Has she tried changing his formula?' asked Bea, greatly daring.

'What? No, of course not. Here . . . Nicole, you'd better take the phone because I've got to go, yes, yes, I must. Yes, I know all that, but you must realize . . . Anyway, mother's found Mouse.'

Nicole's voice came on, tearful, complaining. 'I do realize it's awkward, and of course he's got other toys, but he just won't settle and I'm sure he would if he had Mouse. If you've got it, couldn't you just bring it over? I've just got to get some sleep before his ten o'clock feed or I don't know what I shall do!'

Bea loved her little grandson. One look into his blue eyes, and she'd been his slave. She longed for the day when Nicole would allow her to play with the child, or feed him; or even bathe him. So far Bea was only allowed to help by doing the shopping and cooking and generally keeping the flat tidy, which she did when she had cover for herself at work. But go over there now? Hadn't she done enough for them for one day?

Nicole sobbed into the phone. 'It's not that I don't love the little rascal, but I'm not as strong as I might be.' For that, read 'not as young as I might be'.

'I'll be with you in about an hour, maybe hour and a half,' said Bea, slamming the dishwasher shut. Upon which the doorbell rang. 'Must go, Nicole. Someone at the door.'

Chris had presented her with a bouquet, but Chris's father clearly thought that a bottle of bubbly was a better bet. Had he come to badger her into looking for Tomi, too? Bea didn't appreciate all this pressure. 'Look, I'm going out in a minute. Driving. So I can't drink.'

He walked straight past her into the sitting room. 'This won't take long. And I'm not driving, so I can drink.'

She fetched a glass for him from the kitchen while he popped the cork. CJ – as he was commonly known – was about her own age, but looked as if the faintest of breezes might blow him away. He was a grey man; grey hair, grey

suit – rather a good suit actually. An unremarkable presence
if he wished to blend into the background, but an incisive
profile if he wanted to take charge of the conversation.

'I thought you were too busy even to exchange the time of
day with your son,' said Bea, feeling sour.

He grunted – which might mean anything – and poured
champagne.

She said, 'I haven't even had a chance to look at Chris's
DVD yet.'

He held out his hand for her copy, slotted it in under the
television set, and pressed buttons. Picking up his glass, he
retired to the settee, still holding on to the remote control.

Bea rolled her eyes. Men who walked in and comman-
deered her remote control were, to her mind, overbearing
brutes. That included her son Max, who believed that, even
today, a woman couldn't be trusted to change a television
channel.

The credits rolled. A girl in a white sweater and jeans was
helping an elderly woman to dress, in what looked like a
council flat. Then she was playing a violin, busking in the
open air and collecting money in the violin case laid on the
ground before her. She wasn't a beauty, but had an interesting
face. Dark-skinned for a European, fair for a Nigerian. Tomi,
presumably.

Each scene was short, lasting only long enough to register
what the girl was doing and then passing on. One minute
Tomi was teaching a small child to play the violin, then –
dressed in a workmanlike overall and cap – she was dishing
out school dinners. The clock registered time was passing.
The girl, now back in sweater and jeans, was rehearsing in a
flat with some other musicians, then playing at a party, wearing
a long red dress. Back to the council flat. The violin was in
its case in one corner, while Tomi – back in white sweater
and jeans – fed a paraplegic woman in a wheelchair. Finally,
Tomi was in evening dress with her violin case under arm,
returning home after an evening out, fitting her key into the
door. Was it all a dream? Which was reality?

The DVD ended. 'Interesting,' said Bea, 'if confusing.'

CJ switched off the power. 'I've never met the girl. Have
you?'

'No.'

'Chris wants her for his next film. Something about people having the wrong shadows. Sounds weird. Might be just unusual enough to work.'

Bea tried to be tactful. 'Why are you concerned? If he doesn't find her, he loses his star performer, abandons film-making and has to go back to uni. That's what you want him to do, isn't it?'

'We're magnetic poles apart, him and I.' He turned the television on, found a football game, muted the sound. 'I thought you could do a bit of digging. If you could prove the girl's gone off with a delectable hunk or returned to Nigeria . . . ?'

'You don't think that's what's happened?'

He sighed, poured himself another glass. 'No.'

She blinked. 'You expect me to prove . . . what?'

'You're the expert. Take a look at her belongings, see what you can find out about her. You know what to look for: women's stuff, diaries, calendars; any trace of drug-taking. Letters, her laptop, her mobile.'

She didn't tell him she'd been thinking along those lines already. 'What you're saying is that if the library books aren't back at her flat, then she never returned there after she left Chris?'

'That hasn't occurred to Chris yet. He thinks they're there somewhere, and that he just didn't find them. Of course, they may be. He didn't get on with her flatmate. Would you be willing to have a go?'

'If they're not there? And if her passport is?'

Silence. He switched off the television set, drained his glass and got to his feet. 'Must go. Early start tomorrow.'

Bea persisted. 'What if . . . ?'

'I'll ask around, see if a suitable body has turned up anywhere. Don't bother to see me out.' He hardly made a sound as he left. Even the front door closed with a muted click instead of its usual thump.

Bea looked at the clock, shoved a cork in the neck of the bottle and put it in the fridge for later. She scribbled a note for Maggie, picked up her handbag, collected her big coat from the rack in the hall, set the house alarm, and followed him out.

A chilly night. Overcast. She switched the heater on in the car. She wondered if she ought to have provided herself with

a notebook to record what she learned at Miss Drobny's. It
might have been helpful. Perhaps next time she'd remember.

Friday evening

Miss Drobny – Ms Drobny? Mrs? – lived in a basement flat
in Holland Park. It wasn't as fashionable an area as Bea's part
of Kensington, but it was doing nicely, thank you. Number
twelve was divided into three flats, and there was a party in
progress on the top floor. The ground floor was semi-basement,
its windows dark.

Bea's house was also three floors, plus an office in her
semi-basement, but the scale was different. Bea's house was
late Georgian with tall windows, high ceilings and cream paint;
this one was brick built and squat. There was a light over the
front door, which was fortunate since the steps down to the
basement were steep.

Bea negotiated the steps, rang the bell and waited.

A thickset woman opened the door. A grouch with more
than a hint of a moustache. 'You are . . . ?'

'Mrs Abbot. And you are Miss Drobny? Ms? I'm sorry I'm
a little late, but I brought your money.'

The woman ushered Bea inside. 'Miss. Did you bring cash?'

'Won't a cheque do? I have cards to prove my identity.'
She handed over one of her business cards.

Miss Drobny slammed the door shut, casting a darkling eye
upwards. 'They have parties every weekend. No peace.' She
twitched her head, indicating that Bea follow her down a
passage encumbered with cardboard boxes, to reach a brightly
lit living room at the back of the house.

The furniture was mismatched, mostly oak, probably from
second-hand shops. The room smelt clean; it had been dusted
and hoovered recently. A small television set was showing a
film with subtitles. A film made in Miss Drobny's own
country?

Brown curtains, brown and grey carpet, a brass vase
containing peacock feathers on the mantelpiece. Weren't
peacock feathers supposed to bring bad luck? The fireplace
was not in use, but had been fitted with a reasonably up-to-
date gas fire. There was no central heating, but a large overnight
storage heater took the chill off the air. In one corner was a

somewhat rickety bookcase overflowing with CDs, DVDs and paperbacks. Had the missing library books ended up there?

A meal for one had been eaten on a table drawn up under a curtained window and a cup of coffee was poured out, ready to drink. Bea was not offered any coffee, which was just as well as she didn't drink coffee in the evenings.

Miss Drobny had short, stumpy legs. She was wearing a tight black sweater over a short black skirt. Her tights were also black, no ladders or holes. Her shoes were cheap but well polished, and her black hair had been newly washed. She wore a trace of lipstick, which was the wrong shade for her sallow complexion, but which showed that she cared about her appearance to a certain extent. She probably didn't earn much. Possibly sent money back home to her family? No boyfriend? No rings on her fingers. No fiancé.

She pointed to a wooden chair with a removable cushion on it. Bea sat, unbuttoned her overcoat and got out her cheque book. 'How much . . . ?'

Miss Drobny had the amount written down on a piece of paper, which she handed over. 'One month's rent? For that I keep her room.'

Bea nodded, wondering if her hostess had exaggerated the rent. Probably not, as it seemed reasonable. She wrote out the cheque and handed it over. 'This is all most distressing. I do hope Tomi turns up soon, but if she doesn't . . . I know you've had to think ahead and clear her things out of her room. I can see that her disappearance must be putting you in a difficult position. For one thing, there's not a lot of storage in these flats, is there?' She remembered the boxes in the hallway.

'That's so. It is a big problem.'

'Perhaps you'd like me to store Tomi's things for you, until we know what's happened to her?'

'You pay her rent, and I keep her boxes for one month. What is your interest in her?'

'My son Oliver is best friends with Chris, the lad who put her in his film. They're both worried about her.'

'That Chris. Humph. He thinks he's funny. Too much money, not enough sense.'

Bea laughed. 'I agree. He's an idiot in some ways, but clever in others. Did you see the film he made of Tomi?'

'He puts ideas into her head about being a big film star,

earning pots of money. Tomi is stupid. She believes him, and look what happens!'

Jealousy rears its ugly head, right? Tomi was charismatic, and this woman would be lucky to attract the attention of a failed farmer. How on earth had the two women managed to live together peaceably? Perhaps the arrangement had been recent? Perhaps they'd had a series of rows, and this woman had done away with Tomi? No, kill that thought. Miss Drobny did not know what had happened to Tomi.

Bea said, 'I don't think Chris did away with her, if that's what you mean. She's not his type. He only likes blondes . . . that way, I mean. No, he really is worried about her. You are too, aren't you? You've seen enough of the world to realize she could be in danger.'

Miss Drobny failed to thaw. 'She is silly girl. I tell her straight. All those men taking her to places she cannot afford, they are up to no good. But she wouldn't listen to me, oh no!'

'What do you think has happened to her?'

A frown. A helpless gesture with pudgy hands. 'This man she is gone away with, she does not give me his name. I know her old boyfriend, Harry. Nice enough in the English way, but with no understanding of what it is to leave your home and make a new life in another country. He says to me, will I clean his flat, and I say he should clean it himself. I am not his slave.'

'No indeed. You already have a job, of course?'

An emphatic nod. 'I have a good job with big food preparation company. I have a college degree back in my own country, you understand.'

Indeed. It was a big step up from cleaning flats. 'So you don't think she went off with Harry?'

Again, the hands twisted and fell apart. 'She texted me she had a new friend.'

'Anyone can text a message. It need not have been Tomi.'

'It was from her mobile phone. I have no landline here, you understand, so we use mobile phones all the time.'

'Can you give me the number?'

Miss Drobny recited it by heart, and Bea made a note of it on a page in her diary.

'The day after she texted me, I try her phone, but she does not reply. I try it many, many times. So yes, I am worried about her.'

'It's hard to know what to do about it, in a foreign country.'

Miss Drobny nodded. A small grey cat with a thin tail appeared from nowhere and jumped on to her lap. She stroked it, and the cat settled down. 'The cat from upstairs. She does not like noise. At party time she comes down to me.'

'Nice,' said Bea, who had been adopted by a stray cat herself. She felt sorry for Miss Drobny. 'I am going to try to trace Tomi. You will help me, won't you?'

Miss Drobny sighed, but nodded. 'It is best to know.'

'Right,' said Bea. 'So, let's start with what we can find out here. Are any of her books still in your bookcase?'

Miss Drobny heaved herself out of her chair, depositing the cat where she'd been sitting. 'These are my books, some from home, some for learning English. Tomi buys books from charity shops, and she borrows from library. All trash. She calls them romance.'

'So where are her books?' Bea scanned the contents of the bookcase quickly. Nothing from the library.

'I put them in this.' Miss Drobny dragged one of the cardboard boxes in from the hall and opened it up. There were paperback books in plenty, all romances. Bea sifted through them. No library books? No. Yes! Two romances, both overdue.

'No other library books at all?' said Bea.

'None,' said Miss Drobny. 'I thought to take those back to the library for her and then I say to myself, "Better not. Perhaps the police will come one day, and they will want to see everything."'

'You tried the police?'

Miss Drobny shook her head. 'That Chris said he told them and they do nothing. I tell myself, "Wait. Something will happen." And now you come.'

Friday evening

Claire hummed as she gave the baby his last feed for the night. He was a poppet, a sweetie-pie who was so adorable she'd like to eat him up.

It was going to be a wrench to part with him, but his parents were going abroad and she couldn't go with them or she'd lose her chance to walk down the aisle to the strains of the Wedding March. Not that she'd got her boyfriend to the point of popping the question yet. What he didn't know was that she couldn't have any babies herself. What she could have was untold wealth. Three down, seven to go.

Baby's eyes had closed and the bottle had fallen away from his mouth. The little darling. She put him over her shoulder, and he brought up his wind. She was good at that. And at disposing of people who got in her way.

THREE

Bea turned back to her search. Some magazines: fashion and film stars. A calendar with handwritten appointments inked in to the end of the year. Tomi's handwriting was big and loopy and she used a pen with black ink. There was also a calendar for the following year, peppered with more engagements. Parties, people's birthdays, a check-up at the dentist's, a concert here and a play there.

Her boyfriend Harry's birthday in February was ringed and underlined. Someone's wedding was pencilled in for mid-January. There were envelopes addressed to Tomi, which contained cuttings torn out from magazines, free offers for this and that, hair products mostly. She also had a collection of holiday magazines, nearly all for the Mediterranean.

Ah. A bible, a paperback modern edition. Well used. Tomi hadn't underlined anything or made notes in the margin, but there were several bookmarks and pieces of paper stuffed into it.

Miss Drobny said, 'She is a Christian, as I am. Tomi's parents are – how you say? – lukewarm Christians, but Tomi is red hot. You are a Christian, too?'

'I try to be one, yes. Would you mind if I borrowed her bible? There are notes in here which might help me.'

Miss Drobny shrugged. 'If she doesn't turn up, the police will want it.'

'Understood.' Bea put the bible aside and dived back into the box to retrieve one last item, which was an address book: large, solid and too big to carry around in a handbag. 'She was last seen carrying some library books. They're not here. Let's see what else we can find, shall we?'

'Cosmetics.' Miss Drobny carried in a hefty make-up box and dumped it on top of the first one.

Much what you'd expect. Mid range, not expensive. Hair care. Did Tomi braid? She'd had braided hair in the video.

There was a switch of false black hair in a separate bag, presumably for evening events.

'Clothes.' Miss Drobny dragged the first two boxes back into the hallway, substituting first one and then a second suitcase. Bea went through both meticulously. Most of the clothes had been dry-cleaned and were pristine. Tomi was not the sort of girl whose clothes lived in a stir-fry on the carpet. Most had labels from supermarkets; trendy, but not expensive. Bea recognized the jeans and top the girl had worn in the video, also the long evening dress in dull red jersey.

A separate bag contained dirty clothing, which was presumably intended for the washing-machine, plus some used towels. There was a stack of underclothes; some warm jumpers; three jackets, all clean, nothing in the pockets. A long black coat, warm. A bag full of pull-on hats; some gloves.

No violin. Had that been a prop supplied by Chris? 'Did she own any musical instruments?'

Miss Drobny shook her head. 'She was not musical. In the film she mimed playing a violin.'

Underclothes and tights had been rolled up and kept separately. The girl had worn long woollen nighties, but also possessed some lighter silky pyjamas, perhaps for sleepovers? Tomi had felt the cold. The flat did feel slightly damp. Shoes and boots were in a sports bag. Nothing expensive, nothing down-at-heel.

Bea sat back on her heels. 'Any more?'

One last box produced toiletries. There was a manicure set, bubble bath, some tiny bottles of good perfume. Tampons, aspirins, paper hankies, throat lozenges, digestive remedies, something for a sore throat. Oh, and a small radio. Also three huge handbags, all empty except for the odd receipt and some used paper tissues.

While Bea investigated the handbags, Miss Drobny dragged the boxes back into the hallway and brought back a large, old-fashioned laptop. 'Her boyfriend gave her this. He couldn't find the connecting leads and the batteries have run down. Typical of him to give her something that needs attention. He said she could easily buy some new batteries, but they're expensive and she isn't technical. She used it for a while, but when the batteries finally gave up, so did she. She told me her parents were going to the USA for a holiday. I am thinking every day that they will phone her, but if her phone is not working, what will they do next?'

'They'll get someone – perhaps a friend of theirs or a business acquaintance – to come round here to see what's wrong. No one has come yet?'

Miss Drobny shook her head. 'I think their email address is on her laptop, but I don't want to buy new batteries for it. I have a good job, but not enough money for extras.'

'I know someone who might be able to make it work,' said Bea, thinking of CJ, and of Oliver. Oliver loved a challenge when it came to computers. Bea sank back on her heels. 'What was she wearing when she left, do you know? What handbag was she carrying?'

Miss Drobny raised her hands in the air. 'She wears jeans at weekends. I think, yes, her green things are not here. She has a green sweater and a jacket which is leather, though not real, also green. And her green handbag. She bought it from a stall in Portobello Road. It is fake, but looks good.'

The party on the top floor was just getting into its stride. The whole house shook. The little cat jumped off the chair and tried to climb up Miss Drobny's leg. She picked it up, stroked it, calmed it, held it against her.

Bea commented, 'No passport, no bank statements, no official documents. Did she have any credit cards?'

A frown. 'Yes. She is at the same bank as me. She has some store cards, too.'

'May I see her room? I'm wondering if she hid her passport and cheque book somewhere?'

Miss Drobny led Bea back down the hall and into a room whose windows would overlook the steps leading down to the front door of the flat. 'This was hers. I have cleaned it, of course.'

So she had. The room smelt clean. And damp. There was a night storage heater, but it had been turned off to conserve electricity. Brown furniture again. Green curtains at the window, which presumably was below ground level? A reasonably modern single bed, chair and table, chest of drawers, and a wardrobe. A door in a recess opened to reveal a tucked-away washbasin. Centre light, separate reading lamp. Small bookcase, empty. The bed had been stripped, the duvet folded over, pillows on top of it, Indian cotton cover over all.

Bea lifted the bedding and the mattress to look underneath. Nothing.

There was nothing left in any of the pieces of furniture, either. Bea checked, taking out the paper which lined each drawer and cupboard to make sure, even though she believed Miss Drobny would have been thorough.

There was a crash outside in the road. Someone upstairs threw open a window and shouted down to the people in the street. Party-goers or comers.

'Tch. I have complained,' said Miss Drobny. 'They take no notice.'

The carpet was a square mat. Bea flipped up all four corners to see if Tomi had kept anything beneath it. Nothing. Not even fluff.

Bea looked at her watch. She was due at her son's flat in ten minutes and was going to be late. The little cat wriggled through the half open door and leaped on to the bed, which creaked.

The wardrobe? Bea stood on the chair, and there it was: a large envelope with all Tomi's private papers in it. Passport, bank statements, letters from the Home Office confirming her right of residence, college certificates. No credit cards. Bea looked at the passport photo and showed it to Miss Drobny. 'That is her?'

'Yes.' Miss Drobny shook her head. 'If her passport is here, she did not go away to France. I am getting a bad feeling.'

'Me too.'

Someone banged on the front door of the flat. Miss Drobny went out into the hall, sighing. 'Is always the same. They think they get into the party upstairs through my front door.'

She opened the door to merry cries of, 'You took your time!' from a couple of men who seem to have taken drink already. Bea buttoned up her overcoat, eyeing the laptop. She wondered if Miss Drobny might allow her to take it, because when Oliver returned home, or CJ came round, one of them might be able to make it work.

While Miss Drobny was directing the newcomers upstairs, Bea had another thought; would Miss Drobny let her borrow Tomi's address book? Presumably her parents' home address would be in it. What was Tomi's last name? On the other hand, perhaps everything ought to be left here for the police to look at.

Miss Drobny let someone else into the hall. Two people. First came a hard-faced middle-aged woman, expensively got up, with a pallid clone of a daughter in tow. The older woman's eyes were all over the place. '—difficult to find, and she must be near the Central Line, of course, because of her job, but this might do, I suppose. I would be prepared to pay three months' rent in advance for a suitable . . . But I'm not at all sure that this—'

'It looks perfectly all right to me,' said the daughter, who was perhaps not as young as she'd looked at first sight. 'It's better than living out in the sticks.' And, to Miss Drobny, 'OK to look around?'

Silently Miss Drobny led the way to the big sitting-room at the back of the house. The older woman followed to look Bea up and down and register the fact that she was well-dressed. One of Us, in fact. 'Are you . . . ?'

Bea shook her head. 'A visitor. Just going.'

'Oh. Nothing to do with . . . ?' The newcomer threw her eyes upwards. More and more people were ringing the door-bell and tramping up the stairs to the party. 'That's what's attracting my daughter. Parties mean people. I suppose I can't blame her. She's just out of a long-term relationship which was always going to end in tears, as I told her on day one, but she couldn't see it.'

Bea twitched a smile. She'd known Nicole wouldn't be the best wife in the world for Max on day one, as well.

Then came another thought. Had the parties been an attraction for Tomi, too?

Miss Drobny was getting on well with the newcomer. 'From here it will be an easy journey for you to work. Do you cook?' Throwing open a door. 'The kitchen is small.'

'Heavens, no. I have a takeaway, or buy something ready-cooked. I can have a shelf in the freezer and use the microwave?'

A nod. 'The bedroom is back this way.'

There was another outburst of laughter from the top flat, and something – a bottle, hopefully empty – crashed down into the garden. The two older women winced, exchanged resigned shrugs. Bea said, 'I wonder how late they keep it up.'

'My daughter won't care.'

There was a bump and a bang in the hall and the daughter reappeared, rubbing her shin. 'Well, Mother. I don't think I can do better for the money. The bathroom's small, but there's a shower, and I'm not going to be in much, am I?' So, to Miss Drobny, 'When can I move in? And what is all that stuff in the hall, anyway?'

Miss Drobny looked at Bea, and Bea looked back. Miss Drobny needed a flatmate, but Bea had paid her a month's rent. Theoretically the flat should remain vacant for another three weeks. Also, if the police were going to get involved, Tomi's things ought to stay where they were. Except that they'd already been packed up and removed from her room.

Bea wanted that laptop. 'Those things belong to someone who's moved out. I've offered to store them for the time being. I can take some of them with me now – if that's all right with you, Miss Drobny? – and I can collect the rest tomorrow.'

The daughter was pleased. 'Well, if that's the case, I can move in tomorrow. I haven't much beyond my clothes and a few bits and pieces.'

Miss Drobny frowned. 'If Miss – er – would take a seat in the sitting room, I'll just have a word with my friend here before she leaves.'

Ah. Miss Drobny didn't think Tomi's stuff ought to be moved? As the living room door closed on the potential flatmate and her mother, Bea said, 'You think Tomi's stuff should be left here. I understand. You can find me at the address on my card. I promise to see the police get involved if she doesn't turn up by tomorrow morning. Will you let me take the laptop? I know someone who might be able to get it working again, and I do think her parents ought to be informed, don't you?'

'I don't know. I'm not sure what to do for the best.' But she made no demur when Bea picked up the laptop and walked off with it.

As Bea left the flat, she came face to face with two more young men and a couple of leggy blondes who, even on that chilly evening, weren't wearing much. They were trying to find the party. Bea told them where to go. Repressing a shiver, she put the laptop on to the passenger seat, got into her car, and switched on the heater. Thank God for an efficient car heater. Would there be a frost again tonight?

She was going to be later getting to Max's flat than she'd promised. And she must ring CJ.

For some reason the traffic snarled up around Earls Court. Bea told herself to be patient. There was no point in leaning on the horn. If a traffic light had stuck on or off, it wouldn't help to get in a state about it.

Nevertheless, she did feel rather anxious as she drew up by the block of flats in which Max and Nicole lived and hauled herself and the raggedy Mouse out of the car and up in the lift. Her back twinged, reminding her that at her age she shouldn't have tried to heave Tomi's belongings around.

And, oh dear, she was rather late.

Nicole opened the door to her. Nicole was in a frenzy; blonde hair wisping all over the place, make-up long gone, smears of baby talcum on her grey sweater. The strict regime she was following gave her no time at all for herself.

'Where have you been? I thought I could rely on you, and look at the time!'

The baby was wailing somewhere in the background. The television was on, muted. Baby paraphernalia was spread around the floor. Untidy. Unnecessary.

Bea bit back words of censure, reminding herself that new mothers did get worn out, and Nicole wasn't in the first flush of youth. Or the second, come to think of it. Pippin wailed. A disconsolate, heart-rending wail, which sounded as if he'd lost all hope that life could ever take a turn for the better. It wrung Bea's heart to hear him cry like that. She ought not to have gone to see Miss Drobny. She ought to have come here first.

'He won't sleep till he's got his Mouse. I didn't know what had happened to you. I rang you, and you didn't even bother to pick up the phone!'

Bea felt guilty. 'Sorry. An emergency. I'm here now, and here's Mouse. Can I help with anything now I'm here?'

'Haven't you done enough?'

The door slammed in Bea's face. She tried to laugh. Blinked. Well, that was that. Not needed. In the way. It gave her stomach ache to think about it.

Better go home and get a good night's sleep. Except that she had something important to do before she slept that night, hadn't she?

She got back into her car and found her mobile phone.

'CJ? Sorry to ring so late, but I've been round to see Tomi's flatmate. Her passport is there and so is her laptop, which has no power cable and flat batteries, but I managed to bring it away with me. Chris's library books are nowhere to be seen, nor any credit cards, cheque book, or mobile phone. She was probably wearing a green leather jacket, sweater, jeans, and carrying a large green handbag. Without her passport, she couldn't have gone abroad—'

'On a private boat, perhaps?'

'You're clutching at straws. She's dead.' Bea grimaced. She hadn't known she was going to say that. It might not be true. Possibly.

'Where are you? I see you're on your mobile phone.'

'Ten minutes from home, bath and bed; but I suppose you want to collect the laptop?'

'You're trusting I can wave a magic wand over it? Right. But I can't spend much time on this at the moment. When's Oliver due back?'

'Wednesday next week.'

A sigh. 'We can't wait till then to report her missing. All right, I'll set things in motion from here.' He disconnected.

Bea shut off her own phone and drove home. CJ was not in sight when she arrived. Should she leave the laptop on her doorstep? Probably not. Ah, here he came, in his unremarkable but souped-up car, flashing his lights at her as he double-parked. She took the laptop over to him even as he wound down his window to accept it. He said, 'I'll be in touch,' and drove off.

Fine. She might as well go straight up to bed and try to sleep because tomorrow was going to be another long day.

Before she did, she went down to her office to make some notes about what she'd learned at Miss Drobny's, in case Chris asked her something and she couldn't remember. Then she booted up her computer to see if there were any reply from Oliver. And there was.

Tomi's missing? That's not like her. If Chris says he's worried about her, then there's something to be worried about. What do the police say?

I wish I were back home now and could help you

*look for her. Have you tried the hospitals? She's the last
person to down tools and walk off like that.*

*I plan to get away on Wednesday, if you can collect
me then. I'm afraid I do have a lot of stuff to bring back.
Tell Maggie I'll see her at home. Let me know roughly
what time you can get here. Chris did pass his driving
test, but he hasn't a car of his own and CJ won't let him
drive his.*

*The more I think about it, the more worried I am about
Tomi.*

I'll ring you later. Love, Oliver.

Another vote for action. Had Chris tried the hospitals? Yes,
he'd said he had. Had CJ got on to the police about Tomi?
He'd said he would. Hadn't Bea enough to do without looking
for a girl who'd strayed from home?

She switched off the computer and stumped up to bed. *Dear
Lord, deliver me from worrying about something that doesn't
need worrying about. Or, if You do think I have to worry about
it, then let me have a good night's sleep first? Please?*

*Oh, and thank You for everything else that's good in my
life. Oh dear. I don't feel in the least like praising You tonight.
I'd better read my bible for a bit . . . which reminds me . . .
what about Tomi's bible, which I left there? Oh well. I'll think
about that tomorrow.*

Friday night

'Rock a bye, baby.' Claire could sing it in her sleep.

*It was hard to leave her babies at six every evening, but it
prepared the young mothers for the moment that Claire moved
on, and it gave her time to herself, to plan for the future.*

*When she'd first realized that her beloved was going to be
out of town for some days, she'd been devastated. Only later
did it occur to her that this gave her freedom to pursue the
Grand Plan without hindrance. In some ways she thought her
loved one even more childish than her babies, although of
course she never said so. She would never have imagined he'd
need so much care and attention. But there . . . it was all going
to be worth it in the long run, wasn't it?*

How many more days to D day? Not long now.

Three down and seven to go. The red tide of excitement rose in her. Who should she target next? Harry? Yes. Harry.

A pity they hadn't found Tomi's body yet. It might be necessary to tell someone where she was. How about a text message to Chris, luring him to the spot? She could send another to the police, who would catch him red-handed. Yes, why not?

FOUR

Saturday noon

Saturday mornings were sometimes, but not always, quiet at the agency. This Saturday they were busy with clients coming in for interviews, and only two of Bea's staff were in to answer the phones. It was at times like these that Bea really missed Oliver, who seemed to be able to do three things at once. Maggie was no help with the agency work, whisking in and out to meet a contractor here and a new client there.

It was after twelve before Bea could spare the time to think about Chris and his troubles. She got him on the phone and, before she could say anything, he asked, 'Have you found her?'

'Not so fast. And no. Your library books are not there, but her passport is. You did try the hospitals, didn't you?'

'It's serious, then? I kept hoping . . . All right, I'll try the hospitals again and ring you back.'

She started to say that his father was already on the case, but he'd put the phone down. As she did the same, it rang under her hand.

'CJ here. I've done a spot of ringing around. The police say there's no unidentified body turned up in the London area that could be your girl. I've asked them to spread their enquiries wider.'

'She's not *my* girl. I've asked Chris to check the hospitals again. I assume he's capable of that.'

'Possibly. I have to go out in a minute, but I'll drop by your place on my way. I got Tomi's laptop working, copied the entire hard drive, and overwrote it on to a spare laptop for you. I haven't the time to go through it myself, but I thought you could get young Oliver on to it.'

'He's not back till Wednesday.'

'This is an emergency. Can't he get back sooner?'

'Would the university consider it an emergency?'

'Oh. Very well.' He disconnected.

Bea smoothed back her hair, then realigned the fringe to lie across her forehead. She inspected her fingernails, trying to remember when she'd next booked in to have a haircut and a manicure. She thought it might be in ten days' time. Could she fit it in earlier, perhaps? No, they were always booked solid.

Oh, well. It was a fine, frosty day with a brilliant blue sky. Soon, perhaps, the trees would break open their buds and they could believe that spring was on its way. It had been a long, hard winter.

She could do with some time to herself, but suspected that she wasn't likely to get it.

She swivelled her chair round so that she could look out of the French windows and up through the branches of the sycamore tree at the bottom of the garden. If she looked hard, she could see the tiny buds swelling on the tips of the twigs. Through the branches she could also see the spire of St Mary Abbot's church, pale stone against the blue sky. Victorian. High church. It was not really her style, but a constant, everyday reminder of what a difference it made to her life to know God . . . and what God might or might not want her to do in any given circumstance.

What He didn't want her to do was to get cross with Nicole and Max. Bea had a horrid feeling that she'd been less than kind to them the previous night. She'd been put on the defensive and had reacted by criticizing them. Slap on wrist. She must try not to find fault, but help them in whatever way she could. Perhaps soon they'd let her hold Pippin and give him a cuddle.

What did God want her to do about Tomi?

Whatever it was, Bea didn't want to listen. She'd more than enough on her plate as it was. She could do with some fresh air. A walk in the park, maybe have tea in the Orangery. Their scones were first-class. If she did that, she'd be out when CJ dropped another load of work on to her.

She really didn't see why she should be dragged into this affair. It was nothing to do with her, was it? No. If she got a move on, she could be out of the house before CJ reached her.

The front doorbell pealed. She closed her eyes, pretended

not to hear it. Then sighed, pushed herself out of her comfort-able chair and went up the stairs to let CJ in.

'Must rush. Here you are. I've made a note of the parents' email address, so that we can contact them as soon as – if – we hear anything. Let me know if you find anything else of interest.' He thrust a slimline laptop at her and dashed back to his car, which was double-parked.

Bea considered dropping the laptop on to her stone doorstep, which would hopefully put it out of commission, but knew she couldn't do that. She was a creature of habit, wasn't she, trained to obey the Voice of Duty? She would go out for a short walk, and then put in an hour or so on the laptop. She was going out that evening, anyway, so couldn't give it much time.

She made the mistake of booting up the borrowed laptop straight away and never got out for her walk.

It didn't seem that Tomi had used it much. A few emails to her parents and friends – Bea took a note of their email addresses in a notebook. She couldn't find the notebook she'd used last night, so started a new one. There was a lot of spam, which Tomi hadn't bothered to delete; reminders about library books she'd ordered, which were now in and waiting for her to collect them; some query about her subscription to a Health Club; and so on and so forth. Nothing particularly interesting. Bea switched to the 'Sent' box.

The girl's style had been chatty, friendly and, now and then, ungrammatical. Most of the emails were to friends, with a weekly one to her mother. None to her father. Tomi chatted about how she was getting on at work – nicely – and where she'd been with Harry, the boyfriend who Chris said had now moved on to someone else. She'd been to an art gallery with a different friend – unnamed. Not Harry? – and to some dance or other, very swish. She'd been worried that her old red dress mightn't have been up to scratch, but it had passed muster. She wondered about buying some more clothes if this whirl of activity went on. Possibly second-hand?

Health Club. Chris and Oliver belonged to the Health Club down the road, didn't they? Maggie had had a subscription for a while. Bea wasn't sure whether or not Maggie still used it, because it was rather posh. Expensive.

What was Tomi's salary? There wasn't anything on the

laptop about that. She'd worked for a magazine, hadn't she?
There must have been something in the paperwork at her flat
about it, terms and conditions, etcetera.

Bea made herself a cup of tea before delving into the files
which Harry had left on the laptop before handing it over to
Tomi. He'd deleted them, but they were still hanging around
if you knew where to look. Bea could imagine Harry's lordly
attitude as he handed his old laptop over to Tomi. 'Play about
with this one, if you like. I've got a new one.'

The phone rang. It was Chris, sounding strained. 'I phoned
round all the hospitals again. She's not there. So where is
she?'

Bea didn't reply. What was there she could say?

Chris gave a little cough. 'Sorry. Think I'm going down
with something. Can't settle to anything. When's Oliver due
back?'

'I'm fetching him on Wednesday.'

'Not till then? I went round to Harry's just now. Tried to
talk to him about Tomi, but we . . . we've never really got
on. There was a bit of a confrontation, I'm afraid. He's,
well, everything I'm not. Dependable, earning a mint, public
school background, upper class right back to the umpteenth
generation. Thinks I'm a charlatan.'

'Surely not,' said Bea, who had sometimes thought along
those lines herself. 'What you mean is, you were tugging Tomi
one way, and he wanted her to conform to his background?'

'He wasn't thinking of marriage. He liked showing her off:
black is beautiful, causes heads to turn, my girl has been the
star of an art-house film. You know? Plus she worked on a
magazine. She ticked all the right boxes as a girl to be seen
around with, but she said he never took any notice if she
expressed an opinion of her own.'

'You saw different things in her.'

'I liked her.' Frustration in his voice.

'You think she's dead, too?'

Silence. The phone clicked off.

Bea went back to the computer to continue searching
through Harry's emails. Lots of spam. Sent emails, arranging
meetings. Business? Looked like it. There were draft reports
in legalese on projects in the Middle East. More reports on a
different set of businesses. All work-related. Nothing recent.

Nothing personal. No nice chatty letters to friends saying how he'd been getting on with Tomi.

In-box. A couple of emails from friends, new email addresses, phone numbers, that sort of thing.

Bea turned the computer off. If there was anything there, it was going to need a better brain than hers to access it.

The front doorbell rang. There was no one else in the house, so she went up the stairs to answer it. It was Chris, looking gaunt. Normally he wore cheerfulness like a mask. It was interesting to see how worry had hollowed his cheeks, making him look a lot older.

'Suppose Harry killed her?'

Bea blinked. 'Come inside. You're letting the cold in.'

He stepped inside the front door and let her close it behind him. 'Look, will you come with me to see him? This morning when we spoke, well, he took a swing at me and I retaliated. I annoy him, you see. Nothing whatever in common. I was angry that he could forget Tomi so quickly. I suppose I overreacted.'

Bea could imagine it.

Chris jingled keys, shifting from foot to foot. 'I might have said, well, I suppose I did say . . . But she, his new girl, she's the daughter of someone important, and he's ambitious, aiming to climb the corporate tree, you know what I mean? Though I could have told him that this particular girl's well beyond his reach, and however much she plays around with a good-looking man, she always goes back to a dim-witted youth with a title. She's got far too much sense to tie herself down to Harry. If you see what I mean.'

'So?'

'So, what if Harry thought it would help him with Hermia? Yes, silly name, her parents were fixated about *A Midsummer Night's Dream* if you ask me, which of course you didn't, but . . . Where was I? Oh yes. Suppose Harry thought he had a better chance with Hermia if he got rid of Tomi? Suppose there was a row and he hit her or something? Killed her by mistake? He would panic, of course, and put her body somewhere, I don't know where. Tipped her in the river, maybe.'

Ridiculous nonsense. 'I doubt it, Chris.'

He screwed up his face. 'I can't just do nothing, can I?'

'Have you told your father what you think?'

A hunched shoulder. 'He said I was barking mad, but we're at opposite ends of the spectrum, aren't we? It's automatic that he thinks I'm wrong. You're different. You take your time and think about things. So, will you come with me to talk to Harry?'

'Why should you think that—?'

'You got Miss Drobny eating out of your hand, didn't you?'

'Well, but—'

'Look, come with me now. Have a word with him, ask him about Tomi. See how he reacts. I trust your judgement. Oliver's always saying what a good judge of character you are. I promise that if you think Harry's got nothing to do with Tomi's disappearance, I'll not mention it to the police.'

'Police? But we don't know yet that anything's happened to her.'

'Don't we?' His mouth set in a grim line.

She hesitated. 'All right. I'll get my coat. Where's my handbag?'

'Are these your car keys?' He picked them up from the chest in the hall. 'I'll drive. I know the way.'

Bea opened her mouth to tell him she wouldn't trust him with the keys to a piggy bank, never mind her car . . . Her only experience of being driven by him before had given her a bad case of the shakes, but Oliver said Chris had at long last passed his test. Perhaps he'd learned by now how to drive without giving his passengers a nervous breakdown?

But no. She had a better idea. 'Sorry, Chris, I'm not insured for you to drive. If you insist on this wild goose chase, I will drive and you will tell me where we're going.'

He gave in with a bad grace and instructed her to twist and turn through back streets until she wasn't entirely sure where they were. Somewhere north of the Bayswater Road was the best she could do.

Ah, a mews. Gentrified. Expensive. As she parked the car, he got out to ring a doorbell beside some closed garage doors. Some of the original mews buildings had been modified, adapting what had originally been intended for use as coach houses into garages, and later on into ground-floor living rooms. Some – not many – had retained the space to garage their owners' cars. As this one had.

Chris indicated a low-slung sports car parked nearby.
'Hermia's.'

'Won't it be awkward, asking him about Tomi, if Hermia's
there?'

He shrugged. The door opened.

'What the—! Get the—!'A tall man in a dressing gown
tried to close the door, till Chris put his foot in it.

This was Harry, presumably. A cut-glass accent, curly blonde-
to-red hair, bony face. Late twenties? Bea could imagine him
looking down his nose from under a Guards helmet. Officer
type, definitely.

Harry made a second attempt to close the door. Chris leaned
on it, smiling slightly, but not in a friendly way. 'We need a
word.'

'And who might you be?' Harry was tall enough to look
down on Bea.

'My name is Mrs Abbot and I'm also trying to find Tomi.
Chris thinks you might be able to help.'

'Who is it, Harry?' A voice from above. Roedean? Also
crystal clear, but warm. Not a soprano, but an alto.

'Chris and some woman looking for Tomi.'

'Oh?' Denim-clad legs appeared at the top of the stairs.
'Well, don't let the cold in. Come on up.'

A tiny hall, carpeted stairs leading to the first floor, Spy
cartoons on the walls. Harry led them up the stairs and into
a small living-room overlooking the mews. Furnishings by a
good department store; John Lewis, perhaps? The walls had
been painted a warm apricot; there were matching low leather
chairs and settee, a large TV on the wall, and Scandinavian
rugs on a pale carpet. Newspapers had been strewn about the
place; a mobile phone was at the ready. Glass coffee table,
of course. Coffee mugs and a cafetière. The surface of the
coffee table could have done with some attention. Nothing
shows dust like a glass table top.

The girl was something else. No, not a girl; mid twenties,
perhaps. Tallish, but stocky rather than slim. Minimum make-
up, dark hair cut in a severe bob. She reminded Bea of Miss
Drobny; perhaps it was her air of knowing exactly what she
was doing? Not pretty, but striking. Her nose a trifle large?
A Jewish background?

She was wearing an expensive heavy sweater in mottled

grey and white, denims, and beautifully cut brown boots. A
soft fawn leather jacket had been tossed over a chair nearby.
Money.

Harry picked up a mug of coffee, without offering any to
his guests, and threw himself into a chair. 'So what now? Has
the silly girl turned up at last?'

Chris ground his teeth, but replied in an even tone, 'No.
We're all worried about her. So why aren't you?'

Harry shrugged, sending Hermia a glance which invited her
to be amused by this charade. 'So what? And did you have
to bring your mother with you?'

This stung, as it was meant to do. If Harry knew anything
about Chris, he'd have known his mother had died young.

Chris held on to his temper. 'I asked Mrs Abbot to come
because she's been through Tomi's things and found her passport, which proves she didn't go to France. Don't be afraid;
I won't hit you again.'

An insult that also hit home. The mug of coffee Harry
was holding jerked, and he swore, shaking hot liquid off his
hand.

Had Chris – who was not all that tall, or heavy – actually
managed to land a blow on Harry? Was that a reddish graze
on Harry's chin? Bea flicked a glance at the girl, who looked
amused.

Harry reddened. 'Diddums, then. Has his ickle bunny girl
deserted him?'

Chris moved his shoulders within his jacket, but kept his
temper. 'Tomi was special, but never my girlfriend. You ought
to know that. You went out with her for what – three months?
As soon as the film won a prize.'

Harry contrived a laugh, inviting Hermia to share his amusement. 'A five-minute sensation. Yes, she was an amusing little
totty to have around for a while, but no one could be serious
about her. Or you. I hear you dropped out of college to make
your little video, using money you'd borrowed from your
father. Not much of a future in that, is there?'

'Oh,' said Hermia, frowning. More to herself than anyone
else. 'So you're *that* Chris, are you?'

Chris wasn't looking at her, but concentrating on Harry.
'Look, Tomi's missing. I know she texted you to say she was
taking off to France with a friend, but she couldn't have gone

because her passport's still here, and she's not picking up messages left on her mobile.'

'Gone back to her roots, I suppose. Like a rabbit to its burrow. Sudan, Nigeria, Sierra Leone? Take your pick.'

Chris turned away with a gesture of frustration.

Bea took up the questioning. 'Could you tell us when you last saw Tomi and what she was wearing at the time?'

'Really, I'm not responsible for the girl. Now if that's all, perhaps you'd leave as we have plans for the rest of the day which don't include you. Either of you.'

Hermia picked up her jacket and retrieved a small diary from a pocket. 'Two weeks last Saturday I was at a party with some friends. Harry came in, moaning that Tomi had gone off with someone else. Does that help?'

Harry scowled. 'She stood me up. After telling me she was going shopping for something to wear to the party, too.'

'That helps,' said Chris, ignoring Harry. 'I saw her on the Saturday morning. We went to the library together and took some books out, some of which she was carrying for me. That was the last I saw of her. So between Saturday morning and Saturday evening she went missing, and no one's seen her since.'

'She got a better offer, I suppose,' said Harry, yawning. 'Now if you don't mind—'

'A better offer than you were likely to make to her?' said Chris. Then stopped, for Hermia had made a slight but definite movement, frowning, communicating . . . what?

Bea looked from one intent face to the other. She could feel the air in the room becoming supercharged with . . . sex? No, not sex. Though perhaps there was sex in it.

She tried to work it out. There was a recognition on Hermia's part that she was interested in Chris, and that he had suddenly realized it. Despite the age gap, something was definitely going on between them.

But Chris only goes out with blonde cuties!

Hermia was not a blonde and had never been a cutie, but she had brains and integrity and a cool intelligence, which would make her a better partner than any number of blonde cuties. There was money in her background, too; something which Harry was said to appreciate, but which probably wouldn't weigh with Chris at all.

Bea's brain slid on and on. If Chris and Hermia got it together, would they not argue? Yes, probably. Would she tire of him if he failed to fulfil his early promise of bright young film-maker? Yes, probably. But what if what she was feeling for him now developed into a deep, true love? She'd mother him through his bad times, admire the persistence with which he'd overcome so many problems to produce his first film and appreciate his warm and loving nature. She'd discount his charm, of course, and probably fall in love with his father and . . . would there be enough left, if he failed in his career, to keep them married?

Marriage? What was she thinking of? Chris was nineteen years old, living off his father and the kudos of a one-shot video, while Hermia came from old moneyed stock. Bea could imagine what her family would say if she invited Chris home as a prospective husband. Besides, didn't she have some pea-brained aristocrat in tow? Someone with a title?

Bea shook her head to clear it. She was imagining things.

Hermia ran her hands up through her hair, fluffing it out into a softer style. She picked up her jacket. 'Well, Harry; I can see you're hardly dressed for our planned run in the country, so I'll be on my way.'

'What? But—'

'See you around.' She turned to Chris. 'Can I give you a lift somewhere?'

'I came with Mrs Abbot.' He stood back to let her pass down the stairs ahead of him. 'I don't have a car of my own yet.' Was he setting out his own stall?

Hermia opened the door to let them out into the mews. 'How can I help you look for Tomi? I saw your film. I was impressed. She's a lovely girl.'

Hermia had used the present tense. Bea noted it. So did Chris. He said, 'I'm so afraid something's happened to her. I tried the hospitals, and my father's tried the police. Nobody's reported a body that could be hers.'

'Your father's Cecil Cambridge, the computer guru, isn't he? My father knows him. Have you got any PR shots of Tomi that we can use to jog people's memory?'

'Back at home, yes.'

'I'll give you a lift, shall I?'

'But – Mrs Abbot . . . ?'

'I'll take myself off, then,' said Bea. 'Let me know how you get on.'

'Yes. Thank you.'

Eye drawn to eye, like a sleep walker Chris got into Hermia's expensive car and was driven away. Kidnapping? Well, no. They both knew what they were doing. Probably.

Bea got into her own car and flicked on her mobile.

'CJ? Can you spare a minute? No, nothing earth-shattering – well, it is in a way. You know a girl called Hermia? Or her father?'

'Both. Yes.'

'She's just annexed Chris. Popped him into her car and driven off. With intent.'

'What do you mean, *intent*?'

'Well, on his side, I should say he recognizes an intelligence equal to his own, an earth-mother figure, and is eager to have sex with an adult.'

'What? You're not serious. She wouldn't. I've known her since she was a baby and . . . What on earth would she see in him?'

'Integrity? She likes the way he's pursuing his quest for Tomi. Also, perhaps, she sees that furthering his work could give a purpose to her life. She won't act hastily. However attracted she may be, she'll turn him inside out, test his potential, and decide whether or not he's worth more than a quick fling.'

'But she's supposed to be marrying—'

'Mmhm. And Chris is only nineteen.'

'He's twenty next week. But still. It's preposterous. Couldn't you have stopped it?'

'How? When did you last stop Chris doing something he wanted to do?'

A sigh. 'I've got news. Thames Valley Police have found a body. It might be Tomi and it might not. What did you say she was dressed in?'

'I told you. Green jacket and jumper, jeans, boots. Big green handbag. Where is she?'

'Out near the M25, in some bushes on a country road. She's been there some time.'

'A natural death?'

'Suspicious circumstances, I'm afraid. Someone phoned in

to say they'd been walking their dog and found it, but didn't leave their name. They're asking Tomi's flatmate to identify the body. I'll be in touch.' He disconnected, and she drove home, concentrating hard to avoid an accident.

Saturday afternoon

'Hi, Harry. How's tricks? I was thinking, if you're going to the party at Von and Simone's tonight, you might be able to pick me up, because the Mini's playing up, and my beloved's otherwise engaged this weekend.'

'Not going. Don't feel like it. Bloody Hermia's given me the air.'

'Oh, you poor thing. How's about I pop round and you tell me all about it. Shall I bring a bottle?'

'Might as well.'

Claire's brain was whirring. Excitement rose in her. What good fortune to find him depressed. One of her special drinks and he'd be asleep in minutes. This one ought to be a suicide: dressing-gown cord round his neck, haul him up, let him dangle. If Hermia had indeed chucked him, there was all the reason in the world for him to kill himself.

FIVE

There were lots of jobs Bea knew she ought to be doing, but she didn't want to tackle any of them. Oliver had promised to ring, but so far hadn't done so. She missed him. It would be good to have him back again.

Maggie was out. The sky glowered at Bea, promising rain, sleet or snow. In March, for goodness' sake! It didn't often snow in London, but when it did, life became difficult. Post was delayed, train services disrupted, airports closed. Shops ran out of milk.

Bea rummaged in the kitchen, looking for something quick and easy to cook for supper. She came up with ducks' breasts marinaded in something spicy. They'd go all right with rice and perhaps some calabrese. She'd put in an online order for food supplies recently, and Maggie had been cooking up a storm against Oliver's return, so there was plenty in the freezer, but nothing Bea really fancied.

The office was silent; the staff had packed up and gone home. The answerphone light was blinking. Bea eyed it with dislike and left it to blink. It was probably Nicole, wanting her to do some shopping or cleaning for them while Max was away. Enough! Although she must admit to being anxious about poor little Pippin. If only they'd listen to her . . . But no, they were never going to admit that Granny knew best, were they?

The landline rang, and she answered it.

'Bea? I tried to ring you earlier.' A man's voice brought her back to the present. Piers, her first and long ago ex-husband. 'You haven't forgotten about tonight, have you?'

'Of course not,' she lied, eyeing with disfavour the ducks' breasts now defrosting on the worktop. Going out with Piers, a much-sought-after portrait painter, was always interesting. He'd been an unsatisfactory husband, tom-catting around from the day they were married, but of recent years had proved himself a good friend. 'Where are we going?'

'Someone gave me some tickets for the *Messiah* at the Albert Hall. Not my usual scene. What do you think? We could eat somewhere local afterwards, or before.'

The front door banged and in marched Maggie, bringing a blast of cold air with her. 'Yoo-hoo! I'm back.'

'Fine by me,' said Bea, distracted. 'Whatever.' She covered the phone over to say to Maggie, 'They've found a body, might be Tomi's.'

Piers' voice was sharp at the other end of the phone. 'What's up?'

Maggie dropped her bag on the floor. 'What?'

Bea turned back to the phone. 'A girl's gone missing. Someone Maggie and Oliver know. They've found a body which might be hers.'

'You want me to help?'

'Doing what, Piers? The police will deal with it.'

Maggie sat down on the nearest stool with a bump. 'Really?' Her eyes were enormous.

'Sorry, yes.' To Maggie. And to Piers, 'Look, Maggie's just come in, and we're both in shock. Can I ring you back?'

'I'll come round.'

'No, don't—'

He'd already clicked off. Bea replaced the receiver on her landline phone and put her arm around Maggie. 'It might not be Tomi.'

Maggie shuddered. 'If it isn't, then where is she?'

Bea held the girl close to her. Maggie burrowed her head into Bea's shoulder and huffed. Then pulled away, swiped her hand across her eyes and got up to put the kettle on. 'I'm dying for a cuppa. How about you?'

'I can't think. Yes, I'd . . . No, better not. Piers is coming round. He's supposed to be taking me out, but I'd forgotten and got those ducks' breasts out of the freezer for supper.'

'It's Saturday night. I was going to a party, but . . .'

They stared, not at one another, but at the defrosting ducks' breasts.

Maggie said, 'Where did they find her?'

'Beside a country road.'

'It's not Tomi, then. She's not exactly a country person.'

'No.' Bea didn't argue. CJ had sounded very sure.

'I'll cook these for supper,' said Maggie. 'There'll be enough

for three. Piers will like home cooking for a change.' She
looked at the clock and reached for her apron. 'I don't think
I'll bother going out again tonight. It's been a stressful week,
what with this and that. I'll knock up a pudding for us, shall
I? Carbohydrates. Cold winter food. Keeps you going.'

'Yes. Thank you, Maggie.'

'If you feel too tired to go out with him, you don't have
to, do you?'

Bea felt like saying 'I'm not that decrepit,' but kept her
mouth shut. They might pretend all they liked, but the image
of Tomi lying at the side of a country road was weighing them
both down.

Piers arrived, wearing lightweight clothing despite the chill
in the air outside. He often wore black, partly because it was
fashionable, but also because it suited him. While he'd never
been handsome, black did set off his mop of greying black
hair, slightly twisted nose and olive complexion. He didn't
wear suits, of course. At least, not the usual pinstripe city-
style jobs. He wore silk shirts over denim in the daytime and
silk over well-cut black trousers in the evening. His jackets
were always made to measure.

His son Max had all the good looks in the world – though
he was running to seed a little lately – but he'd none of Piers'
immense charm, alas.

'My dear.' Piers kissed Bea on both cheeks. 'My beloved
Maggie.' Another hug and a kiss. 'So tell Grandpa what's
happened.' He made a joke of it, but he was pleased to have
a grandchild and had already set up a savings account for little
Pippin . . . which had caused Max to remark, sourly, that a spot
of instant dosh would have been even more acceptable.

Bea forced herself to smile. 'Nothing yet. Rumours, people
panicking. It may all be a storm in a teacup. Would you like
to share supper with us before we go out?'

He was not fooled, but was intelligent enough to accept
that they'd decided to make light of whatever it was that was
bothering them. 'So, do we sit through the *Messiah* tonight?
I must admit it's years since I heard it. I very rarely go to a
concert or listen to the radio. I work in silence, as you know.
Even the tinkle of a mobile phone irritates me.'

'Who gave you the tickets? Someone who wants to widen
your horizons?'

'In every way, probably. Not that I'm tempted. She's patron of something in the music world, can't remember what. Would you like to come too, Maggie? I dare say we can find another ticket for you.'

'No fear! I'm partying tonight,' said Maggie, making up her mind to it. 'What, sit in a cold concert hall all night, when I could be out having fun?'

'They tell me that fun and music are not incompatible. What sort of music do they play at your parties nowadays?'

Bea and Maggie responded to his lead as best they could. It would be hours before they had any firm news, wouldn't it?

Sunday morning

Bea awoke to the music of the Hallelujah Chorus still ringing in her head. A talent for playing music hadn't run in her family, although her grandfather had had an enormous collection of seventy-eight records, which he'd played on an old wind-up gramophone. As a child, one of her jobs had been changing the discs every four minutes for him. He'd loved the *Messiah*, and they'd played something from it at his funeral. Bea couldn't remember hearing it much since then, but the tunes had all come back to her last night.

She'd tried to shut out all thoughts of Tomi lying dead in the country while the music washed over her. Only when Piers urged her to her feet did she remember that the audience always stood for the Hallelujah Chorus. Tears came then, unbidden, as that great melody thundered through the vast concert hall. She'd thought at the time: this is a requiem for Tomi.

Which was absurd. She'd never even met the girl and wasn't at all certain of her death. Nevertheless, she'd wept. And, waking with the music still pounding through her head, she knew she now desperately wanted to find the girl, alive or dead.

A girl's body had been found in a country lane. If it was Tomi, then what had she been doing there?

Bea threw her arms above her head and stretched, thanking God for her own robust health. Also for good friends, and for work.

She could feel in her bones that this day would be difficult, so she prayed aloud, 'I trust You to see me through it.'

The morning light seemed different. She pulled back the curtains. Ah, so it had snowed in the night. It wouldn't last long, of course. She lingered to marvel at the patterns which the snow had made on the sycamore tree, and how it had placed a soft white cap on every bush in the garden below. There were footprints in the snow; a fox? Birds had hopped here and there, and so had a cat.

The bedroom door opened, and Maggie brought in a cup of tea. 'Chris is here. Hung over and in a panic. Wants to borrow the car. As if! I said you weren't up yet.'

Bea glanced at the clock. It was a good half hour before the time she usually rose. She pressed her fingers to her eyes. 'Did he spend the night on the front doorstep?'

Maggie shrugged. She was wearing what looked like a man's woolly pyjamas, and huge bunny rabbit slippers. Her eyes were shadowed, and her hair was all over the place. She hadn't slept well, either. 'He's in a terrible state. Do you think he wants to confess to murdering her or something?'

Little fingers of dread played around the back of Bea's spine, and she shuddered. 'Unlikely. He's overreacting, as usual.'

Maggie nodded and left. Bea drank her tea, showered, and dressed. It was Sunday morning and she'd intended to go to church. She didn't often go – perhaps once every six weeks – but this was one day she'd intended to do so.

Surveying her still trim figure in the pier glass, she wondered if this particular shade of greyish-green – almost eucalyptus – really suited her. A cream jumper with a cowl neck was fine over her new dull green trousers, but the gold-embroidered waistcoat was perhaps too much of a good thing? Too upbeat for what the day might hold? She changed it for a brown suede jerkin.

Chris would play the Tragedy King, of course. He might even convince himself that he was responsible for Tomi's death. Blame himself for everything.

Please, tell me what to say and do, Lord.

Why was it that some people seemed to have been born without common sense? But perhaps if Chris had been more evenly endowed with talent, he wouldn't have the imagination to make films?

He was crouched on a stool in the kitchen, fingers in his mouth. Hadn't shaved, of course. He started up when he saw Bea.

'Mrs Abbot, I need to borrow your car. It's really important. I don't know who else to ask.'

Bea exchanged glances with Maggie, who was dressed in a heavy duty jumper and cords. No make-up. Maggie looked worried. Bea supposed she did, too. She tried not to let Chris's anxiety infect her. 'What do you want to borrow it for?'

'I can't tell you, but it's really important. Please?' He made an immense effort to calm himself and to speak quietly. 'I don't know who else to ask. Dad said he'd k–kill me if I . . .' He swallowed hard. 'If I took his car without permission.'

Bea took orange juice out of the fridge and poured three glasses full. He shook his head, tried to smile and failed. 'Do you have any aspirin? I've a terrible headache.'

His eyelids were at half mast, and his skin looked pasty. Were those the clothes he'd worn yesterday? No, the shirt was different. Bea got out a packet of aspirin and poured a glass of water for him.

Maggie said, in a small voice, 'Breakfast, anyone?'

'Yes, please,' said Bea, needing sustenance.

He shuddered. 'No, thanks. Look, Mrs Abbot, I know I'm being unreasonable, and of course you can always say no, and I'd understand, because you don't know what . . .' He gagged, wiped his mouth with the back of his sleeve. 'Sorry. Not totally "with it" this morning. The thing is, a friend needs me to collect him . . . her . . . from somewhere in the country, and there's no public transport that . . . Or perhaps you could lend me enough to take a minicab out there? No, that won't do, because if she's not there or . . . I can't think straight.'

He began to pace the kitchen. Maggie held up a carton of eggs and a pack of bacon for Bea to see. Bea nodded, getting out the muesli and cornflakes. Perhaps, if she stocked up internally, she'd feel strong enough to work out what was upsetting Chris.

Oh! Something cold slithered up and down her spine. The country? Someone wanted collecting? Him or her?

Tomi?

But Tomi was dead, wasn't she? Bea looked at Maggie,

who looked back at her, registering alarm and surprise. Bea noticed that her own hands were trembling as she opened the pack of muesli and poured some out for herself and Maggie.

'You mean Tomi phoned you and asked her to collect her?'

'Yes. No. I mean. I can't think straight.' He clutched his head with both hands. 'She texted me: COME AND GET ME. FULMER LANE. TOMI.'

Fulmer Lane. CJ hadn't mentioned Fulmer Lane when he'd reported that the police had found a body, had he? Calm down, Bea. Think this through, step by step. She poured milk on to her muesli.

Winston, their furry black cat, appeared. Chris picked him up to stroke him, and then put him down again. 'My head's killing me.'

Bea tried not to let her voice wobble. 'A text message is not necessarily genuine.'

'I know that. I'm not stupid. At least, I know I'm not thinking clearly at the moment – this headache – but I can't just ignore it, can I? Yesterday I was sure she was dead, but now . . . You must see that I've got to find out what's going on.'

Maggie looked very pale, but was making a good job of spooning muesli into her mouth while setting some bacon on to fry.

Bea put the kettle on to boil and spooned coffee grounds into the cafetière.

'Fulmer Lane. Where is that?'

'It's just off the A40, a turn off near the M25, leads down to a pretty village called Fulmer. We go out there to a pub for drinks in the summer, sometimes. But Tomi hasn't any transport, and neither have I. Why should she be out there, anyway? That is, assuming she's alive.' He clutched his head again. 'Am I going mad?'

'No. You're confused because you haven't enough information. What does your father say?'

'I don't know. I crashed out on a friend's couch last night and only read the text when I got up this morning. I tried to phone him, but he never answers the landline and he turns his mobile off at night. I was walking home when I remembered you lived closer and might lend me your car.'

Bea tried to think clearly. 'Your father told us late last night that a body had been found in a country lane near the M25. No identification as yet.'

Chris groped for a stool and sat on it, breathing heavily, eyes closed. 'It's Tomi, isn't it? She texted me, I didn't pick up, and now she's dead. If I'd gone out there last night, maybe she'd still be alive. What happened to her? A heart attack? No, no. She was so strong. I can't believe it!'

'Your father said the body had been there some time and that there were some suspicious circumstances.'

His eyes flew open. 'So it wasn't her who texted me.' His eyes flickered around the room. 'It was from her mobile phone. I recognized the number. I thought . . . hoping against hope.'

Bea cleared her plate. Pushed the orange juice towards him. 'Extremes of hope and despair can kill you. Let's not jump to conclusions, right?'

He downed the orange juice. Winston leaped on to his lap, and Chris held him close, huffing into his fur.

Maggie broke eggs into a saucepan. Bea pushed the plunger down into the cafetière.

Chris said, 'Whoever texted me wanted me to rush out to see if Tomi were still alive. It was a trap, wasn't it? I was supposed to be found there by the police, who would jump to the conclusion that I was responsible for . . . Do they think she was murdered? Is that what you meant by saying there were suspicious circumstances?'

'We don't know anything for certain as yet. Luckily you have the text message as evidence that someone used her phone last night. Do you think you could eat something now?' Bea put four pieces of bread in the toaster.

'Not after . . .' He shook his head at the packet of muesli, but accepted a mug of strong black coffee instead. He grimaced, trying to smile. 'What you must have thought when I landed on your doorstep! Oliver's right, and you're the one person we need when the world turns topsy-turvy.' He pulled out his mobile. 'I'll have to tell the police about the text message, won't I? I wish I could remember who Tomi went off with, the last time I saw her. I must have been one of the last people to talk to her.'

A plateful of crispy bacon and glistening scrambled eggs arrived in front of Bea, and she tackled it with relish. 'Let's try to reconstruct what happened. Close your eyes, and think

back. It was a Saturday. Noontime? You'd been to the pub with
Tomi, and then you went across to the library to get out some
books. You got out more than you could carry, so she offered
to carry some for you. Two, three?'

'Two, but they were big ones. Coffee table type books.'

'Someone came up to talk to you. Or was it someone in a
car?'

He was impatient. 'Not in a car. He was walking up from
the High Street, had been doing some shopping for the
weekend. He lives in a flat just up the road from there.'

'Let's recreate the scene for you. How was he dressed?'

'Dressed? How should I remember? He's called—'

'Of course you can remember how he was dressed. Sit
down. Do you want sugar in your coffee? Or perhaps some
more orange juice?'

'What? What does it matter how he – I suppose, yes, brown
jacket, grey denims, boots. A scarf. It was a really cold day.
We were all huddling up against the wind. He was in a hurry
because of it. He'd just come from getting in some food at
Marks & Spencers, said there was a party on that night just
off the Brompton Road, and was I going, and I said yes, probably, and though the wind was bitter, the sun was bright, and
he was wearing these shades, wrap-around, heavy side pieces.
I thought they didn't really suit him, but I wouldn't mind a
pair. I'd forgotten that.'

'His name?'

'Brian. A bit of a bore about . . .' He clicked his fingers.
'Horse racing. His father owns one leg of a horse. Brian's
always on about it. I turned away from the sun – yes, that's
right, the sun was in my eyes – and I turned away from Tomi,
and she said she'd seen someone across the road and would
talk to me later. That's the last I saw of her.'

'You didn't see her cross the road?'

He shook his head. 'No, not really. No.'

'Tomi knew Brian, too?'

A shrug. 'I can't be sure, but I don't think so. On the other
hand, we meet all sorts at parties. It's like we're all in different
circles, and some of them intersect.'

'Yes, I can see that. You may need to find out where Brian
lives, to confirm your story. How do you know him?'

'Someone at the Health Club introduced us. He said his

father's horse was running that weekend. We'd nothing much else on so we went to watch and the horse won and there was a party afterwards. The way it is. You know?'

Bea thought of the party at Miss Drobny's house. 'Are these parties open to everyone?'

'Not really. People bring their friends, sometimes. If it gets on Facebook then it can get out of hand. When it's at our place Dad goes away for the weekend, but since the last one I've promised him I'll keep the numbers down and pay for the cleaner to come in afterwards.'

'How did you meet Tomi?'

He was vague. 'At a party somewhere, about a year ago, I suppose. She wasn't with Harry then, was she? Maggie, you were there, weren't you, with Oliver? Something vaguely theatrical. Can you remember?'

Maggie tried to help. 'It was at Von and Simone's, wasn't it? There was this leggy blonde you were going out with at the time, who invited you. Oliver and I came along because we were all going on to some crazy comedy show in a pub afterwards. The blonde didn't want to come, so you shed her and invited Tomi instead.'

'I remember.' Chris pulled his coffee towards him and drank it black. Quiet descended on the room. Winston the cat jumped from Chris's lap to Bea's, to be fed the last scrap of bacon.

Chris said, 'What do we do now?'

'We try your father's phone again, and if he's still not in, we contact the police.'

Sunday morning

Claire smiled to herself, painting her toenails bright red. Beside her was an array of mobile phones. Tomi's. Harry's. Leo's. And hers.

Their weight at the bottom of her handbag reminded her of how much she'd achieved so far, and of what still remained to be done. Every now and then she turned them on to listen to their friends' frantic messages: 'Please call, please ring me.' That amused her.

She'd used Harry's mobile to tell the police where Tomi was to be found because she wanted them to think he'd been responsible for Tomi's death. Then she'd texted Chris using

Tomi's mobile, asking him to pick the dear girl up. Claire hoped he'd acted on it and been found by the police cradling Tomi's body. That would muddy the waters nicely.

Claire didn't like Chris much. She'd met him a couple of times at parties, but he'd never taken any notice of her, even though he was supposed to be passionate about blondes. He deserved to be hassled for that. Not that he was on the list, exactly.

Not like the others.

She put her head on one side to consider the particular shade of nail varnish she'd used. Would her beloved like it? He was a trifle old-fashioned, liked his girlfriends in high heels, short skirts, and giggles. But his wife? Perhaps he'd prefer something a little more restrained? It was a problem, how much to tone down her behaviour to catch him.

No more babies. Aaah. Well, maybe they'd adopt.

Meanwhile, her time was nearly up with her present employers. She'd been booked to go on to a wealthy family in Knightsbridge, but the woman had miscarried, so Claire wouldn't be needed. Where should she go next? She could pick and choose her jobs nowadays. Perhaps a titled family? Or a millionaire's? Or a pop star's? She must call into the agency, see what they'd got to offer.

SIX

Sunday morning

Before Bea could ring CJ, he rang her.

'News,' he said. 'Not good.'

'We suspected the worst. We have Chris here. He got a text from Tomi's phone this morning.'

'What! I'll be right round.'

'Was that—?' said Chris.

'Yes. Why don't you wash and brush up before he gets here?'

Chris blundered out while Bea helped Maggie put the dirty dishes in the dishwasher. Maggie found her big handbag and started to apply make-up. Bea stood at the window overlooking the garden. A few fluffy clots of snow drifted out of the sky, but didn't settle. The sun tried to break through heavy clouds, and the temperature rose. If it got much higher, the snow would vanish.

The bells would be ringing for the church service any minute now, but Bea wasn't going to get there this morning, was she?

Maggie came to stand beside Bea. They put their arms around one another. Maggie sighed. Bea wondered whether at some point in the future it would be Maggie supporting her, and not the other way around.

Maggie said, 'I keep thinking of Tomi lying out there all by herself. Was she . . . you know?'

'Raped? I don't know.'

'Horrible, to happen like that. All alone. Screaming, probably.' She shuddered.

'I wish Oliver were back.'

'Wednesday.'

The doorbell rang, announcing CJ's arrival. Chris thundered down the stairs, and Bea ushered them all into the sitting room. 'Coffee?' Being bright. No one accepted.

CJ glared at his son. 'Where were you last night?'

Chris's shoulders rose defensively. 'A party. The usual. I stayed overnight. Yes, I drank too much, I've got a hangover, and before you can say it, yes, it serves me right.'

'Bea said you'd had a text?'

Chris handed his phone over, and CJ nodded. 'Not from her, of course. She's been dead for ten to fourteen days – probably died the day you last saw her.'

'Not raped?' Maggie feared the worst.

'No. That would have been understandable, I suppose. The police will want to see you, Chris. I'll go with you. Her death's official now, but we'll have to wait for an autopsy. It's not clear how she died.'

Chris straightened his shoulders. 'I understand. Shall we go now?'

CJ didn't take his eyes off his son. 'Who in your lot introduced Tomi to drugs?'

Chris was startled. 'Drugs? Well, I suppose, yes, one or two took this and that, party style, you know. Are you saying that . . . ? But Tomi never—'

'You've admitted you all experimented.'

'No! I didn't because it would take the edge off things and—'

'Doesn't getting drunk do that, too?'

'Yes, but . . . I don't usually, you know that. As for Tomi, she thought people who took drugs were stupid. There was a row at a party once when someone was handing out pills. She came over to me, asked me to see her home, said she'd slapped a man's face when he'd offered her—'

'Who was it?'

A shrug. 'I didn't see. I was in the other room when she stormed in, woman on the war path. I didn't take it seriously. After all, lots of people—'

'Who? Names!'

'I can't. None of my friends, except maybe a couple of times to prolong the party spirit, you know. Are you saying that Tomi died from taking drugs? I don't believe it.'

'The police will need names.'

'It's that serious? But –' he gestured wildly – 'this is ridiculous. Tomi did not do drugs.'

'Just one dose would be enough for someone who hadn't done it before.'

Chris collapsed on to the nearest chair. 'I've heard that the first time can be fatal. But no, not Tomi.'

'They all say that,' observed CJ, stone-faced.

Maggie was hugging herself. 'I second what Chris says. Tomi didn't do drugs. If anything, she was more judgemental than I was about it, talking about slippery slopes and beginning small and ending up dead. She wouldn't do drugs.'

Bea filled in the dots. 'Was it, perhaps, done to her?'

CJ looked hard at Bea. 'What makes you think that?'

'Everything that everyone has said about her. Searching through her belongings, piecing her lifestyle together. There was nothing in her medicine kit. No syringes, no unidentified twists of powder. Nothing. So how did she die?'

He twisted his lips. 'There'll have to be an autopsy. There was a syringe sticking out of her thigh.'

There was an indrawn breath from Maggie and Chris. Chris shook his head, over and over. 'No, she wouldn't. She didn't. This is just not right!'

Bea said, 'If she died a fortnight ago, then who sent the texts from her phone? And where is her phone?'

Silence.

Bea went on, 'What was she wearing? Were Chris's library books with her?'

CJ shook his head. 'Pass.'

Maggie put her hand to her head. 'Why would anyone want to kill Tomi?'

Chris shot out of his chair. 'Harry! He's the only one who had a motive. He needed to get rid of her, so that he could make up to Hermia.'

'You've tried that line already,' said Bea. 'Hermia gave him a sort of alibi.'

'Yes, well; he laid it on thick, didn't he? To impress her? He could have killed her before the party and dumped her, then cried into his beer to attract Hermia's attention. Why not?'

'It feels wrong, that's why not,' said Bea. 'What happened between you and Hermia yesterday?'

'Hermia had other fish to fry last night, some important charity dinner or other.' He grabbed Bea's handbag, extracted the keys 'Let's get going. I'll need a witness, so you'd better come, too.'

CJ was, uncharacteristically, dithering. He wanted to get his son to the police, of course, but Chris had forgotten all about that. Bea reached for her big coat. 'Give me back my keys, Chris. You know perfectly well you're not allowed to drive my car. Come on, CJ, let's see what all the fuss is about. Maggie, do you want to come, too?'

Maggie shook her head. 'I don't think he would have needed to kill Tomi to shake her off. Whatever he may have thought, she wasn't that keen on him. Look, I've a cracking headache. I'll see you later. Give me a ring when you find out what's happened.'

Bea didn't think Maggie had a headache but, as the girl was obviously keen to do something else, there was no point in querying it.

On a Sunday morning, the mews was creepily quiet. Nothing moved, except for a well-fed cat. There were several parked cars. The sound of traffic on the main road outside was muted.

Bea parked her car outside Harry's door. Hermia's distinctive sports car was nowhere to be seen. Snowflakes were still descending at intervals in half-hearted fashion. There was a light dusting of snow on the ground, but no footprints led to or from Harry's door. His windows upstairs were closed and the curtains drawn. Had he had a heavy night, not got up yet?

Chris rang the bell. Nothing happened.

He thumped the door. Kicked it. It swung open. 'That's odd.'

CJ caught his son's arm. 'Let me go first.' CJ climbed the stairs in the shallow grey light and the others followed him into the living room on the first floor.

'No one here,' said Chris, pushing his way between them and opening doors. A tiny kitchen, very clean. A shower room, and loo.

Bea homed in on a laptop, up-to-date version, open and running, but on a screen saver. A bottle of wine stood nearby, open, with a used wine glass.

'Don't touch anything,' said CJ.

Too late. Chris tried to open the door into the bedroom, and failed. Something resisted him as he tried to open it.

'What the . . .!' said Chris, and he gave an extra big heave. The door rebounded on him. 'There's something behind the door. Help me to—' Another heave and he got his shoulder and head round the door, took one long look, retreated and let the door slam to in his face. 'Oh.'

'Harry?' said CJ, getting out his mobile.

Chris swallowed. 'His face is . . . He's very dead. Hanging from . . . Oh God!'

He dived for the loo, and they heard him throw up. CJ thrust his head and one hand round the door, and returned. 'Icy cold. No point trying to cut him down.' He got out his mobile. 'Cambridge here. Is Inspector . . . ?'

Bea turned away to look out of the window. *Dear Lord, what is going on? I'm not a betting woman, but I'd lay odds that there's a suicide note on that laptop. I don't like anything about this. It doesn't feel right.*

'Don't touch anything,' said CJ, clicking off his phone. 'The police will be here directly. We'd better wait downstairs in the car.'

Chris came out of the loo, looking shaky. 'I pushed this and the bedroom door open.'

'They'll take your prints for comparison.'

'We were both here yesterday morning,' said Bea. 'I'll try to remember what either of us touched.'

'Anything different?' CJ, very sharp.

'There were newspapers all over the place then. They're in the waste-paper basket now. There were two coffee cups on the table, one each for Harry and Hermia. A cafetière. No wine, bottle or glass. He was wearing a dressing gown over pyjamas, slippers. The laptop? I think it was on the floor in a case by the television.'

'Anything else? I trust your eyes.'

'He had a mobile phone with him. The latest. It was on the coffee table with . . . Let me think . . .' She closed her eyes to recall the scene. 'There was dust on the coffee table. It has a glass top, difficult to keep clean. There were some crumbs on the floor; he'd been eating a croissant for breakfast, perhaps? Since then the floor's been hoovered and the table top cleaned. The doors leading out of this room weren't open when we came yesterday, so I didn't see inside the other rooms.'

'Thank you, Bea. Will you two wait downstairs now?'

Sunday afternoon

Police. Paramedics. A doctor.

Bea and Chris sat in her car. Bea turned the engine on, so that they could get warm.

The snow stopped. Started again without really meaning it. Later footprints smudged earlier footprints. Bea tried to ring Maggie, but the line was engaged. Bea knew that once Maggie got on to the phone, she might be on for hours. Eventually Bea got through and said they'd be some time, as Harry had been found dead. Maggie was shocked and wanted to know details.

More police arrived. After conferring upstairs, an inspector asked Bea and Chris to accompany them to the station, so that their statements could be taken. It looked open and shut; suicide, of course. But still, better to be safe than sorry, eh?

Bea made a statement, telling the police what she had seen. She asked what message Harry had left on the laptop and where his mobile had got to. They smiled and said she wasn't to worry about all that, leave it to them, they knew what they were doing, etcetera.

The station was warm enough. Fingerprints were taken. 'For elimination purposes'. She didn't think she'd touched anything at Harry's, but supposed she might have done, without thinking. On further consideration, no, she really didn't think she'd touched anything. Fingerprints still had to be taken. She was given a cup of tea.

Chris was taciturn, monosyllabic. Polite. CJ was nowhere to be seen. He was 'known' to the police, in the best possible way, of course. He was some sort of expert, called upon in emergencies. Bea thought that sometime she might ask him to define 'emergencies'.

Bea considered that if anyone had done anything to Harry – and of course that was a big 'if' – then his visitor, if he'd had a visitor, must have been and gone before the snow started in the night. What time had the snow started? It had been snowing for some time before she got up.

Finally Bea and Chris were allowed to go. Bea rang Maggie to say they were on their way, a police car transferred them back to the mews, and Bea drove herself and Chris back home. Her home. She wasn't particularly surprised to see CJ arriving in a taxi, just as she parked her car outside her door.

Bea half expected CJ to collect Chris and remove himself, but he drifted in with them, frowning. Chris seemed to be in a world of his own; a grim world, to judge by the look on his face.

Inside the house the central heating was ticking away, the lights were on in the kitchen, and there was a smell of something good cooking. Hurray.

Maggie had been busy. She'd spread herself all over the kitchen table, with large sheets of paper in an untidy pile in front of her and a mug of coffee at her elbow. There was no sign of the headache she'd claimed to have earlier.

Bea looked at the clock. Breakfast seemed a long time ago.

Maggie said, 'Ready for a cuppa? Cheese scones in the tin, butter in the fridge. I've some lamb shanks in a casserole in the oven. Ready about six, if you can wait.'

Bea put the kettle on. Chris looked as if he still had a headache. Eyes half closed, he peered at what Maggie had been doing. 'What are you doing?'

'I've been ringing around. I tried everyone who knew Tomi, told them the news and asked did they think Tomi had ever taken drugs. No one thought she had. I told them how she'd died and, like me, they were shocked and then got angry, thinking of someone doing that to her. Shock and anger loosens tongues. So I asked each one if they knew who might have tried her with something – for fun, you know.'

She picked up the top piece of paper. 'This is Simone's list, for instance. She gave me a couple of names, but it was all for recreational stuff, very mild, hardly illegal at all. So we talked about people who gave parties, and I asked her who she usually invited and how many people gatecrashed them, and we chatted for a long time about that, and I got quite a lot of names. She even gave me some telephone numbers.

'Then I tried other people I'd met with Tomi. Mostly they were from your team, Chris, people who'd been involved in making the film. Some I knew quite well, and some I didn't, but they all go to parties, or nearly all of them, so I yakked on and got more lists of people they invite, and one or two more names, people who have a reputation for pushing drugs. I started a new list with each person I spoke to.'

'Good grief!' Chris was impressed. 'That must have taken hours.'

'You've been away for hours. Some names come up on everyone's list; some, I've never heard of.'

Bea picked up a couple of lists and compared names. 'There must be a hundred names here.' She spotted a discrepancy, looked at Maggie, who was all wide-eyed innocence, and decided not to mention what she'd seen.

Maggie shrugged. 'We need Oliver and a computer. He could sort it out. He rang, by the way. I said you were out and told him what had been happening. He's mad keen to get back to help us, said could you collect him about noon tomorrow instead of waiting till Wednesday, and I said I thought you might. He'll ring back later to confirm. Oh, and Nicole rang, too. I said you were out and she sounded really angry; wanted you to go over there and cook a meal for her or something. I said you'd ring her when you got back, but that might not be till late and she should get a takeaway.'

Oh dear. Bea's hand went to the phone. If Nicole really needed her, she must go. At once. She hesitated, took her hand away because it was too late for her to go over there today. She'd ring Nicole back as soon as she could.

Maggie realigned her pile of paper. 'I spotted a couple of names of possible drug pushers which come up fairly regularly, but I don't know either of them. In fact, I got two different spellings for each one, so there may be four people there or two or three, or . . . whatever.'

CJ bent over her shoulder, lifted up the top couple of sheets and glanced down them. If he'd noticed what Bea'd seen, he said nothing about it. 'This is incredible. It would have taken the police hours to find so much out, and these people probably wouldn't have talked openly to police, anyway. You haven't got phone numbers for everyone?'

'No, and a lot of it is hearsay; two people said they'd heard that if you wanted something to liven you up, you could invite so-and-so because he had some pretty good stuff for sale, but then they'd say they hadn't tried it themselves, of course. They'd probably deny it if asked direct, or if they were asked tomorrow. It was the shock of Tomi's death which made them indiscreet. Also, I suspect that those who denied all knowledge of drug availability might know a lot more about it than some of the others. Might even sell it themselves. Maybe I'm being fanciful.'

'You're a wonder,' said CJ. 'May I have these?'

She got up to fetch a large envelope for him from the side. 'I've run off some photocopies for you. I liked Tomi. I'm not much good at office work or computers or anything, but I thought this was something I could do for her. So the police finally let you go?'

Bea shuddered. CJ pinched in his mouth. Chris said, 'We had to give statements to the police because we found Harry, dead. It looks as though he committed suicide.'

'What?' Maggie couldn't believe it. 'He's the last person, I'd have thought.'

'What makes you say that?' CJ, putting her under a microscope.

Bea dished out plates, knives, scones and butter. Put the kettle on.

Maggie looked bewildered. 'Well, I suppose I oughtn't to say that, but Tomi did talk about him quite a bit, and she said he was always so pleased with himself. He only ever talked to her about what he was doing, and what he wanted to do. If Tomi ventured an opinion he cut her off at the knees. I asked her why she continued to go out with him, and she said he'd been quite an experience, but she was probably going to move on sometime soon.'

Chris hunched his shoulders. 'He left a suicide note on his laptop.'

CJ took a stool, helping himself to a scone. 'His body was found hanging from a dressing-gown cord via a hook behind his bedroom door. A chair had fallen over beside him. There was indeed a suicide message on his computer. I believe the police will think he killed Tomi after an argument, stuck a syringe into her to make it look as if she'd tried drugs, and dumped her out in the country. They think it was he who sent the texts from her phone, to give himself some sort of alibi and stave off enquiries from her friends and workplace.'

Bea made a big pot of tea. 'So where's her mobile? And where's his? Did they find them at Harry's?'

'They haven't finished searching yet. If they don't find them, they'll say he got rid of them after texting the police and Chris last night.'

Maggie shook her head. 'I suppose that makes sense. How horrible. I don't think he treated her well—'

'Plus,' said Chris, 'he was all over someone else as soon as she was out of the way.'

Maggie nodded. 'But why would he want to commit suicide?'

'The only person he ever loved was himself,' said Chris. 'He didn't love Tomi, and he didn't love Hermia. He fancied being seen around with them, that's all.'

'Nevertheless,' said CJ, round a mouthful of scone, 'I think the police will accept the easy option. Maggie, just to tie up loose ends, did Harry have access to anyone selling drugs?'

'Well, I suppose we all did or could have done. I mean; they are around if you want them. Someone told me, ages ago, that you only had to ask and someone would know someone who could help you.'

'Can you point out any names of people Harry might have had contact with?'

'I suppose so.' She rustled through her papers, then pushed them away from her. 'No, I don't believe it. None of it. If Tomi died of a drug overdose, then someone else gave it to her without her knowledge, and if Harry committed suicide, then I'm a . . . a Polish plumber!'

'Agreed,' said Bea. 'CJ, what can we do to help?'

'Nothing, my dear. Let the police deal with it from now on.'

'Tomi's parents?'

'I've given the police her laptop. That gives them her parents' email address, and the police will inform them of what's happened.'

Bea poured out tea. 'What about Miss Drobny? She's still holding all Tomi's belongings.' And has already let her room again.

'They'll see to all that.'

Chris stared at his empty plate. 'I know you'll say it's not rational, but I feel responsible. My vanity caused me to drop out of university, where I might have learned something useful, just so that I could show off and make a film. To do this, I made use of my friends and trespassed on my father's good nature. My inflated ego! I thought myself no end of a genius when I won that prize. I thought the world was going to beat a path to my door, asking me to direct the next Hollywood blockbuster. Idiot that I am!

'On top of that, as the police have pointed out, I've been making a fool of myself rushing around after Harry, actually hitting him. Stupid! Stupid! And now what? I've no job, no place at university, no stomach for making another film, no car. Not even a mobile phone, as I had to leave mine with the police. I can't help feeling Tomi wouldn't have died if I hadn't picked her out to star in my film. I feel responsible. And you tell me that I can't do anything to put things right?'

There was a long silence while Chris looked out over the snowbound garden, and CJ looked at him. CJ would want Chris to return to university, of course. Would he? No, thought Bea; probably not. And if he does, I'll think less of him.

Chris shook his head, more at himself than anyone else. 'I got into the film-making without thinking it through, without any proper training. But I do have a flair for it. I think I'd better sign up for some courses, or get a job as a gofer with some film company or other. Start at the bottom.'

Bravo, thought Bea. 'There is something else you can do, Chris. I'll bet you've got some unused footage of Tomi. You could splice it together with the best bits from the film and put it all on a DVD for her parents.'

Chris nodded and helped himself to a scone. The lines of strain around his eyes remained, but he tried to smile. 'Wouldn't you know, I put Hermia's phone number on my mobile and said I'd ring her tonight. Now I can't even do that.'

Maggie pushed one of her sheets of paper towards him. 'Oh yes, you can. I've got her number here. Simone gave it to me.'

Sunday evening

'Hush a bye, baby . . .' Claire rocked the baby in her arms, smiling to him. He smiled back, well fed, clean and sleepy. 'Time for bed, little one'.

She'd agreed to work this evening, while his parents went out. In a few days' time she would pass out of his life for ever. Did she regret moving on all the time? Yes, sometimes, but the future was rosy.

She'd dropped in on the agency that morning to see if there was anything of interest, and they'd offered her a couple of places which weren't suitable because they wanted her to live in.

Her darling boy would be back soon and was taking her out on Wednesday. Hurray. She knew she had a mountain to climb still; his friends weren't all that keen on her, and there was always the childhood girlfriend in the background, though she wasn't as much of a threat as she had been. Not since Claire had introduced him to her way of making love.

She laid the baby down in his crib. He protested, but not much. She watched him fight off sleep, and fail.

She tidied the room, thinking that since she had two more nights to herself, she could use it to tackle someone else on her list. Excitement rose in her. Who should it be? Little Nick, probably. Dapper little Nicky-wicky, with his high-pitched, penetrating voice and bottom-pinching habits. He wore pinstriped suits with silk ties, but never picked up the tab in a restaurant or paid for his round in the pub. Took home a giant's salary, ran a Porsche, but kept the central heating turned down really low at home. He complained about the housekeeping bills and told his wife to buy her clothes in charity shops. No wonder she'd filed for divorce and was currently pursuing him for everything she could get in the law courts.

Claire would bet on his having stashed lots away in offshore accounts somewhere, just so's his wife couldn't get at it.

Yes, little Nick should be next. Little Nick should be easy.

SEVEN

Sunday evening

Chris and CJ stayed for supper, of course. They talked about Harry for a while, before moving on to discuss Oliver's return home and what sort of training Chris might go in for. CJ and Bea were mostly silent.

Oliver phoned, and Bea arranged a time to collect him. Later, she rang Max, who might be back from the Midlands by now, only to find he'd switched to his answerphone. She left a message, but no promise to dash over there to housekeep for them, because she was going to be busy the following day. She ached to think of the baby, her darling little grandchild, wailing unhappily to himself, but there . . . her interference had only made matters worse, hadn't it?

Only when their guests had gone, and Maggie was packing dirty dishes into the dishwasher, did Bea approach the delicate question of who had helped Maggie with her research. It would have been easy for the girl to say she'd had a friend call who'd volunteered to help, but Maggie hadn't mentioned it, which might mean that Zander – her on-off boyfriend – had been involved.

Zander was an intelligent, handsome man of mixed race, who'd found himself a job he liked and was climbing the career ladder. He was sensible, sensitive and serious about Maggie.

Maggie had been brought up by a petite, fluffy mother who'd denigrated her tall daughter at every turn. Maggie's father had disappeared into the woodwork when his daughter was two, which – having met the mother – Bea didn't find surprising. Maggie hadn't had much sense of self worth even before a short-lived marriage to a man who'd carried on criticizing her where her mother had left off.

In her late twenties, Maggie ran as fast as she could from commitment to men.

Zander patiently followed. An interesting situation. Bea's money was on Zander in the long run.

'So,' said Bea, 'if you didn't want us to know that Zander had helped you, why didn't you give him a black biro to match yours, instead of letting him use a fountain pen with blue ink in it?'

'Mm?' Maggie blushed to the roots of her spiky hair. 'Oh. Well. I told him about Tomi, and he offered to help. So he took some names, and I took others. I'm afraid my phone ran out of credit so I used your landline for a while. He put some more money on mine, so it's working again now. Sorry about that. I'll repay you, of course.'

'Nonsense. Thank you, Maggie. I'd never have thought of ringing around like that and getting people to talk, and I'm glad Zander wanted to help.'

'He's not my boyfriend.'

'Of course not.' Tread carefully here. 'But he's a very good friend and I like him.'

'So do I. Not *that* way, of course, but as a friend. He said that what we did was like dropping a stone into a pond. The ripples would fan out and reach all sorts of people who knew Tomi in different ways, and that some of them might then phone back to whoever told them about her death, and they might then contact us. The only thing is that the landline might be busy for a while, maybe even a few days.'

'All right by me, but won't it interfere with your work schedule?'

Maggie stretched and grimaced. 'I'll make it up somehow. If Oliver comes home tomorrow, maybe he can help me out. That is, if he's not above such things, what with doing so well at uni and winning prizes and stuff.'

Bea was anxious. 'Perhaps we ought not to ask him to help?'

'Nonsense,' said Maggie. 'He was fond of Tomi, too.'

Monday morning, Cambridge

The weather was atrocious, making it doubly difficult to stow all Oliver's gear into the car. It was just as well that Maggie hadn't come, for there wouldn't have been any room for her.

Oliver looked well, and Bea thought he might even have grown another half inch. She wanted to put her arms around him and give him a hug, but this handsome young man, so poised and confident, didn't bear much relation to the skinny little outcast whom Maggie had dragged home over a year ago.

Bea found herself talking about the weather. Absurd.

He seemed to feel awkward with her, too. After all, she wasn't his birth mother – whoever she might have been. In his second term at uni he'd immersed himself in some weird and wonderful research project which was totally beyond her understanding, but which was already gaining him kudos in his rarefied field of higher mathematics. He'd moved further away from the nest, and she wasn't sure he'd still welcome a hug and a kiss.

When all his bits and pieces had finally been stowed inside the car and his bicycle lashed to the roof rack, she looked up at the sky and grimaced. 'Shall I drive the first leg?' The snow had turned to sleet. The main roads had been gritted and the motorway would be all right, but the rain made driving difficult.

Oliver had passed his driving test at the first attempt but, like other university students, used a bicycle to get around town. He wouldn't have driven a car for some months and might be rusty at the wheel.

As they fastened their seat belts, he gave her a big smile. Only then did she relax. 'You're growing up so fast.'

'You look just the same. You never change.'

She laughed and shook her head. She had her bad days, like everyone else. 'Tell me how to get out of this one-way system.'

'Turn right at the end here. I've had Chris and CJ emailing me, both worried about Tomi. Have the police been informed? What do you think has happened to her? Can you tell me exactly what's going on? Keep going. I'll tell you when to turn left.'

'I wish I knew. It started when Chris wanted me to find his library books. No, it started before that, but this is hearsay, right? Needs checking.' She proceeded to tell him everything she had heard and learned. And, as they left the city and approached the motorway, she went on to tell him what she'd seen and heard for herself.

It started to rain in earnest, and he suggested taking over the driving. They changed over at the next motorway services, but she didn't continue her story until she was sure that he could cope with the difficult driving conditions.

' — and there it is. The official line is that Harry killed Tomi and, when her body was discovered, killed himself. Her parents are being informed and will no doubt remove her effects from Miss Drobny's place in due course. Maggie has produced lists of names, one or two of whom might have been dealing with drugs at some time, but that's all they are: lists of names. Chris refuses to go back to university. He says he'll pick up the pieces of his film career, try to get himself some training. CJ seems to be holding a watching brief.'

'Inconsistencies?'

Bea stared ahead. Driving in heavy traffic in a rainstorm was not easy, yet she felt safe with Oliver at the wheel. He was a few months younger than Chris, but much more dependable, and intelligent in an entirely different way.

'Things I would like the police to look at? Missing mobile phones. Tomi's and Harry's. At least, Harry's might have been somewhere at his place, and I just didn't see it. On Saturday morning there was dust on the table at Harry's and crumbs on the carpet. By Sunday the crumbs had been cleaned up, the dust removed. Would someone about to commit suicide bother to do that? Oh, I don't know. It's probably all right.'

He drove on in silence. Only when he was parking the car outside their house did he speak again. 'Would you like me to look at what was on her laptop?'

'I looked and couldn't see anything significant. But yes; you'd be better at it than I.'

'It was brilliant of Maggie to tackle Tomi's friends. Would you like me to look at her lists?'

'You're on holiday now. Making sense of Maggie's lists would take up a lot of your time. Are you sure?'

'I liked Tomi; she was a very real person. And thank you for looking after Chris for me. He needs someone. An anchor? I'm putting it badly.'

Bea laughed. 'Be prepared for a new, earnest, down-to-earth Chris, who may be in the process of acquiring a proper girl-friend.' She got out of the car and stretched. A tiresome journey, and she was both hungry and thirsty. What had she planned for lunch? She couldn't remember.

The pavements glistened with slush. If the temperature

dropped tonight, there would be ice everywhere tomorrow. As she bent to help Oliver unload the car, they were surrounded by people shouting a welcome, hugging and kissing Oliver; everyone was talking at once. Maggie was there, and Chris. Of course Chris would be there. Zander was taking a box of books from Bea, while yelling at Oliver that it was about time he came home. There was CJ, wryly smiling, removing Oliver's laptop from his grasp. Maggie was dancing up and down, shooting questions at Oliver while disentangling his bicycle from the luggage rack, and here came Miss Brook up from the agency office. Surprise, surprise! 'My dear boy, how good to see you again!'

Oliver was laughing, too, as a chain of people removed his belongings from the car and bore them into the house. Bea had a bundle of bedding in her arms, which was taken from her by someone, she wasn't sure whom. Then she was being urged up the steps and into the house, where everyone seemed to be talking at once. CJ was opening a bottle of bubbly, wouldn't you know, and Maggie screamed something about bringing food in from the kitchen, and dear Miss Brook was holding on to Oliver's arm and shaking it, trying to tell him all about the new girl they had working for them. Chris was bobbing up and down like a jack-in-a-box, yelling that they must have a party that night, of course they must!

Babel. But after the champagne had been drunk and Maggie's individual pizzas consumed, the crowd dispersed; Maggie and Zander went back to work, as did Miss Brook. CJ took Chris away, and the house was quiet again.

Some of Oliver's belongings had been whisked up to his room on the top floor, but some had been left in the hall. Bea toiled upstairs with a box of books, to find Oliver standing at the window, surrounded by piles of belongings which were clearly not going to fit into the available storage space. He turned to her and held out his arms. She hugged him tightly. There were tears in his eyes.

He said, 'I never in all my life . . . I never dreamed . . . Such a homecoming. Better than at Christmas, even.'

'Don't look back. This is your home and we are your family now.' She thought of Max, of her frosty daughter-in-law and tiny grandson, and held back a sigh. In some ways

Maggie and Oliver were more of a family to her than her own flesh and blood.

'I've always called you Mrs Abbot. I can't call you by your Christian name.'

'I don't care what you call me, as long as you treat this as your home. I was afraid you'd grow out of us. Silly me.' She flicked a tear off her cheek.

He tried to smile. 'I was afraid you wouldn't want me here any more.'

'Silly.' She gave him another hug, then looked around her. 'What are we going to do with all your stuff?'

The phone rang downstairs, and she had to leave him to answer it.

It was Max, who had returned home desperate for Bea to fetch something from the shops for Nicole, who'd gone back to bed to try to catch up on some sleep. He'd tried to get Nicole's mother to come down to look after them for a while, but she was too busy with preparations for some dinner party or other. Was a dinner party more important than one's grandson? Well, really!

'Yes, of course I understand, Max, and I would come, but not this afternoon. I simply can't get away today.' She started to think how she might manage it. 'Perhaps if I ask Miss Brook to . . . No, she's got her hands full. I've been out all morning, you see, collecting Oliver from—'

'I would have thought you'd give me priority.'

'Yes, I do. I will.' She grimaced, thinking she was going to have to work late again tonight, if she took more time off now. 'I'll be over as soon as I can, for an hour, no more.'

'Surely you can do better than that. I wouldn't ask but . . . I can't bear it when Nicole cries, and Pippin just keeps on wailing. I'm at my wits' end.'

Greatly daring, she said, 'I could get you a day nanny.'

'You know Nicole can't give him up to anyone else.'

'I'll see what I can do.' Bea sighed. Replaced the receiver. Rubbed her forehead.

Oliver had come in behind her, noiselessly. 'Shall I help Miss Brook out for a couple of hours?'

'No, no. That's not your job now. But I have to go out. It's Pippin, you see.'

'Let me help. I'd like to. I'll take a look at Maggie's lists, too.'

'It's your first day back. I wouldn't have thought . . .
Anyway, your life must be so different now.'

He laughed. 'I know which side my bread's buttered. If I
don't muck in, I'll get no supper from Maggie, right?'

'She's out on a big renovation job. It's my turn to cook.'

'Now I know I'm back. Everyone dashing out in different
directions, no time to cook, and nothing in the freezer. So it's
my job to organize a takeaway, right?'

'Nonsense. Maggie and I have been filling the freezer with
food prior to your return. There's a big chicken pie with
home-made stuffing balls currently defrosting in the kitchen
for tonight's supper. If I'm not back in time, would you be
a dear and pop it in the oven at six o'clock? Maggie'll do
the vegetables when she gets back.'

'I'm impressed.'

'Remind me sometime to give you some cooking lessons.
No man should be launched on the world without knowing
how to boil an egg.'

She picked up her coat, her handbag – where were her keys?
Oliver handed them to her. She made it to the hall, hesitated.
'I suspect Chris might join us and possibly CJ.'

Oliver nodded, making shooing movements. 'Understood.'

She got to the front door, turned back. 'And possibly
Zander?'

'Very possibly Zander. We're all going to the pub afterwards.
It's Chris's birthday, remember.'

She hit her forehead. 'I'd forgotten. You're not holding a
party?'

'We're organizing something for later on in the month. Go,
Mrs Abbot, go! Before your son rings again.'

She went. At Max's place she tidied, hoovered, and dusted.
Did some shopping. Made up Pippin's formula while wishing
she had the nerve to substitute a different one; but no, she
couldn't do that, could she? Instead, she followed Nicole's
instructions to the letter.

With gathering anxiety, she noticed that Pippin was fretful,
and not – at least to her eye – putting on weight. And Nicole?
Instead of resting, Nicole was either hanging over Pippin's
cot or on the phone to her guru, going through a checklist of
the regime the baby was supposed to be following. Pippin
wailed. Nicole wept.

Bea set her teeth, cleaned the shower tray, took out the rubbish. Another thing; Nicole wasn't eating properly. Bea knew, because she'd done the shopping and the washing up, and although Max might have eaten a takeaway curry, Nicole certainly hadn't.

Bea ironed for half an hour. Nicole was using proper nappies, which was much greener than the expensive nappy pads sold in supermarkets, but was labour intensive. Nicole said all Pippin's nappies must be ironed before use, but it wasn't Nicole who was having to iron them, was it? Surely no one ironed nappies nowadays, did they? Bea almost chucked the iron at her daughter in law. Max was out. Of course.

Finally, Bea said she had to go, and Nicole wept once again. She always seemed to be in tears at the moment.

'Look, Nicole,' said Bea, trying to moderate her tone from firm to gentle. 'You're making yourself ill, going on like this. If you go down with a bug or have to be hospitalized, what will Pippin do?'

'If you'd only help me, I wouldn't get in such a state.'

'I am helping you. I have been. As much as you will let me help. It's not enough, is it? And I do have my own business to run. Why don't you let me find you someone to come in and look after you every day? Just for a few weeks? Then you can relax and devote yourself to Pippin.'

'You're saying that I'm a bad mother?'

'No, of course you're not. I can see you'd lay down your life for Pippin. But—'

'Then don't interfere. I can't stand it. Every time you come here, you criticize me; maybe not openly, but behind my back to Max.'

Bea held on to her temper. Then she softened. 'My dear, every grandmother thinks they know best, and of course things change and I'm not up to date with the latest in child care. But I do see that all is not well with you, and Pippin is not putting on weight, is he? Don't you think that—'

'I'd like you to go now. Please.'

Nicole stood up and went to the front door to let Bea out. So Bea had to go, frustrated, unhappy, not knowing what to do or say. Except pray. *Dear Lord above, help!*

She drove back home, slowly and with great care. She was

exhausted. There were more showers of rain, and the temperature had dropped. The roads were slushy, the pavements becoming treacherous.

The house was quiet when she let herself in. No Maggie banging around in the kitchen. No messages on the answerphone. She checked that the security grilles were all locked into place and drew curtains against the night.

She descended to the agency rooms, to find them empty. Miss Brook and her team had gone for the day, but someone was talking . . . laughing . . . loudly. In Bea's own office. Ah, of course. Oliver's old office had been taken over by Maggie, so he must be using Bea's. Yes, he was.

Oliver was sitting at her desk, entering data into her computer while listening to Chris, who was striding about, animated, gesturing, full of life. '—so you see, it's all to play for, really.'

Oliver grinned at Bea. '"Who's been sitting in my chair?" said Mummy Bear.'

Bea hadn't thought she could laugh, but did. 'We'll get Maggie to move some of her stuff out of your office tomorrow. Her method of filing is to cover every surface in sight with papers, but she actually does most of her work on the kitchen table.'

'Mrs Abbot, Mrs Abbot!' Chris, bounding up to her. 'Guess what? Hermia thinks she might be able to swing some funding for me to start my next film.'

Would Hermia fund it herself? N–no, possibly not. But she certainly had access to money. Bea smiled, tried to be bright. 'That's excellent news, Chris. And, by the way, happy birthday, too.'

Chris was halfway up the stairs. 'I bought another mobile this afternoon. It's in my overcoat. I think. I'm going to ring around, see how many of the crew might be available.' He disappeared.

Oliver exited the programme he'd been working on and shut down the computer. 'Mrs Abbot, Miss Brook and I agree you've been overdoing it. Business is in boom time, says Miss Brook. She says you need to take on another part-timer, someone who can keep Maggie's work straight as well as coping with some of the agency work. Oh, and she's forbidden me even to think of doing anything in the office. She seems to think I've suffered a sea change, and that agency work is now beneath me.'

Bea's head was aching. 'My dear boy; knowing you, you'll do exactly as you please, no matter what anyone says.' She rubbed her forehead, went to look out at the garden . . . except that it was now dark outside. She checked that the safety grille over the windows was locked there as well and drew the curtains.

Oliver straightened some papers on her desk. 'I've had a quick look at Maggie's lists of names while Chris was yakking at me. You realize that they weren't particularly open with you about taking drugs themselves?'

'I did wonder, because he's the sort to experiment with anything and everything, just to see what it's like. I'm not sure about Maggie.'

'Chris has an excellent constitution,' said Oliver. 'No ill effects. Once he'd experienced this and that and could evaluate the results, he filed the information away and moved on. Maggie tried cannabis, didn't like the results, hasn't tried anything else. Both know where to get drugs from, but won't tell. I . . . Well, it's not my scene.'

Of course not. Oliver was too fastidious. Wouldn't willingly hand control over himself to anyone else. 'You know who supplied them?'

He pointed to a couple of names, which he'd underlined. 'I've heard tell. These two names are on most of the lists. CJ rang earlier, said he'd be round to see what I've found, if anything. He's waiting for the result of the autopsies.'

'Did you know Harry?'

A shrug. 'I met him at a party once. Not my sort. Tomi said he was just a little boy inside, playing at being grownup. I couldn't see it myself.' It was a long time since Oliver had grown up. In years he might not match Harry, but in experience, oh yes. 'He didn't treat Tomi as a person, but as a Barbie doll. Which she wasn't.'

'How did they meet, do you know?'

'A party at the top flat above where she lived; they have parties there almost every weekend.'

Ah. Yes, of course. Bea had experienced the fallout from the party in the top flat when she'd called on Miss Drobny.

'He – they call him "Von", which I think is a reference to the fact that his parents came from northern Germany originally – works at the BBC, doing stunts. His partner

Simone works there too, in the wardrobe department. They know all sorts. One of Chris's old girlfriends knew them, and invited him. Chris took me and Maggie along once, but we didn't last long. He shed the girlfriend, collected Tomi and we all went on to see a comedy turn in a pub somewhere. I never went back, but Chris did, I think. It was too noisy for me.'

'Interlocking circles,' said Bea. 'What's the common denominator?'

'Girls and boys come out to play; have fun, don't take it seriously. Bring a bottle; don't make a scene or throw up till you get outside. See the girls home safely, and if you strike lucky, make sure you both know what you're doing.'

'So you can be invited to one party by a friend, and the next week you know of another party somewhere else, and maybe invite the first host on to the next party?'

'You probably wouldn't do that, no. But you might see some of the same people at the next venue. Some people never host a party. Others keep open house every weekend. Quite often a crowd meet up at a pub and move on to wherever there's word that they're welcome. Sometimes the news of a party goes up on Facebook, and then hundreds may come. That's not usual, but it does happen.'

'In private houses?'

'Usually not, because that's when people you don't know gatecrash and houses get trashed. In the summer you get outdoor gigs, in a field somewhere if the weather's good.'

'Out at Fulmer? Is that why Tomi was left in a lane near Fulmer?'

'I hadn't heard of one out that way, no. Chris, Maggie and I went out to a pub in Fulmer last summer a couple of times. Pretty place. Quiet. Good beer.'

'Tomi wasn't with you?'

He hesitated. 'I think she came with us once, but I didn't always want to socialize, so she might have gone out with them at other times as well. But that's not the sort of party you're thinking of, is it?'

'Chris holds parties sometimes?'

'He used to.' Cautiously. 'Until one night there was some damage. I think the carpet and an armchair had to be replaced, and a table repolished. His father said Chris must limit himself to small numbers in future; ten, I think he said. Not sure that Chris had any more parties after that, though he wants to arrange something special in a couple of weeks' time to celebrate his birthday.'

'Neither Maggie nor you are really involved in his film-making, but you'll be invited to his birthday party. How many other circles does he access?'

'He makes friends easily.'

Which was more than Oliver did. On the other hand, friends like Maggie and Zander were good for all weather conditions, which might not apply to those whom Chris gathered around himself.

Bea sighed. 'I give up. Let's have supper, shall we?'

He switched off lights, held the door open for her to precede him. 'I envy him, really. I've stood on the sidelines, cold stone sober, watching him walk into a party and become the focus of the room. I've tried to join in, but I can't. I'm a regular party-pooper, they say.' He smiled, disguising discomfort. 'Same applies at uni. Luckily there are other people there who prefer jazz and conversation to getting drunk. Some of us are really into modern jazz, all curved bits and wobbly pieces. Not everyone likes it, but I'm learning to appreciate it. I promise not to play it too loud.'

'My dear boy! That's wonderful. This house is so well built that if you shut your bedroom door, I won't hear it. Or if I do . . . Well, I can always buy some earplugs, can't I?'

'No, no.' He reddened. 'I can mute it. So . . . shall I put the pie in the oven now?'

Monday evening

'*Nick, is that you? Claire here. I'm just on my way home, but the Mini's playing up again and, as you know, my beloved's not around. I wonder, didn't you say you knew some garage that would look at a car and not charge an arm and a leg?*'

'*What? Who? Oh, Claire. Caught me at a bad moment, I'm afraid.*'

'*You sound as if you're going down with something. Not the dreaded flu?*'

'*No, no. It's – the thing is, you won't have heard, but it's quite a shock. Harry's dead. I had to phone him at work about*

*something, only to hear he hadn't come in. They phoned me
back later. He pulled the chain, committed suicide. Yesterday.'*

'*What? You mean Tomi's boyfriend, Harry?*'

'*Who else? Anyway, he'd given her the chuck, hadn't he,
and the rumour is – not that I believe it, mind you—*'

'*I'm shocked. Oh, oh!*' *Stifled tears. Beautifully done.
Effective.* '*Oh, I'd better not try to drive when I'm crying. Oh
dear, I nearly crashed into the car in front.*'

'*Claire, are you there? Are you all right?*'

'*Yes, I suppose . . . Oh, that's terrible. Can I park here? I
don't think I'm safe to drive. Oh, I'd better leave the car here,
take a taxi home. Oh, if only my beloved were back. I can't
bear the thought of being alone, all by myself, when such
terrible things are happening. You men are so strong, can
cope with anything, but oh dear, whatever shall I do?*'

'*I'm having a stiff drink, I can tell you.*'

'*I don't like going to the pub by myself. Oh dear, oh dear!
And yet, tonight of all nights, I wouldn't mind—*'

'*Where are you?*'

'*I think . . . Just round the corner from you. Yes, that's right.
In the next road. Lucky to find a parking place at this time
of night. Oh, I'm all of a tremble, silly me.*'

'*Why don't you pop round, then? We can drown our sorrows
together.*'

A sniff. Blow nose. '*Ten minutes? You are so good to me,
Nick!*'

*Turn off engine. Check make-up. Locate bottle of good stuff
in handbag. Practise a mournful look, put on the Little Me
persona, damp down the excitement. Nick should be a doddle.
His bitterly fought divorce was going to make the perfect
excuse for suicide.*

EIGHT

Bea wasn't particularly surprised to find that there would be a full house for supper. Maggie and Zander, CJ and his son Chris, herself and Oliver, plus Winston the cat. Winston had his own dish of cat food on the floor but liked human food as well.

Six made a tight fit around the kitchen worktop, but they managed. Whoever was nursing Winston prevented him from actually eating off their plates, and he managed to beg enough titbits to satisfy himself.

Bea did suggest, half-heartedly, that they use the proper dining table in the big room, but was shouted down. Perhaps CJ might have been more comfortable on a proper chair instead of a stool but, as he'd invited himself, it didn't matter, did it?

'Tell me,' said Bea to Zander as he was stacking the dishwasher, 'I'm trying to work out how people with different interests get to know one another. For instance, how did you come to know Tomi?'

'I was in the pub up the road with Oliver when Tomi came in with Harry. While Harry got their drinks, Oliver introduced me. I'd seen her before somewhere, but couldn't place her for a while, and she felt the same. Eventually we worked out that we'd both been at a church International Evening. She'd been on the tea urn, and I was stewarding. We didn't attend the same church, but it was another link.'

Bea tried to work out distances. 'The pub up the road is some way off Harry's place and even further away from Tomi's.'

'It's fashionable,' said Oliver. 'Harry liked to be at the right place at the right time. He knew some of the others who go there. Brian, who lives up the road—'

Chris jumped in. 'That's who I was talking to, when I last

saw Tomi. I wonder if we can get hold of him, ask him if he remembers who she went over the road to see?'

'Hold on a minute,' said Bea. 'How did Brian know Harry?'

Chris shrugged. Zander looked puzzled. 'I don't know Brian, do I?'

Maggie clattered knives and forks into the dishwasher. 'I think I know Brian by sight. How do you know him, Chris?'

'Through the Health Club. Father owns a race horse. You remember him, Oliver?'

'Vaguely. But—'

The landline rang, and Maggie swooped on it. 'I'm expecting one or two people to ring back about Tomi. I said after supper, and so . . . Yes, it's me. Hi. You got my message?'

CJ collected Bea and Oliver with a flick of his eyebrow. He was the only person Bea knew who could dominate when he chose and be invisible at other times. She led them out of the kitchen and into the big living room. He shut the door and gestured that they should take a seat. Even in Bea's own house, he acted as if he were the host. 'A word. Not to go outside these four walls. Can I trust you?'

Bea and Oliver nodded. Of those left behind in the kitchen, Chris had a leaky tongue, and Maggie could be indiscreet at times. Probably only Zander could be trusted not to betray a confidence.

CJ steepled his fingers, looked over them. 'The autopsy on Tomilola. She was drugged with barbiturates – probably sleeping pills – then given an injection of heroin. Either would have killed her.'

The room was quiet.

A murmur from Oliver. 'Murder?'

CJ nodded.

'Rape?' from Bea.

CJ shook his head. 'No interference. Fully clothed as per your report of what she was wearing when last seen. No sign of a struggle. Her handbag was beside her, also the library books, which are – I'm sorry to say – rather the worse for wear since the weather has been inclement. Her credit cards were in her bag, but no cash or notes.'

Oliver said, 'If it was a robbery gone wrong, why did the murderer leave the credit cards?'

'The police believe that Harry took the cash because it was untraceable, and its absence would make it look as if Tomi's death were a robbery gone wrong. They think he might not have known how to sell the credit cards, which is why he left them behind.'

'Humph,' said Bea.

CJ ignored that. 'Tell me; what would *you* expect to find in a young woman's handbag nowadays?'

Oliver shrugged, but Bea concentrated. 'House keys, credit cards, wallet, travel pass, purse for change. Make-up, hair-brush, mirror, etcetera. MP3 player of some kind? Tissues, letters, bills – paid and unpaid. Perhaps a book of puzzles, or an electronic game? Pens, pencils. Something to read? Mobile phone, of course.'

'Anything else?'

'Address book and diary; something small enough to carry around with her. There were large ones among her belong-ings at the flat, but I think she'd carry smaller ones around with her for every day.'

Oliver agreed. 'She had both.'

CJ frowned. 'There was no small diary or address book. Everything else you've thought of is there; except for the mobile phone, of course.'

'Which the murderer took to use for himself? Or herself? Whichever. He or she used Tomi's phone in the first place to make people think the girl had gone off to France, then to lure Chris out to Fulmer late on Saturday or early Sunday. And we know she was dead by then.'

CJ looked at the clock. 'My bedtime. We'll keep in touch, right?'

Oliver wasn't ready to let go of the subject yet. 'What about Harry?'

'Autopsy tomorrow.'

Bea said, 'Did they find his mobile phone?'

'No.'

'I've heard,' said Oliver, 'that murderers sometimes collect trophies from their victims. I wonder if that's what's happening here. I mean, a murderer might well take Tomi's phone to use for themselves, but why take Harry's as well?'

CJ said, 'The two deaths may not be connected.'

A vague thought connecting mobile phones and diaries swam

around at the back of Bea's mind, but she couldn't make sense of it. Trying and failing to pin it down, she saw CJ out of the house. Oliver went to join the others in the kitchen, from which came the sound of laughter and voices. Someone was talking on the phone? Someone – Zander? – tapping on a keyboard. Entering the new data?

Bea decided not to interfere. She returned to the sitting room and went to sit at the table at the far end. She settled herself, leaning back to look up at the portrait of Hamilton, her second and much loved husband, which had been painted by Piers, who had been her first. Piers had swum back into her life of late, but Hamilton had gone on ahead, and she missed him terribly.

Hamilton had been accustomed to sit at that table to play patience with real cards. He claimed it freed his mind to operate on the back burner, while his conscious mind concentrated on moving cards around.

Bea tried doing the same thing. She got out a double pack of patience cards and dealt them out, eight cards across and eight down. Bottom cards face up. Turn over the rest of the pack in threes. Aces up and build on them.

She couldn't get the game out. Finally she put the cards away and looked up at the paint and canvas which was all she had left of her second husband, apart from memories. So many happy years. Hard work. Honesty. Laughter. Wisdom.

The eyes in the picture still seemed to be telling her that he loved her and valued her above rubies. She knew that if she got up and moved around the room, the eyes would follow her.

Hamilton had managed Max much better than she had. Max had looked up to him as to a father. Piers had never been much of a father, had he? Although, to give him his due, he did care for his son nowadays.

Nicole. Oh dear. What to do or say? Had Bea damaged even the fragile relationship they'd achieved over the years? The problem was – and here Bea had to talk severely to herself – that she had never really liked the girl. That afternoon, for instance, Bea had wanted to take Nicole by her bony shoulders and shake her till she rattled. Or slap her. Either. Or both.

Bea grinned. Of course, she wouldn't really do it. But oh, how she'd like to.

She scolded herself, half-heartedly. Bad girl, slap on wrist! Perhaps she'd better put in some praying time about Nicole.

Her mind wandered, and she found herself thinking of the girl Tomi, dying in a country lane. The method of her death spoke of premeditation. First stupefy with drugs, and then polish off with an injection.

Some medical knowledge there?

Bea turned her head to the door. The youngsters were leaving the house for the pub to celebrate Chris's birthday. She loved Oliver and Maggie dearly, but it was good to be alone for once. She let the silence fold around her and was soothed.

When she found herself yawning, she went up to bed and read for a while. Winston the cat followed her up and settled down to give himself a good wash and brush up. She stroked him absent-mindedly, and he gave her hand a good licking, too . . . which made her laugh.

She might doze off, but wouldn't be able to fall into a deep sleep until Oliver and Maggie were safely back home again. She heard them come in and checked the time on her bedside clock. Half eleven. Not bad.

She continued to read for a while, half hearing some music, but not being able to place it. Maggie always hooked herself up to her player when she wanted to listen to music. Could it be Oliver playing his radio? Ah, he'd mentioned he was into some modern jazz. Gracious me. But the sound was not too obtrusive. Quite sweet, in its own way. She didn't find it objectionable.

She put her book on the bedside table and in doing so knocked her bible to the floor. Bother. Various postcards acting as bookmarks had fallen out. More bother. She scooped them up and then, holding her bible, stared into space.

Her darling husband had had several bibles and had used them all at different times, but this had always been his favourite so it was the one Bea read every night – well, most nights, anyway. During his last illness he'd given it to her, writing in it a note 'with all my love'.

So, what had happened to Tomi's bible? When Bea had been looking through Tomi's belongings she'd picked up the bible, noted that there were various pieces of paper and cards stuck in it, and laid it aside to inspect later. According to Miss Drobny, Tomi's parents weren't strong Christians and might not want the bible. Probably the police had taken it, along with everything else belonging to the girl.

Only, if Tomi were anything like Bea, she might well have popped the odd note or even a photograph into her bible. It might be worth finding out.

Tuesday morning

The sky was bright blue, the sun shone, and the snow had melted away, leaving roads to turn a sluggish grey and then to dry. It was supposed to be an ordinary working day, but it didn't feel 'ordinary'. Maggie and Oliver told Bea what they were planning to do that morning, and Bea failed to register a word they said. She'd woken up knowing exactly what she'd done with Tomi's bible. She'd been half sitting and half crouching on the floor over Tomi's boxes, had wanted to have another look at the bible and so had put it behind her somewhere. On the floor? On a chair? In the hurry and bustle that had occurred after that, she'd forgotten the bible. It might still be there.

Of course, there was no reason to suppose it was important, but Bea felt driven to pursue the matter. Leaving Maggie and Oliver to squabble over the last piece of toast, she rummaged around in her bag to find Miss Drobny's telephone number. With any luck the woman hadn't left for work yet.

'Mrs Abbot here. I was hoping to catch you before you went off to work. Can you spare a moment? I've been wondering how you've been getting on. Is your new flatmate working out all right?'

'We manage. She will only stay for a while, I think. For the present, it's OK.'

'I understand. Have the police been?'

'Yes. It is a shock to hear Tomi is dead, though I think she must be. I was afraid I would be sick when I see her body, but it was not hard. Poor girl! So sad. The police look through her things, take all the paperwork and say her people can have the rest. My new flatmate is not happy to have all

Tomi's things still here. Also Tomi's parents telephoned me when they heard from the police. They want everything kept for them.'

'So what will you do?'

'I am putting all her things in storage and keeping the bill for the parents. They come to London soon, and then it will be finished, I hope.'

'Yes, of course. Now I remember your saying that Tomi's parents were not committed Christians. Do you think they will want her bible, because a friend of hers would really appreciate it? I seem to remember having left it somewhere in your sitting room, where it must be frightfully in the way.'

'I found it when you had gone. Do you want it still?'

'I would love to have it. Do you think I might collect it some time?'

'When do you come? I am off to work in a second, but I can leave it outside the front door if you like.'

'That would be very kind of you. I'll be over in half an hour.'

She clicked off her phone, only to discover Oliver was giving her an old-fashioned look.

She said, 'Sentimental of me, I know, but I didn't like to think of her bible thrown out in the rubbish. What did you say you were going to do today?'

'If it wasn't rape – and it wasn't; if it wasn't robbery – and clearly it wasn't a straightforward robbery – then why on earth was she killed? I can't get my head round it.'

'Neither can I. We're missing something. I'm going to collect her bible now. What will you do?'

'Look at what was on her computer.'

'All old stuff.'

'Did you connect it to the mains, see what new emails might have come in recently?'

Had she done that? She couldn't remember. 'Best of luck, Oliver.'

'Well, before I touch it, I'm going to finish correlating the information Maggie and Zander have collected and give the police the names of the people we believe may have been pushing drugs. That's one positive thing we can do.'

'It's a mess, isn't it?' Bea put on her big boots, collected keys, handbag and warmest coat, and left to collect Tomi's bible.

The house in which Tomi had lived was quiet and dark today. Presumably all the tenants had gone out to work by now. The steps down to Miss Drobny's flat were dripping with melted ice, but Bea managed them without taking a tumble. A used envelope containing Tomi's bible had been propped against the front door. Good.

Bea hefted the envelope in her hand. If she returned home, she'd find the agency rooms buzzing with queries and she'd be drawn into dealing with them as soon as she opened the door.

Also, there might be another call for help from Max; she dreaded hearing his voice nowadays. Don't think about poor little Pippin! She wrenched her thoughts away and took a deep breath. She couldn't help Pippin at the moment, and she needed to inspect the bible in peace and quiet.

She drove some way back towards home, found a parking space, and took her prize into a pleasant corner café. The windows had steamed up, but the Gaggia machine was working, the tables were clean and the place was almost empty.

She ordered a skinny latte and drew the bible out of the envelope. It seemed Tomi had bought it for herself, for there was nothing except her name on the title page. She'd had a firm signature and used black ink. Not a fountain pen, but a good ballpoint.

As Bea had noted earlier, the bible had been well used. A few pages had become dog eared, but Tomi had smoothed out the creases and there were no torn corners or other defacements.

There were half a dozen slips of paper marking various places in the bible, mostly in the Psalms or the New Testament. There were a couple of museum or art gallery postcards; one was of Dali's Crucifixion, in which Christ looks down on the world below. Another was of a Florentine angel. Both were cards which had been sent through the post to Tomi; holiday cards from friends at work? Bea skimmed through the messages on the back. Yes, that's what they were. Presumably the police would have contacted Tomi's workplace by now?

There were bible references scrawled upon a couple of slips of paper. Had the girl been asked to read the lesson in church sometime? It looked like it. There was just one piece of A4, folded over to fit inside the maps at the back. Something printed off a computer:

'I hereby promise to pay Leo one pound (£1) per week for six months. I promise to abide by the rules we agreed. I understand that I forfeit my share if I fail in any respect.'

Underneath were the words: 'Signed: Libra' and a space, followed by the words 'Witnessed' and 'Dated'. Neither the date nor the signatures had been filled in.

Presumably this was Tomi's copy of some sort of agreement with a person called Leo. Bea turned the paper over. There, in writing which matched Tomi's on the title page of the bible, was the name 'Leo' followed by a telephone number.

Was this, perhaps, some form of blackmail? No, surely not. Not for a pound a week. It wouldn't be worth it.

Perhaps a syndicate of some sort had been formed at work? Everyone put in a pound a week and some lucky person – chosen by lot each week – scooped the jackpot. If fifty people played, then someone got fifty pounds. Perhaps Tomi had joined a syndicate to play the football pools? Or the National Lottery? No, that wouldn't be like Tomi.

Ah, Bea had a better idea. This would be some kind of charity for which Leo was collecting. Save the Planet, Go Green, rescue abandoned pets, that sort of thing. Highly commendable. Except that the terms of the agreement didn't quite fit. Why the time limit?

Well, perhaps the charity wanted to raise a specific sum for something: to supply fresh water to an African village, or to purchase a heart monitor. Yes, that might be it. One pound a week seemed about the right sum. But what was that about Tomi forfeiting her share if she broke the terms of the agreement? Her share of what?

Bea read it again. 'Leo' was a man's name. Fine. Bea didn't know anyone called Leo, but presumably Tomi did and the name would crop up somewhere on Maggie's lists or in Tomi's diary. The small purse diary, which was missing, or the big one back at the flat?

Bea took a short cut and dialled the phone number on the back of the agreement. The phone was switched off: 'Please leave a message.'

'This is Mrs Abbot here. My son was a friend of Tomi's. I understand you have some sort of agreement with her. I'm not sure whether you are aware of it, but tragically she died a while back. The police will have the details, or you can ring me on . . .' And here Bea dithered whether to give her home or mobile number. The battery on her mobile was running low, so finally she gave the Abbot Agency office number.

That done, she returned to her scrutiny of the document. It was supposed to have been signed by someone called 'Libra'. Not by Tomi.

Ah. Libra and Leo were two of the signs of the zodiac, weren't they? So it was possible that they were nom de plumes, and that Leo's real name was something quite different, such as Ponsonby Smythe. He was probably male and, if you fitted the name to the personality behind the zodiacal name, Bea thought he might well be the leader or instigator of whatever arrangement it was they'd made. Leos were usually leaders, weren't they?

On the other hand, Librans were supposed to be level-headed, all-for-justice type of people. Could Tomi be described like that? Mm. Possibly. Perhaps it was her birth sign? Chris might know.

Bea sighed. Since the paper was not signed in any way, the 'Libra' referred to might not be Tomi at all, but someone completely different. Ah, but if so, why had Tomi stowed the paper in her bible? Putting it there must mean it was important.

It was a puzzle. Why the talk of 'rules', for instance? What rules? The whole thing smacked of mumbo-jumbo and secret societies, which wasn't like Tomi at all.

Bea read the form again. She held the paper up to the light. Reasonable quality paper, such as was used in millions of printers attached to computers. Watermark? No. Evenly printed in black, no colour. Font size twelve, Times New Roman, which was the most common. The printer was in good condition.

Bea put the paper back in the bible, popped the book back inside its envelope, finished her coffee and returned home.

Tuesday afternoon

Claire helped her employers to pack. Tomorrow morning early they'd be off to the airport and tenants would be taking over their flat. Unfortunately the new people didn't need a nanny, or Claire might have offered herself for the job.

Baby was sleeping peacefully, so Claire helped clear out cupboards and wash them down. She often said she didn't mind what she did, and it was true; she was frequently given clothing and cosmetics which were almost new, and which she couldn't possibly have afforded to buy on her salary. And medication, of course. All sorts. Even the hard stuff, now and then. She had to promise to dispose of the drugs safely, and promise she did.

Disposal was another matter.

She smiled to herself, cleaning round the shower in the en suite. She'd been running a little low on sleeping tablets, had used the last on dear little Nick the previous night. So it was really good to be able to replenish her stock.

Dear little Nicky-wicky. She'd played blindfold with him till he didn't know which was the floor and which the ceiling. Then she'd taken off the blindfold and given him a push . . . Oops, over the banister he'd gone. Tumbling head over heels. Poor little Nicky-wicky. If anyone had heard him fall, she'd have been ready with a sob story of trying to stop him committing suicide, but no one had stirred. So she'd cleaned up, left an appropriate note on his laptop, and had been safely tucked up back at home before her darling boy rang. He missed her terribly, he said. Good. He was looking forward to tomorrow evening. Even better.

She wasn't sure what she'd do about another job. Perhaps visit the agency again to see if there was anything going? Nothing too taxing, of course. After all, it wouldn't be long now . . .

It was only after she eventually got home and was playing with her mobile phones that she noticed someone had left a message on Leo's old one. That sent a chill through her. Whoever could it be?

Who was this Mrs Abbot? What was her son's connection to Tomi? Was she a threat? Or just a curious neighbour who could safely be ignored?

NINE

Tuesday afternoon

Bea put in a couple of hours' work down in the agency rooms before making some leek and potato soup plus ham sandwiches for lunch. Oliver had cleared his desk in the office which Maggie had been using – well, the one she'd been using in theory – and was totally immersed in computer-geek mode. Bea took him a mug of soup and a pile of sandwiches, which he reached out for without taking his eyes off the screen.

There was no sign of Chris, which was something of a surprise. No sign of Maggie, either; but to be fair, Maggie had said she really must find that wretched plumber and screw his head off that day or the new en suite would never be finished in time. Bea's money was on Maggie, who might run a mile from a man who had sex on his mind, but brought her projects in on time and within budget. It was a good sign that she'd allowed Zander to help her look for Tomi's killer.

Which reminded Bea of the paper she'd found in Tomi's bible. She pulled it out and found a clear folder to put it into. Perhaps there might be fingerprints on it which would help the police? Her own included, of course. She reread the paper and still couldn't make sense of it. While she was making some photocopies of it she heard her front doorbell peal. Oliver wouldn't go upstairs to answer the door when he was working; he never did.

Besides, Bea recognized that peal. It was either the police being heavy-handed, or CJ making sure he was let in.

It wasn't the police.

CJ wasn't carrying a bottle, but he had news. She took him into the sitting room, where he drifted around, hardly disturbing the air.

'You have bad news?'

He sighed, sat down, addressed the fireplace. 'The police have a great many important cases on. They are under stress

and undermanned. They are very happy to pursue the drug
dealers named in Maggie's lists. They see no prospect of a
conviction for the murder of Tomi since Harry admitted culp-
ability before he killed himself.'

'Oh. Did he really commit suicide?'

'There was a note to that effect on his laptop. According
to the autopsy, he took some drugs, put the cord of his dressing
gown around his neck while he sat on a chair behind his
bedroom door, fell off the chair – or pushed it away – and
strangled himself. Scuff marks on the carpet indicated that
he'd tried to pull himself up, but had tied the rope too tight
and so failed. He was probably out of it, anyway; comatose
from the drugs he'd taken.'

Bea sank into a seat. She was shocked. 'So they aren't
going to pursue either case?'

'No. Officially Tomi's case is down as a murder which was
committed by Harry, who needed to ditch her in order to curry
favour with Hermia. The call alerting the police to where
Tomi's body might be found came from Harry's mobile phone.
Case proved.'

'But, according to Maggie, Tomi wasn't all that smitten by
Harry and was preparing to move on.'

'Hermia has been questioned by the police, who says she
did agree to go out for the day with Harry last Saturday, but
wasn't serious about him. When she found he'd not even bothered to get dressed in outdoor clothes, she changed her mind
and went off with Chris. She cited witnesses, so you may be
asked to confirm that she did just that. The police have already
been round to ask Chris if he'd confirm that Hermia left with
him and was with him most of the day. Which he did. In the
early evening he saw her back to her place; confirmed by her
flatmate. Hermia then changed into evening wear and went
on to some charity "do" or other, as a partner to her old friend
Lord Fairley.'

'So her on-and-off boyfriend has a title? I suppose that
explains his attraction for her.'

'Don't be so cynical. He's a decent enough sort. Her appearance at the function is confirmed by a hundred people. She
stayed overnight with her host and hostess somewhere out in
the Home Counties. Confirmed.'

'So she dumped Chris to return to the titled one? Well, well.

You know that Chris is still in touch with her?' Bea sighed. 'I don't understand her. Does she play fast and loose with everyone?'

'Possibly. But she's in the clear as regards Harry's demise.'

'They're not trying to make out that Chris killed Harry, are they?'

'They did ask him where he was on Saturday night, but luckily he met up with some friends in the pub immediately after he left Hermia, so he's in the clear. No, the police are quite happy to leave it that Harry murdered Tomi and then committed suicide.'

'Humph!' said Bea, 'Which leaves Hermia believing that she was responsible for his death. She'll have a guilt complex from here to eternity.'

'She's a very well-balanced young lady,' said CJ, non-committally. 'On past form, she'll rise above it.' Of course, CJ would be pleased if Hermia had dumped Chris.

Bea said, 'I don't like it. Do you?'

'It's a neat enough outcome.'

'There were no prints apart from his on the laptop?'

'Only his. However, I was involved in another case some time ago where I was asked whether or not the defendant had left a damning message on his laptop. I did an experiment using the tip of a pen to depress the keys. I found I could type whatever I liked that way, and it hardly disturbed the existing fingerprints. On the other hand, I found there was a certain irregularity, a lack of rhythm in the key strokes, a hint that the message might have been typed by someone who was not an experienced keyboard user.'

'What you're saying is that someone else might have put the suicide note on his laptop without disturbing fingerprints Harry had put on it before?'

A hesitation. 'It is not easily provable. My evidence wasn't accepted in the case to which I refer, though it didn't make any difference to the result of the trial in the long run, since there was plenty else to convict the man.'

'So it's possible that Harry didn't type that message himself? Right. Well, what about his mobile phone? That was missing. Or have they found it somewhere? Also, the floor and table top had been cleaned. Surely that's proof that someone else was there after we left.'

CJ cleared his throat. 'Someone else might have been there quite innocently, perhaps even tried to divert him from committing suicide. When Harry hung himself they might have panicked, decided to remove all trace of their having been there, cleaned up and scarpered.'

'I don't believe that, and neither do you.'

'I'm not sure what I believe. What I do know is that there are no grounds for the police to look any further. They received the lists of names which Maggie put together and will give special attention to those who may have been dealing with drugs. That's about it, as far as they are concerned.'

Bea produced Tomi's bible and the original agreement. 'This might help to muddy the waters. It's Tomi's bible, which was left out of the boxes of her belongings by mistake. I don't think the police have seen it. I thought there might be some sort of clue in it as to how Tomi was thinking, and I found this paper in the back. I haven't the slightest idea what it means, but you might be able to work it out.'

He scanned the paper, looked at the back of it. 'Who's "Leo"?'

'The person who organized this game, or whatever it is they were playing? I tried his phone, left a message to ring me.'

'What!'

'Not a good idea?'

He frowned, shook his head. 'Well, it's done now. Probably this hasn't got anything to do with her death and Leo is not in any way involved, but I think I'd have been happier if you hadn't phoned him. Suppose he's the drug dealer who supplied the dose which killed her? Did you leave your name?'

Bea felt herself pale. 'I did. I never thought.'

'Well, well. It's probably nothing. Is there someone called "Leo" on the list of names Maggie got for us?'

'I don't think so. I'll check.'

Oliver tapped on the door and slid in. He could be as pussy-footed as CJ when he chose. 'I'm glad you're here,' he said to CJ. 'Did you get the latest emails that came through on Tomi's computer? I'm particularly thinking about those from her parents, who've been worrying about her. What are the police doing about it? Shouldn't they have been in touch with her people by now?'

CJ said, 'They have been. Her mother and father are flying over later this week.'

'Why did you ask me to check on her emails, then?' Oliver was not pleased. 'Anything else been happening that I don't know about?'

Bea said, 'Tomi's parents have been in touch with Miss Drobny, asking her to keep her things for them. She's putting everything in storage, which seems sensible to me. Apart from her bible.'

CJ handed Oliver the agreement. 'Here's something new. What do you make of it? It was in the back of Tomi's bible.'

Oliver read it, shook his head and shrugged. 'A charity appeal.'

Bea said, 'When is Tomi's birthday? Do you know?'

'Last autumn some time? I seem to remember there was some sort of celebration when they finished putting the music on the film, and it coincided with her birthday.'

'So she could have been a Libran?'

'I don't think she put much stock in that sort of thing.' He turned the folder over. 'Who is this Leo? Can he cast any light on things?'

CJ held out his hand for it. 'It's a forlorn hope, but I'll give the original to the police and check it out myself. I have to tell you, Oliver, that the police have closed the case. They think Harry killed Tomi because she'd become a nuisance and he was after Hermia. When Tomi's body didn't turn up straight away, he phoned the police to tell them where she might be found, and then killed himself. The phone call to the police definitely came from his phone. There really is no point in taking the matter further.'

'What? I don't agree. Surely they don't believe . . . I can see how it might look like . . . No, I just don't believe it. What about the text from Tomi's phone to Chris? Where is her phone, and where is his?'

Bea gave a little cough. 'I had a thought about that. I think the killer took the mobiles to conceal the fact that he'd rung his victim to make an appointment earlier. The caller's number would automatically come up on the screen, wouldn't it? So it was necessary to take the mobiles away after the murders. That might explain why Tomi's diary is missing, too. The killer might fear Tomi had jotted down that she was meeting so and so that day, which is why her diary is nowhere to be found. What about Harry's diary? Is it still there?'

'I'll check. But even if it's not there, I doubt your theory is strong enough to move the police to action.'

'It sounds right to me.' Oliver was more positive. 'We'd better ask Chris if Tomi took a phone call when he was with her that morning.' He looked at his watch. 'Chris is out now, at this very minute, trying to track Brian down. You remember Brian? The man who met Chris and Tomi in the street the last time he saw her outside the library? Chris knows roughly where he lives, in one of those big red brick blocks of flats up the road from the library, so he's going to see if he can find him—'

'Brian will be at work, won't he?'

'Yes, but if Chris can find someone who lives there, they may know which flat is Brian's, or even where he works.'

Bea said, 'There must be a hundred flats in those blocks, and they're all six storeys high, aren't they? Would any one person know anyone else, even if they used the same staircase or lift?'

'I know that, but Chris needs to try everything. You understand?'

'Wouldn't it be easier to track him down through the Health Club? He's a member, and so are you and Chris.'

Oliver struck his forehead. 'I'm not using my head, am I? Sorry. Yes, of course it would be easier. I'll see if I can catch up with him, stop him wasting time. We can go down to the Health Club together, make up some story about needing to contact Brian urgently. They're not supposed to give out addresses, but – we'll think of something.'

CJ got to his feet. 'Just remember that the case is closed in the eyes of the Law.'

'Is that justice?' Oliver tried to smile.

'You may not think it is, but it is the law.'

Bea pushed her hair back, and then swept her fringe across her forehead. 'We'll feel better when Tomi's been buried, no doubt. Meantime, it's back to work for me.'

'And for me,' said CJ, making a soundless exit.

Wednesday evening

The front doorbell rang, and in came Chris and Oliver, pushing a protesting man in his mid thirties before them. After a tiring day, Bea was not amused to see them.

Chris turned on the charm. 'I know, I know, Mrs Abbot. You've had an awful day with cleaners pretending they can cook, and butlers downing the port instead of decanting it. You've had society hostesses crying on your shoulder because they've no staff to run a charity event for six hundred, and your feet are killing you. But this –' he indicated his captive – 'is Brian.'

Bea had to laugh. 'How do you do, Brian. What can I do for you?'

'It's not for you, it's for Tomi,' said Oliver, steering them all into the kitchen. 'Will supper go around?'

'No, it won't,' said Maggie, pointing a spatula at them. Maggie was frying something and in no mood to admit intruders. 'Out of my kitchen, this minute.'

Chris changed direction and pushed Brian ahead of them into the sitting room. Bea laughed, shrugged and followed.

'I'm sorry, Brian. When these two take the bit between their teeth . . .'

'If I could help, I would.' Brian had a brawny physique, but perhaps not too many brains. He was dressed in a brown suit under a camel-haired overcoat. Tidy, but probably not a city type. He might, perhaps, work for an estate agent? What was it that Chris had said about him? Health Club. Yes, but there was something else, too. Ah. His father owned a share in a racehorse.

Chris pushed Brian into a chair, saying, 'You may think you don't know anything, but you do. After all, you must be the last person who saw Tomi alive.'

'I've told you, I don't know any Tomi and—'

Chris poked Brian's shoulder. 'You were talking to me in the street. I'd just come out of the library, remember? You came up the road from the High Street on your way back home. Now the girl I was with—'

'I don't know where she went.'

Chris turned to Bea. 'You see how he is. We can't get any sense out of him, so we thought you could have a go before we turn him over to the cops.'

'The police? Why? I haven't done anything.' He was not afraid, but he was angry and bewildered.

Bea sat down beside Brian and did her best to soothe him. 'I know you haven't done anything wrong. These two clowns know it, too. They've gone way over the top. Admit it, boys,' she said to them. 'You've behaved very badly. Fancy dragging your friend in here, and yelling at him—'

'We didn't yell, exactly.'

Bea ignored them, to pat Brian's hand. His hand was warm. No gloves. A macho man? Or trying to be? 'I'm so sorry. Would you like a sherry?'

Brian softened visibly. 'Well, I must say . . . Perhaps a small . . . ? I couldn't think what was going on. They practically kidnapped me outside my own front door.'

Bea handed him a glass of sherry and indicated to the boys that they should make themselves scarce. 'We're almost neighbours, then. You know Oliver and Chris from the Health Club, I gather? I'm afraid I don't take any exercise at all. Isn't that awful?'

Brian preened himself. 'Oh well. You probably did when you were younger.'

Bea restrained herself from slapping him and treated him to a wide-eyed look of admiration. Which he accepted. He drank his sherry and almost smiled. Looking around, he observed, 'Quite a nice gaff, isn't it?'

'Sure is,' said Bea, holding on to her smile. 'I must apologize again for the boys' behaviour. Their friend was a tragic loss. You are a man of the world –' was she overdoing it? Probably, but he was enjoying the flattery – 'and can understand how upsetting it is to lose someone you love.'

'Of course, of course.' He sipped sherry, allowed himself to relax, let his overcoat slide off his shoulders. 'It was just, being attacked like that . . .'

Bea shook her head, commiserating. 'Dreadful. Quite frightening, in fact.'

'Oh, well. I wasn't frightened.'

'Of course not. But they shouldn't have acted so high-handedly.'

'It wasn't even as if I could tell them anything.'

'Some more sherry? Yes? I quite understand. She was not one of your circle of friends.'

'That's it. Seen her around, of course. Seen the film, rather good in its way. Amateur, of course, but quite promising, I'd have said.'

'A striking looking girl.'

He nodded. 'Graceful, too. Perhaps a trifle on the skinny side. I like them, you know, a bit more . . .' He waggled his eyebrows.

Bea set her teeth. Of course he did. 'There she was, helping her friend out, carrying this great pile of books for him out of the library—'

'Is that what he said? No, no. A couple of books only. She tried to put them into her bag, one of those huge bags girls carry about with them nowadays, you know? But they were too big. The books, I mean.'

'The blue bag?'

A frown. 'No, green. Or perhaps it was brown. I was wearing my new dark glasses. Could have been blue, I suppose, but I thought it was green.'

'The sun was in your eyes. Of course.'

'No, I was facing north. She came out of the library with Chris. I know Chris, of course. Thought he might introduce me, as a matter of fact, but he didn't seem to want to. He was facing the sun so he moved round a bit, and the girl said something about seeing someone she knew. She waved to him and off she went.'

'Straight into the traffic? Oh dear.'

A gentle laugh. 'I didn't hear any grinding of brakes or shouts. No bumps. She wasn't run over or anything. No, no. She must have got to the other side of the road without causing an accident. Someone said she died of a drug overdose.'

'Oh, you know what "they" are. She was murdered, I'm sorry to say. The police think they've found the person who did it.'

'That's all right, then.' He put down his empty glass, shrugged himself back into his overcoat, and stood up. 'I suppose she got in with the wrong crowd. A sad story, but that sort of thing can happen to young girls who come over here, not knowing the score. And now—'

'You must be going. Of course.'

'If you can keep those two clowns from attacking me again?'

'I promise. And if at any time anything occurs to you . . . ?'

'I'll be in touch. Excellent sherry.'

Bea held on to her smile till she'd got him out of the front door, and then closed her eyes, went rigid and screamed. Silently.

Chris and Oliver watched her from the kitchen doorway, eyes rounded.

'Mrs Abbot, you're brilliant!' said Chris.

Oliver grinned. 'You'd have made a wonderful prosecuting counsel.'

'No, I wouldn't. We didn't learn anything.'

Chris sighed. 'We learned he didn't know anything.' He slumped against the wall. 'I did so hope he'd seen something. Now what do we do?'

'Supper's up,' said Maggie. 'For three. Chris, go home.'

'Chris, before you go,' said Bea. 'Did Tomi take a phone call while you were in the library?'

He put on his most angelic expression. 'The public are requested not to use their mobile phones in the library.' It was odds on he'd been told off for doing just that himself.

Bea almost laughed. 'Well, did she get a call while you were in the pub earlier?'

'Um, yes. Now you come to mention it, she did. She didn't say who it was from, and I didn't ask. Is it important?'

'It might have been the killer making an appointment to pick her up. Otherwise, how would he have known where to find her?'

'Ah. Makes sense. I'll tell my father, shall I?'

Maggie shrieked at him. 'Chris, go home!'

Chris went.

After supper Bea told herself that it was all wrong that she was at odds with her son and daughter-in-law. Perhaps she herself really was out of date and didn't know the best way to bring up a baby. She tried scolding herself.

What do you think you're playing at, upsetting Nicole like this? Is it worth it? Particularly since you're not getting your point across. Wouldn't it be better to apologize and eat humble pie, and even crawl, in order to maintain good relations?

She lifted the phone off the hook, hesitated, and put it back again. She strode about the room. She faced her husband's portrait and asked him, 'Well, what would you do?'

He seemed to smile back at her. He seemed to be saying

that she knew very well what she ought to do, and if it meant apologizing for doing something which she didn't feel sorry about, then she'd better just get on with it.

She had shut the curtains against the night – a nasty, wet, sleety night. The central heating was keeping the house at a pleasant temperature. The side lamps cast a warm glow over the old furniture. Everything within was as it should be – except for her relationship with her son and his wife – and the baby.

Dear Lord, give me patience? Or wisdom? Well, actually, both. I'm troubled in mind and spirit. What would You have done?

Mm. You'd calm and heal everyone in sight. Well, I'm definitely in the market for some peace of mind. Also for the right words to say.

I'm worried about Pippin. It's all very well for me to rant and rave at Nicole and Max, but whether I'm in the right or the wrong isn't all that important. Pippin is. I'm so afraid he's going to . . . No, that's ridiculous. He's not thriving as he might, but I'm sure Nicole's doctor will eventually tell them that a change of formula might . . .

No, I'm not at all sure, am I? In fact, I think their guru is a charlatan who ought to be dragged through the streets on a hurdle to be hanged, drawn and quartered at the Tower of London. Or pilloried in the media. Or something.

All right. I know we're not supposed to judge. I'll leave him to you to deal with. So am I to stand by and let Pippin fade away?

No, I can't do that. I know I'm an old busybody, poking my nose in where it's not supposed to go, but . . . Pippin is dying before my eyes. No, not dying! I didn't mean that. Please, dear God, I didn't mean that.

Please. Help me?

She lifted the phone and pressed buttons. Max answered. 'Oh, it's you, Mother. What do you want now? I've a very important meeting on tonight, and I ought to be on my way this very minute.'

'I just wanted to know—' In the very meekest of tones.

'Haven't you done enough damage? Nicole's so upset she's had to take a sleeping pill, which means I've had to look after my son.'

'Won't you allow me to help?'

'We've asked you to help, but when you come here you make more trouble than you're worth.'

'I am trying.'

'Very. Yes.' He put the phone down.

Bea put the phone down and stared into a future cut off from contact with her family. Her throat ached. Perhaps she was going down with something.

Wednesday evening

Claire listened, and sighed when he sighed – oh dear, how awful! – another of his close friends had died! But there, he still had her, didn't he? She knew how to turn the conversation, how to make him laugh and how to distract him. Just like handling a baby, really.

He took her out to his favourite restaurant. Expensive, of course. He'd always been generous. Then, at long last, he proposed. Would she consider . . . ? Of course she would. She cried tears of thankfulness. He called for champagne to celebrate.

He would introduce her to what remained of his family – a toffee-nosed lot who probably wouldn't be pleased at his choice, but would have to come round to it since he'd been playing the field for a long time – so long, in fact, that there'd been rumours he might be gay and so would never produce an heir. He rang his mother there and then to break the good news and arranged to take Claire down to his home in the country that weekend.

He wanted to know about her family; she'd anticipated this and said that tragically she hadn't anyone, since her parents passed away. Untrue, but she wasn't having him find out about the father she'd never known and her mother's various boyfriends. And especially not about the one who'd made her pregnant at fifteen, which had led to a botched abortion and her inability to conceive again.

She diverted him by telling him about her new job. The agency had rung her only that afternoon to ask if she could take on another family. The name of the client rang a bell. A hollow-sounding alarm bell. A Mrs Abbot, who'd been going round asking questions about Tomi. That needed looking into, so Claire had gone to see the woman that afternoon and had agreed terms.

A good address. A prestigious background. They were in trouble, not doing too well, looking after their first baby. A bouncing boy – except that he wasn't bouncing at the moment. Probably needed his formula changing.

Well, she was the right person for that, wasn't she? And she'd be perfectly placed to take any further action – if required.

Five down and five to go. Would it be too risky to dispose of one more? She damped down the excitement. Perhaps. She'd give it some thought. There was someone on that list whom she detested. Would it be a good idea to get rid of her? Or would that be taking one risk too many?

TEN

C J arrived just as Bea and Maggie were clearing up after supper the following day. Oliver was on the phone, planning to go out with Zander for a jazz session. Maggie said she might join them or not. She wasn't sure.

'A word?' CJ managed to cut Bea out and take her to the sitting room.

'News?'

'Can you spare an hour to visit someone with me? I've traced the telephone number Tomi wrote on the back of her agreement. The phone belonged to a man who lost it some months ago, he's not sure where. He thinks he may have left it in a taxi. No wonder you got no reply.

'"Leo's" real name's Duncan Wylde. He works for a big firm of accountants and has been out of the country for a while, financing and refinancing various businesses that are in trouble. He only got back yesterday, and he picked up the message I'd left on his landline this morning. He phoned me back to say that the agreement we found couldn't possibly have anything to do with his friends' tragic deaths. When I pressed him, he said it was a fun thing a group of them had decided to do for charity. I asked for details. He said he couldn't give them without receiving permission from the rest of the group. I asked him to get permission. He rang me back an hour ago to say he'd be willing to talk to me about it this evening. I need a witness.'

Bea sought for her handbag. 'Your car or mine?'

Duncan Wylde lived in a large first floor flat in South Kensington. Built of red brick, the five-storey terraces boasted tiny balconies in front of tall windows and cavernous porticoes to each doorway. The buildings formed three sides of a square around an iron-railed enclosure which called itself a garden and which probably looked at its prettiest now, with snow capping the trees and shrubs within. Pricey. Exclusive.

Duncan was also pricey. He had the fresh-scrubbed look of a schoolboy under male pattern high-forehead baldness. His hair was taffy coloured and well cut. His skin was clear of acne, his eyes a washed-out blue. He was just above medium height and well enough built, but a tenor rather than a bass. He was dressed to City standards and wore a gold signet ring on the little finger of his left hand. His shoes were highly polished, ditto his teeth.

CJ introduced Bea, explaining how she'd tried the number given for Leo, in her search for Tomi.

'Tomi. Ah. May I take your coats?' Duncan's taste in decor leaned to the antique rather than the modern, which was something of a surprise. Maybe the antiques had been inherited and were too valuable to dispose of? The doors of a lacquered Chinese cabinet stood open to reveal a number of bottles and an array of cut glass. 'May I offer you a drink? No? You won't mind if I do?'

He gestured them to comfortable, overstuffed chairs and poured himself a large whisky. Gulped down about half. Set the tumbler down on a coaster so as not to mark the patina of a mahogany table. Seated himself. Avoided their eyes.

There was good background heating, but also a fake gas-fire in the Adam-style fireplace. The lighting was courtesy of huge side lamps with brocaded and tasselled shades. Everything that wasn't ancient had probably been purchased from Harrods.

CJ and Bea waited, patiently. The carpet was old and had lost most of its colour, but there was a silky Chinese rug before the fireplace.

'The thing is,' said Duncan, 'that I've had to ask everyone's permission to break silence. Some of them are not happy about it. They want me to extract a promise from you that you won't pass on anything I tell you until next Tuesday.'

CJ shook his head. 'You know better than that. More than one crime has been committed.'

'The police don't seem interested, so what harm would it do to keep quiet for a few more days? After that, I promise you, we will all cooperate. It would be a tragedy if the secret got out now.'

CJ said, 'You'll have to trust us. If you can give us a good enough reason to keep quiet for five days, then we will.'

'Very well.' Duncan drained the rest of his glass. He shot his cuffs – gold cufflinks, of course – and sighed. 'You must understand that we weren't drunk exactly, but we had been drinking. It was Harry's birthday. We'd eaten out at a restaurant in the Brompton Road, and then came back here for coffee and liqueurs.

'The birthday boy had drunk more than most and was maudlin. He kept saying his life was a failure because he'd expected to be a partner in his firm by the time he was thirty, and it didn't look like happening. Someone asked what he'd like to happen to improve his life, and he said "to have a big win on the lottery". We all laughed, because none of us played the lottery. Then Hermia said . . .'

Bea blinked. Was Hermia involved in this, too?

'. . . that it was hope that kept us going every day, and why shouldn't we all put some money into a kitty and play the lottery for him? That way he'd have something to look forward to each week. It seemed a brilliant idea at the time. We all clapped and laughed. He cheered up no end.'

He took his empty tumbler to the drinks cabinet and gestured to them, 'Will you?' They shook their heads. He poured more whisky, drank half, returned to his seat.

'Someone suggested – I can't remember who, but it may have been Nick. Yes, I think it was Nick – that we should form a syndicate and arrange to play the lottery for six months. We'd each put in a pound a week, which wasn't going to break any of us, and it would add spice to life. Of course, we didn't really expect to win anything. It was all a bit of a joke. Someone said, "Suppose we do win. It's not likely, but suppose we do?" And someone else said, "Then we share it out, equal shares." You can imagine that by this time we were all practically hysterical. It was a right laugh.

'Julian said he wouldn't play because he had a premonition that his next tour of duty would be his last. He was off to Afghanistan the following week. We tried to jolly him along, you know? "Of course you must play, we all must play. Don't be a wet blanket." So he said he'd play but, if we won anything and he didn't come back, he didn't want his share of the winnings to go to his elder brother, whom he's never liked; with reason, believe me. I suggested that if someone died, his or her share would be put back in the kitty. To which we all agreed.

'Nick said he didn't want it to come out that he'd won anything before his divorce was through, or his wife would grab the lot. He asked us to promise that, if we did win anything, we hold back on distribution till the end of six months, by which time he'd be a free man. Again we all laughed ourselves silly and agreed. We swore ourselves to secrecy, on pain of losing our share of whatever winnings we might have.

'We didn't think anything through, you see? Harry and I drew up a form of agreement there and then.' He gestured to an antique bureau which held an up-to-date laptop and a printer beside it. 'We put everyone's real names down on it and signed it. Then I got everyone to sign a note promising to give so much per week. I ran off copies and gave out one each, to put in a safe place. It was all terribly hush-hush and, well, fantasy.

'We gave ourselves nicknames – mostly from the zodiac. If anything went wrong, if anyone had to change their address or leave the country or something, they had to contact either me or Hermia. She's Sagittarius, by the way. Her birth sign.

'I knew I'd have to be away on business a lot, so I arranged to buy and pay for lottery tickets using random numbers in advance. After two of us died unexpectedly, I reduced the number of tickets I bought each week. I checked the "No Publicity" box, of course. Some paid me the whole lot straight away; some paid monthly. Julian paid me for one month, I remember . . .' He stared into space, then caught himself up.

'Unfortunately I lost my phone somewhere, I don't know where. Probably left it in the pub, just as I was about to go abroad the first time – I've been away three times since we set this thing up. The business hasn't been doing too well, but – enough of that. I got another mobile, but of course the number was different. I emailed everyone my new number, but I suppose Tomi didn't bother to change the number she had on her sheet.'

Bea said, 'Her laptop batteries ran out, and she couldn't access anything for some time before she died. I've seen what emails she received since then. I think there was one from you giving a new mobile number, but she didn't get it and I didn't understand the significance of your message.'

He nodded. 'Ah, I remember: Harry gave her his old laptop, didn't he? He's a bit of a cheapskate. Was.'

Silence. Bea shifted in her seat. 'So, you won?'

'Yes. I was amazed that we'd won anything at all, never mind . . . It was a shock, I can tell you. Anyway, I collected the money, told everyone how much it was and put it in a separate account to wait till the time was up.'

'How did you tell them? By email?'

'No, no. Not secure enough. Hermia had half the telephone numbers, and I had the other half. We spoke to each one personally, when we were sure they were alone.'

'How much did you win?'

He told her. Bea breathed out gently, slowly. Awestruck.

CJ said, 'Hic!'

Bea shot him a look. Had he got the hiccups? Surely not.

'How many of you have died since then?'

'Julian died within a month of returning to duty.' His eyes lost their focus, and he looked tired. 'I'd known him since primary school. I used to help him with his maths homework, and he used to pick me for his football team. He was always so cheerful. He loved being a soldier, was made for it. Survived impossible odds several times. On that last leave of his he was subdued, said he knew he wasn't coming back.'

He straightened his shoulders. 'Shirley; a different kettle of fish. She died in a car accident a month after Julian was killed. Her own fault. She'd had too much to drink, shouldn't have got into her car at all, but she did. She crossed a red light into the path of a juggernaut that was going too fast.

'Tomi; I didn't hear about her or Harry till I was on my way home early this week and my mobile phone started ringing. Everyone rang everyone else. Then Nick died as well. That's five of us gone. The odds have changed, what?'

'Hic!'

'Five? Out of how many?' said Bea.

'Ten.'

Bea breathed out, very slowly. 'Five, out of ten?'

'It makes me wish we'd never thought of it.'

'Hic!'

'CJ, have you got the hiccups?'

He rubbed his chest. 'Sorry, sorry. A weakness of mine. Hic!'

'Water?' Duncan got to his feet. 'Hold your breath. How about a slap on the back?'

'No, no. Hic! I'm so sorry. Absurd thing—'

'A cold key?'

'No, no!' CJ stumbled to his feet, reddening. 'I do apologize. Hic!'

'If you bend over, put your head between your knees—'

'Sugar,' said Bea, looking around. 'A spoonful of sugar. I don't know why, but it always worked when Max got hiccups as a small boy.'

'Sugar?' Both men looked blank.

Bea got to her feet as another spasm struck CJ. He was really suffering. 'Duncan, which way to your kitchen?'

'I'll show you.' Duncan shot out of the door, across a hall and into a modern kitchen, all black marble surfaces and built-in fitments. He opened a cupboard, found a sugar bowl and a teaspoon. 'Would this do?'

Bea took them from him and hastened back to CJ, whose eyes were watering and who was holding on to his chest.

'Get this down you.'

'I d–don't th–think it will d–do any good to—'

'Don't think. Just try it. There.'

Duncan hovered. 'I've heard one can die of—'

'Don't be absurd. Get him some water now.'

Duncan obeyed. Another cut-glass tumbler. Of course. He handed it to CJ, who gulped the water down. Bea and Duncan held their breaths.

So did CJ. Slowly, his colour returned to normal. No more spasms convulsed him. Bea and Duncan relaxed.

So did CJ. He took out a pristine white handkerchief. 'My apologies.' And blew his nose.

Bea laughed from relief.

Duncan smiled. 'How about that!'

CJ said, 'How embarrassing. I do apologize.'

They all three sat down again, smiling at one another. The trivial little episode had banished the awkwardness that had been in the air before.

Duncan didn't pour himself another drink, but sat down beside Bea. 'I must remember that tip.'

'So must I,' said CJ, wryly smiling.

Bea said, 'We used to carry one of those little tubes of

sugar around with us when Max was little. The sort you get in cafés to put in your coffee, right?'

'I must do that in future.'

'The future.' Duncan stopped smiling. 'Do we have one? That's the question. Have we been jinxed? Or worse?'

'Worse?'

He interlaced his fingers, in cat's cradle fashion. 'I'm beginning to wonder if someone isn't knocking us all off, one by one. Because at the end of the six months – which is on Monday next – we're all supposed to meet here again to divvy up the proceeds.'

'How much did you say?'

Gloom descended on Duncan's brow. 'We won nearly forty-one million quid during our second month of play. Because I'd bought tickets for six months, we won another couple of hundred the month after that, and you know what they say, "nothing breeds success like success"? I wouldn't be surprised if we had another win before our time is up.

'I put the lot in a private bank, which is giving us a better interest rate than most. I didn't take risks with it. I didn't play the stock market. It's not my money to play with. Well, a fifth of it is mine at the moment, if I live to collect it. What do you think the odds are?'

CJ and Bea grimaced. Not good.

Duncan said, 'The stupid thing is that none of us who are left really need the money. Well, of course we'd like it. Naturally. But we don't *need* it.'

Bea looked around. The flat was discreet but opulent. Duncan was discreet and opulent. 'You inherited the flat?'

'It was my parents'. Both dead now. It's convenient for work and the shops, but it's always struck me as a trifle on the gloomy side. I'm thinking of getting married; the girl I have in mind daydreams of a detached house in the Home Counties with room to bring up kids. We could sell this place and move out there, while keeping a small flat on for me to be near work; perhaps a bolt-hole in a new block in Docklands, something with lots of space and a view.'

The sale of his highly desirable flat would go a long way towards buying a place in the Home Counties, but if his girl-friend had big ideas, then he'd be looking for a sizeable mortgage, plus the cost of buying a prestigious flat in

Docklands. Mm. Yes, he could do with the money to fulfil that dream.

CJ said, 'You've spoken to the other survivors? What do they think about the death rate?'

Duncan winced at the word 'survivors'. 'They're scared witless, like me. They can't think which of us is trying to kill the others off.'

'You suggested bringing in the police?'

Duncan's eyes lost their focus. 'Four of us would agree to it. One won't. He reminds us that we all signed a confidentiality clause, which we did. So please no police until after the pay-out next Monday. I'm trusting you to keep quiet till then.'

'Isn't he afraid he'll be next?'

Duncan cleared his throat, looked down at his fingers. 'He's – er – very sharp when it comes to finance. He's currently being investigated by the police for something completely different, involving the export of, well, I'm not entirely sure what it is that he's exported, but I strongly suspect, knowing him, that the paperwork may be inaccurate.'

'Arms to Taiwan, sort of thing?'

'Not Taiwan. At least, I don't think so. But yes, that's the sort of thing I mean.'

'He could do with the money?'

A nod. 'Yes, but I don't think it's him that's killing us off. He's a desk-job man, if you see what I mean. And a very old friend.'

'Could he be hiring someone else to do the killing for him?'

'I've thought of that, too. I've thought of nothing else since I heard. It's not him. I've known him since we were at school together, and he doesn't fit the bill.'

'The others are willing to go to the police?'

A nod. 'So am I, though none of us want the publicity. I suggested to each of them that if we don't want to get the police involved, we get a private detective to look into the matter. They all agreed to that, including the one who refuses to let the police know what's happening. I said I knew someone who was discreet.'

'Meaning me?' CJ frowned. 'I'm up to my neck in a big case at the Old Bailey at the moment. Fraud in a big way. I can spare an hour or two now and then, but I can't give you the amount of time you need to sort this out. On the other hand, Mrs Abbot here has an eye for detail and a knowledge of human nature which is unrivalled.'

Bea rose from her chair. 'I run a domestic agency. I don't "do" murder.'

CJ grinned. 'That's what you always say. Then you realize that you've spotted something no one else has seen and—'

'No,' said Bea, reaching for her handbag. 'I've enough on my plate already. Where's my coat?'

CJ was grinning like a basking shark. 'What will you feel like tomorrow when you hear Duncan's been killed in the night?'

'What?' That was Duncan. 'I hope not.' He tried on a smile for size. It didn't fit.

'Oh no, you don't,' said Bea to CJ. 'I'm out of here.'

'Or . . . Hermia?' said CJ.

Bea glared at him. Hermia was a different matter. Bea had met the girl and liked her. Chris liked her, too. It made a difference. She hesitated, but didn't resume her seat.

CJ produced a notepad in a leather holder and a silver pen. 'Duncan, suppose you start by giving us a copy of the original agreement with a list of all those who signed it, complete with telephone, email and street addresses.'

'I'm not at all happy about—'

'How else do you think we're going to prevent any more deaths?'

'But –' a wild gesture with both hands – 'it can't be one of us. We've all known one another for ever, come from the same neck of the woods—'

'So you're prepared for another old friend to drop dead tomorrow? No? Then give us something to work on.'

No reply.

CJ said, 'All right. Start by telling us who was at the birthday party.'

Another wide gesture, but this time one of defeat. 'Myself, of course. I'd only just started to go out with my girlfriend, who's a spot younger than the rest of us, so I didn't invite her. Julian, of course, who was just about to go off to Afghanistan. Then there was Hermia and her on-and-off boyfriend, Lord Fairley.'

Bea sat down again, frowning.

'Harry. He was seeing Tomi at the time and brought her. Nick had various girls after his wife walked out on him, but he was with Shirley that night, though I don't think she thought much of him as a long-term prospect. So the ones who've survived so far are: Hermia and Jamie – that's Lord Fairley – and one of Hermia's friends, called Claudine. She's the deputy head of a big state school, a tough nut, very polished.'

'And one more,' said CJ, who didn't need to use his fingers to do mental arithmetic. 'That would be the old school friend whose probity you don't wish to vouch for?'

'Gregor.' A sigh. 'Married a Greek princess, divorced. Has had live-in partners but . . . Oh, I don't know. Gregor is probably the only one of us who's desperate for money, but this is not like him.'

'Six men, four women. And of those, Hermia and his lord-ship, Gregor and Claudine survive. And you, who've been out of the country for most if not all of the period during which your fellow conspirators died.'

Duncan reddened, but kept his temper in check.

'So, do you want us to investigate, or not?'

A mutter. 'I suppose so.'

'Good. Then if you'll give me a full list, we'll see what we can do to find whoever it is who's killing you off. Meanwhile, I suggest you take all reasonable precautions to avoid being alone. Mrs Abbot will start work tomorrow.'

Duncan lifted his hands, admitting defeat. He crossed to his bureau, activated a laptop, and ran off some sheets of paper on his printer. These he handed to CJ, who glanced at them and gave them to Bea. Names, addresses, and a copy of the original agreement. All present and correct.

It had started to snow again while they'd been in Duncan's flat. CJ turned on the heater in the car, and drove off. Smooth and easy. Like his car. Like himself.

He said, 'You didn't mind being asked to look into the matter, did you? I would do it myself, if my time were not totally taken up with this case at the moment.'

Bea was annoyed. Like Macavity the cat, CJ had a nose for trouble, but when alarm bells rang, he was conspicuous by his absence. 'You don't think I ought to be worried about going after a five times murderer? I notice you weren't offering me a bodyguard.'

'Oh, not five. Surely. Maybe two or three. I think we can discount Julian and the girl who drove her car into a traffic accident.'

'I wouldn't discount anyone at this point in time. Are you sure Julian was really killed in Afghanistan? Or were the rumours of his death exaggerated, and he's now back in London, disguised as a civilian, tracking down all the other members of the birthday party?'

His mouth twitched, which could be annoyance or amusement. 'You want me to check?'

She flounced in her seat. 'I think someone should, yes. And the car accident, too. Shirley something. That's something you could find out about with your police connections, isn't it?'

'Aren't you intrigued by the set-up? I thought you would be, or I'd never have involved you.'

'Humph! Pull the other one. You deliberately involved me in this because . . .'

'Yes?' A bland look of enquiry.

'Because,' said Bea, thinking hard, 'you like solving puzzles. People aren't real to you. Numbers are. You don't get emotionally involved, except perhaps if Chris or one of your old friends is involved. You didn't know any of these people or their families before, did you? Ah, except for Hermia and Lord Fairley. So how well did you know them?'

'I hold no brief for either. I know them slightly, as one knows perhaps a hundred people who trundle along in the charity and business circuits.'

'Give me a thumbnail sketch of Hermia.'

He lifted one eyebrow. 'You've met her. She's been seen around with this and that man in her circle, but always goes back to his lordship. Their families hope they'll walk down the aisle some time this year. It's true that I don't particularly want her playing around with Chris. She's out of his league; too old for him and too experienced.'

'Too rich. If she's won all that money, she might do worse than finance Chris's next film.'

Silence. Bea sighed. 'All right, what about his lordship?'

'Known to his friends as "Jamie". He's from an ancient line which he doesn't seem eager to perpetuate. Not exactly

Brain of Britain material, but masses of boyish charm. An estate in the Shires, a house in Chelsea. Likes to shoot; birds, the winged variety. Part-time job finding country locations for a film company. Too lazy to have a career, though to do him justice, he's said to look after his estate well enough. He and Hermia go back a long way.'

'She's twice the man he is?'

'She has more energy, I suppose.'

Bea thought back over the evening. 'What did you make of Duncan?'

CJ drew up outside her house and parked. 'What did you make of him?'

'I'm not sure. At first I thought he might be gay, but fighting it. Then I thought he wasn't. He's bright enough to have given considerable thought to the problem of who wants to bump who off, but he's not frightened enough to tell us his conclusions. All that guff about Gregor Whatsit was a red herring. I assume you'll be responsible for investigating Gregor?'

'You think so?' He kept the engine running. 'Do you mind if I don't come in? I rather think I've a cold coming.'

She got out and restrained herself from slamming the car door. Just.

What on earth had she let herself in for now?

Thursday evening

Claire sometimes wore a cheap ring on the fourth finger of her left hand when she went to work, to make sure her employers realized she was not in the market for a squeeze from Mister. She'd known Misters wanting her to play around in their bedroom before now. Soon now, there'd be a really good diamond on her hand. Oh yes!

The precaution wasn't necessary in this case. Mr was abstracted, worried, on the phone, papers spread around the living room. Mrs was worn out, overtired and not capable of thinking of anything but her baby, and of getting some sleep.

Mrs explained that when she'd taken the baby to the clinic to be weighed they'd been most unpleasant. It was no fun being an elderly primate, as they called older women having their first babies, and how was it her fault that Pippin refused to thrive no matter how carefully she followed the routine which had been worked out for him? And her mother-in-law was being most unhelpful about giving her a helping hand about the flat and was such an interfering old bitch that Mrs had been driven to distraction.

The people at the clinic had scared Mrs into hysterics, until one of the doctors had taken the trouble to listen to her, and advise – oh, so gently, so kindly – that she could do with a spot of professional help. The name of the Nursing Agency was whisked before the nose of Mrs, and a telephone call had resulted in Claire's appearance on their doorstep.

Claire got all the details without even having to ask for them. So this wasn't the interfering Mrs Abbot who'd left that disturbing message on Leo's old phone, but the daughter-in-law. Well, well! Claire listened – really some mothers were more childlike than their children – and knew exactly what needed to be done. She sent Mrs off to bed and made up an alternative formula for Baby, who took four ounces almost without drawing breath.

Baby looked up at her with large, considering eyes, with-holding judgement. Could he see the tide of red which some-times overtook her? It was only very occasionally that young babies saw it. Calm down, Claire. That's it. Calm down.

This baby had had a bad start in life, that's all. From now on, she'd see to it that he did well. Or not, if things went badly. Fate had handed her a nice weapon to use if the older Mrs Abbot became a nuisance.

Oh, interfering Mrs Abbot, little do you know it, but your grandson's life is in my hands.

ELEVEN

Thursday evening

Bea walked in on a scene of chaos. Had she been descended upon by a crowd of locusts? Every seat in the sitting room was occupied, every inch of table space covered with sheets of paper. There were empty and half empty mugs of coffee everywhere, crumbs from biscuits on the carpet and a pair of trainers, untenanted, just inside the door.

It occurred to her that if she were to continue housing her two young assistants, they must be provided with their own sitting room, preferably soundproof. Tomorrow morning first thing she would investigate how to turn the large junk room in the eaves over to youth.

Her arrival caused heads to turn.

'Oh, sorry!' said a scratty looking youth, removing the trainers and stuffing his feet back into them. 'I think better with bare feet.'

'Um?' said Oliver, who was lying prone on the floor for some reason. Scrutinizing a script? 'You're back, then?'

'Sorry,' said Maggie, trying to sweep the papers on the table into a manageable pile. 'The kitchen table wasn't big enough.'

Chris got to his feet, with one of his most charming grins. 'We were trying to work on a storyboard. Hermia's a genius, but she's also a slave driver.' Bea looked hard at him and realized he knew nothing about lottery wins, nor that Hermia was – on paper at least – a millionairess.

Hermia had been standing at the back window, staring up at the picture of Bea's husband, but now returned to where she'd left her laptop open on the settee. She'd fluffed out her hair and was wearing a touch of blusher as well as lipstick today.

A girl with blazing red hair and high cheekbones had a sketch pad on her knee and was working on it with a soft pencil. Not an actress, but an artist, sketching in possible backgrounds?

Hermia was playing at being a film producer. 'So sorry, Mrs Abbot. We have rather taken over, haven't we?'

Bea wanted to hit Hermia, but refrained. There were other people in the room who hadn't been introduced, but the two women might have been alone. Messages passed from one to the other.

Hermia communicated, without words, that she'd staked her claim to work on Chris's next film.

Also without words, Bea made it clear to Hermia that she was not a happy bunny at this invasion of her territory, and that she objected to Hermia's taking Chris over.

Bea smiled at everyone. 'Carry on, children. Don't worry about me. I'm for a cup of cocoa and early bed. Hermia; a word?'

Hermia snapped off her laptop and followed Bea out to the kitchen.

What Bea wanted to ask Hermia was whether she was serious about Chris or not, but she didn't. Hermia would tell her to take a running jump. Politely, of course.

Bea opened fire from a different angle. 'CJ and I have just been talking to Duncan. He's told us all about the lottery. I understand you gave your permission for us to see what we could do to help.'

Hermia was wearing brown and cream, a cowl-necked jumper over well-cut trousers; cashmere and silk. With a pair of the most beautiful leather boots Bea had ever seen. Bea liked boots and yearned for a pair like them. Before she could stop herself, she said, 'Beautiful boots. Where did you get them?'

'Milan. I do a lot of my clothes shopping there.'

Of course. How parochial Hermia made Bea feel. She mixed cocoa and milk in a mug and put it in the microwave. 'Do you agree with Duncan that someone has been knocking you off, one by one?'

'I don't know what to think.'

'Julian; did you go to his funeral?'

'Yes. Wootton Bassett. The whole town turns out to see the coffins taken through the streets. Impressive.' There were lines of strain around Hermia's mouth that you wouldn't notice unless you were another woman.

'Shirley; did you go to her funeral, too?'

'As it happens, no. I was away. I work for a children's charity, was setting up a big event for them in a friend's house in the country.'

'Which friend?' As if Bea didn't know.

'Lord Fairley. Jamie. He isn't the sort to go round knocking off his old friends.'

'I haven't met him yet. I suppose I'll do so tomorrow. May I ask if your job gives you enough time off to – to—'

'Play around making films with Chris? He says you've been like a mother to him. Very . . . praiseworthy.'

Bea gave a sharp laugh. She took the mug out of the microwave and sipped her cocoa. Too hot now. 'You want to take over as his mother?'

Hermia reddened. 'No, of course not.' She didn't like the implication that she was old enough to be Chris's mother.

Ah, so Hermia did realize there was an age gap there. Eight years? Ten? However, the girl was not to be defeated so easily. She tossed her head, making her well-cut cap of dark hair swing, before it settled back into its usual perfect shape. 'I thought we'd get on to the subject of Chris sooner rather than later. He's got a rare talent, and if I can help him get started, I will.'

'If you're not knocked off next.'

'I could ask him to move in with me, act as my bodyguard.'

'You wouldn't ask Lord Fairley?'

An urchin grin. 'He'd be useless. Shall I ask Chris, then?'

Bea moved in for the kill. 'You've studied him. You know what he'd be like if he knew you were in danger. He'd go all romantic on you and throw himself wholeheartedly into being your bodyguard. He'd want to wrap you in chain mail, incarcerate you in a castle. Suffocate you. You wouldn't be able to stand it.'

Hermia threw back her head. 'Touché. He's very single-minded, isn't he? We'll let him get on with the preparations for his film; he's got a young writer there who's going places, if we can keep him chained to his word processor long enough. Sorry about him taking off his shoes. His feet didn't smell, did they? His artist friend has a good imagination, too. Oliver and Maggie will keep their feet on the ground for them, while I do the finances and chivvy everyone along.'

'Can you find him another Tomi?'

'Tomi was special. But yes, it'll be my job to find a replacement. Never fear, I won't let anything stand in the way of his career.'

'So you'll carry on wrapping Chris in cotton wool until he's made his name. And then what?'

Hermia shrugged. 'Perhaps the magic will last. Hope springs eternal, etcetera.'

'And there's always Jamie to fall back on.'

A sigh. 'I've grown away from him, and he's grown away from me.' She straightened up. 'I've been frank with you. I can't make any promises for the future. Who can?'

Chris came in, recognized the fact that the two women were at odds, and put his arm around Hermia. 'What's up, Puss?'

PUSS! Bea nearly choked. That Chris should give Hermia a nickname was a strong indication of how he felt about her, but that Hermia would accept it was almost unbelievable.

Hermia did accept it. She was nearly as tall as Chris in her high-heeled boots, and instead of using an elbow to push him away from her, she turned within his arm, to look into his eyes. 'I'm accused of cradle-snatching.' No smiles now. She was serious, searching his face for a reaction.

Chris looked back at her, also serious. 'Time will mend that.'

'Mrs Abbot thinks someone's out to kill me.'

Frowning, he looked across at Bea. 'To kill Hermia? Why?' He made one of his intuitive leaps. 'Tomi, Harry . . . You've discovered something?'

Bea appreciated Hermia's tactics, which were designed to bind Chris to her and which were succeeding. 'I've been sworn to secrecy.'

Hermia wasn't having any of that. 'Chris, will you move in with me for a couple of days, till things get sorted?'

'What? Yes, of course, but . . .' He drew back, loosening his hold upon her. 'You have to tell me what's going on first.'

'I don't know that I should.'

Bea realized she'd lost the battle to stop Chris getting involved with Hermia. 'Tell him. He won't be able to keep his mouth shut and the news will be all over the neighbourhood by lunchtime tomorrow, but tell him. Hermia, I'd like to talk to you tomorrow morning, if you're free.'

'I only work part-time. I'll be here at eleven, right? If I last through the night.'

'Don't be ridiculous,' said Chris. 'I'll stick to you like glue.'

Bea took another sip of her drink, which was cooling rapidly. She felt old, old, old. Of course the young ones would cleave to one another. That was the way of the world, and she was ancient, long past her heyday. Also long past her bedtime. 'Make sure the alarm's switched on when you leave.' She tested the back door to make sure it was locked and bolted, and went up to bed. Winston was there already, stretched out on his back, paws in the air. Snoring. What a comfort he was!

Friday morning

'No problem,' said Maggie, stuffing her mouth with a bacon sandwich while she checked over her schedule for the day. 'I'll get the junk moved out of the attic this weekend – although you'd better look it over first – and with a splash of paint, a couple of cheap rugs and an oil heater, Oliver can move his stuff in there, which means we can use his present bedroom as our sitting room. It's not an ideal solution, but it will do for now. Then I know someone who can draw up plans for a loft extension at the back. We could get one more big room out of it, plus a small kitchen. Possibly rejig the bathroom up there as well. Take out the old fitments, install a walk-in shower, extend the central heating – and, by the way, the boiler down here could do with being looked at while we're at it. No problem.'

Bea grunted. 'Cost. Disruption.'

'Mm. I'll manage the project and, being in the business, I know where to get everything. Just leave it to me.'

'You've been planning this behind my back.'

'We thought about it, but we didn't want to say anything till you suggested it yourself.'

Bea gnashed her teeth. 'So holding that party here last night was meant to give me a nudge in the right direction?'

Maggie laughed, blew Bea a kiss and left the house, banging the front door behind her. She returned to fetch her scarf and cap, said the front door step was icy, so watch it! And went out again. Finally there was silence.

A creak of floorboards, and down came Oliver. 'Sorry. Got carried away last night. Hermia's quite something, isn't she?'

'Make your own breakfast and put everything in the dishwasher afterwards.' Bea took her last cup of coffee down the stairs, where the phones were already ringing. It was going to be a busy morning, but first she must try Max to see if Pippin was any better.

The phone rang and rang. Eventually Nicole answered. 'I don't want to talk to you. If it hadn't been for your interference, we'd have got this problem sorted out long ago. It's no thanks to you that he's doing well now.' Down went the phone.

Bea stared at her receiver. What on earth did that mean? Had she been an interfering busybody? Oh dear. Perhaps it might have looked that way, although she had meant well, hadn't she? What did Nicole mean by saying that they'd got their problem sorted out? Had they changed Pippin's formula? If so, then let us rejoice. What else could it mean? Did it matter, so long as Pippin was thriving at long last?

Her thoughts squirrelled round and round, till she realized she was deleting emails without reading them. Concentrate, Bea! You can ring Nicole later and find out what's going on, but for the time being, concentrate on work. The agency was busy enough, wasn't it?

In the middle of a telephone conversation with a tiresome client who rang several times a week, but never accepted any of the agency's suggestions, Miss Brook announced that they had a caller who insisted on speaking to Mrs Abbot there and then, that very minute. 'She's probably from the Embassy, got that manner, you know? Nigerian.'

Nigerian. Tomi was Nigerian. Bea told her caller that she'd ring back later and put down the phone. 'Send her in.'

Tomi's mother. Of course. Tall, dignified, beautiful in middle age, with a long elegant neck and superb clothes. Bea rose to her feet and gestured for her visitor to join her in the group of chairs by the window.

'Mrs Abbot?' The woman remained standing. 'You have something of mine, I believe.' Perfect English.

'I do?' For a moment Bea couldn't think what it might be. 'Ah, your daughter's bible?'

'It is not enough that my daughter is murdered, but that her belongings should be stolen passes belief.'

A soft answer turns away wrath. Maybe. 'I'm so sorry. There seems to have been a misunderstanding—'

'I believe not. Miss Drobny – impertinent creature – tells me you removed my daughter's laptop and bible without her consent.'

'Well, actually—'

'What appalling conduct! To steal from a dead girl.'

Bea held on to her temper with an effort. 'The police have her laptop and the bible. Also the paper hidden at the back of her bible, although they do not know what it signifies.'

'What! Why should they . . . ? But you are the person who stole them in the first place?'

'Let me explain. Please, sit down. Would you care for some coffee?'

'I only care to collect my daughter's belongings.'

'I am sure the police have them safe.'

'I cannot wait. I need her will.'

Bea sank back into her seat. So that was what this was all about? 'As I was trying to tell you, there was a paper in the back of her bible—'

'She told us where to look for it.'

'It's not a will. The police have the original document, but I can supply you with a copy, if you wish.'

'I suppose that when you stole it, you imagined we might cut you in on her inheritance, and so withheld it from her family. Rest assured; nothing is more unlikely.'

Bea began to see where this conversation was leading. 'Ah. You imagine that your daughter was due to share in a windfall of some kind? Unfortunately that is not the case.'

'You defy me?'

'Certainly not. If you will take a seat, I will—'

'I do not socialize with criminals. My daughter's last will and testament, if you please.'

'I am trying,' said Bea, 'to make allowances for a mother's grief. I assume you have already visited Miss Drobny and been to inspect your daughter's property, which she went to considerable trouble to keep safe for you. Did you thank her for all her trouble? Probably not, though you should. It is true that I brought Tomi's laptop and bible back here with me—'

'You confess it?'

'Because at that time we had no idea what had happened to her and hoped to get your email address from her laptop which, by the way, went straight on to the police. The laptop batteries were dead, but they got it working again and contacted you straight away. So much for the laptop.'

'And her bible? I do not imagine you took it to read.'

Bea felt herself flush. 'Yes, I am a Christian, and yes, I do read my bible. Tomi's bible was left behind at the flat by mistake. I collected it, thinking it might contain some notes indicating where she might have gone; remember that at that time it was thought she had run off with a boyfriend to France—'

'Slander! Be sure you will hear from my solicitor about this.'

'There was,' said Bea, gritting her teeth, 'a paper tucked into a map at the back of her bible, which led us to the man who had arranged for a syndicate – which included your daughter – to play the lottery.'

'Yes, yes. She told us all about it when she phoned us on my birthday.'

'She was sworn to secrecy—'

'There can be no secrecy between a mother and her child. We know she was due to receive several million pounds—'

'Indeed. If she hadn't died, she would have done so. As it is, her share goes back into the kitty.'

'What! What are you saying? What lie is this? You are trying to cheat a dead woman? What sort of creature are you?'

Bea got to her feet. 'I will ask the man in charge of proceedings to let you have Tomi's bible and a copy of the contract which she signed.'

'This is fraud! You expect me to believe—'

Bea pressed a button under the projecting top of her desk. 'Meanwhile, I would like you to go.'

'You have the nerve to—'

Bea looked beyond the woman to the door. 'Miss Brook, would you like to see if Oliver . . . Ah, there you are, Oliver. This is Tomi's mother, who seems to think I'm cheating her out of her daughter's inheritance. Would you kindly show her out?'

The woman turned to glare at the ancient but still formidable Miss Brook, and at young Oliver, whose dark good looks gave evidence of his mixed ancestry. 'I don't discuss affairs with servants. Mrs Abbot, you will hear from me. Now get out of my way, you!'

She swept off. Miss Brook raised her eyebrows and followed her out.

Bea sank back into her chair, trying to laugh. Her pulse rate was high. She took a couple of deep breaths.

Oliver hovered. 'Tomi didn't leave any money, did she? What makes her think that?'

'Grief. Greed, pride, intolerance, ignorance. Let the police deal with her. Far too many people know what's been happening for my peace of mind, and I'm going to let you in on the secret, too. Sit down, Oliver, while I fill you in on what's been happening.'

As Bea finished there was a stir in the doorway, and there was Hermia, wearing another cream cashmere sweater, this time over a long dark-brown tweed skirt, plus a different pair of gorgeous boots. Behind her came Chris. He wasn't wearing yesterday's clothes, so must have gone home to change at some point. Neither of them was smiling today.

But, thought Bea, they don't look as if they've spent the night rolling around in bed together, either. Then she told herself that she wouldn't know the signs nowadays. Or would she?

Friday morning

Claire used the keys she'd been given to let herself into the Abbots' flat. Mrs was just about up and moving, but it was clear that cleaning the place up was the last thing on her mind. She was crooning over Baby, playing with his starfish fingers, kissing the top of his head.

Claire thought that Mrs looked poorly and could do with attention from a nurse herself, but that wasn't in the agreement, was it?

Claire took Baby out of his mother's arms to wash and change him. He was a better colour today. Mrs said she'd given him an extra feed in the night. Claire tried to work out whether Mrs meant she'd given him more than allowed for on the previous regime or not. Perhaps it didn't matter.

The Abbot baby was going to thrive with Claire, wasn't he? Or was he?

That was the five million dollar question.
She wasn't sure what the answer was.
Should she leave well alone now? Prudence said yes. But the red tide of excitement threatened to rise up and push her into trying for one last death.

TWELVE

Bea pushed the interview with Tomi's mother out of her mind and turned her attention to Hermia and Chris. 'Please take a seat. I've told Oliver what's been going on. We need him on our side.'

Hermia didn't look pleased. 'Oliver, you do realize what a serious matter this is? I know you are Chris's best friend and I trust you, but . . .' She tried to smile. 'I'm not sure I know who else to trust at the moment. I've been up half the night, telling Chris everything and trying to work out who might want to kill us. Mrs Abbot, I don't think we got off to the best start, and if that was my fault, I apologize. Please, will you help us?'

'Thank you. Of course I'll do what I can. Coffee, anyone? No? Well, Hermia, I've heard the story from Duncan, but I'd like you to tell us what happened from your point of view.'

Hermia took a deep breath. 'It was Harry's birthday. He was depressed. So was Julian, who was due to go back to Afghanistan . . .' Her version of events tied in with Duncan's. She said that while some of the party had imbibed too freely, neither she nor Duncan had done so. 'I've a hard head,' she explained, dividing her attention between Bea and Chris, 'and I was driving. So we each went off with a note of how much we'd agreed to pay, which Duncan suggested we put in a safe place. Tomi and I agreed to put ours in the back of our bibles. I gave her a lift, you see. Or rather, I gave her and Jamie a lift home. Tomi had come with Harry but –' a shrug '– he wasn't fit to drive at the end of the evening. Julian got a taxi and took Harry home instead.

'That was the last time I saw Julian. I've known him since we were at kindergarten. It's a stereotype to say he always wanted to be a soldier, but it's perfectly true; he never wanted anything else.'

Bea said, 'Duncan said Julian didn't want his share to go to his elder brother. Do you know why?'

'He gambles. His family have bailed him out several times. He can't help it, I suppose. If he'd inherited, he'd have gambled the lot away.'

'Understood. So Julian died, his body was brought back to Britain, and you went to the funeral. What about Shirley?'

'She'd lost her licence for drink-driving some years ago, only just got it back. She got rather too merry at Harry's party, but insisted on driving herself home. I thought then that she was asking for trouble, and about a month later . . . kaput.'

'So you don't think either of them were murdered.'

'No, I don't. Tomi, now . . .' She looked at Oliver's wooden expression and Chris's anxious one. 'I don't know what to think. Harry introduced her into our circle, and we all thought she could do better than him. I liked her. We all did. Nick made a pass at her, but that was Nick; it didn't mean anything. He's tried it on with all of us over the years, even before his wife moved out. Afterwards he got worse. I rather think Tomi slapped him for getting too fresh. Come to think of it, that might have been the last time I saw her.

'The following Friday I was at this party, and Harry was there, moaning that Tomi had stood him up and gone off to the Continent with another man. I thought she'd found someone nicer and good luck to her. He asked me if I'd like a day out in the country with him sometime. Last Saturday I had nothing else on till the evening, so I agreed. That's when I met you and Chris. At Harry's.'

Bea reached for her pad. 'Dates?'

Hermia pulled out her diary and supplied them, shaking her head. 'Tomi didn't do drugs. I'm sure of it.'

The dates tallied. Bea tried shock tactics. 'Tomi was filled up with barbiturates, and a needle full of drugs was stuck into her. Either would have killed her. She didn't do it to herself. The police think Harry did it. You knew Harry. Is that likely?'

'No. That was sneaky. Horrible. I'm not saying he couldn't have laid hands on some drugs; he probably could. But to kill her that way? No. Now, if you'd said she was pregnant and expecting him to marry her . . . ?'

'Not pregnant.'

'If she had been, he might have strangled her, I suppose. Ugh.'

'So what do you make of Harry's death? Did he commit suicide because you dumped him?'

Hermia snorted. 'Of course not. He was annoyed, not heart-stricken. I can't think of any reason why he should take his own life, unless there were some underlying medical condition . . . ?'

Bea shook her head. 'None that I've heard of. So if we discount Julian and Shirley, we are forced to consider the possibility that Tomi and Harry died unnatural deaths by some person or persons unknown. What about Nick?'

The girl shivered. 'Ugh. He used to be great fun, but got so dirty-minded I went off him big time. I can accept that he got drunk and fell over the banisters. At least, I would, if it weren't for what happened to Tomi and Harry. What I can't accept is that one of my friends is setting out to kill the rest of us.'

'I think,' said Bea, 'that at first there was no plan to reduce ten to five. The lottery win was a big one and meant that each one of you would have a sizeable windfall. Only, when Julian and Shirley died, it became a whole new ball game. Four million each was fantastic, but five was magnificent. Four meant a new house, a fresh start in business, the wiping out of debts. Five million and you might start thinking about holiday homes abroad; perhaps a yacht, a private aeroplane or a racehorse.

'Suddenly the sky's the limit. Your imagination takes over. What is a paltry four million to you when, if fortune continued to shine, you could buy anything which took your fancy? The insidious voice of envy creeps in; if five million is good, why not seven – or eight? Hermia, what have you been planning to do with your eight million?'

Bea waited while the girl took her time to answer. She looked out of the window, then down at her hands. Finally she looked direct into Chris's eyes. 'When we started this, I didn't expect we'd win anything. Oh, perhaps a hundred pounds that we could spend on a round of drinks in the pub. When we won that big jackpot, I was so excited I couldn't think straight. I fantasized about taking off round the world and booking myself on a flight to the moon. I planned to give some money to charity, of course.

'After a while I stopped thinking about it so much, because I wasn't going to get the money for months. It was hard, not being able to talk about it, except with one another. Claudine and I have been friends for ever. We met up every few weeks and talked about what we'd like to do when we got the money, but it was all so unreal that everyday problems gradually became more important. I decided that, when the time came, I'd ask my father's advice about investments, because he's very shrewd with money. I thought he'd back me in buying a property to rent out. It was fun to think about it, but it didn't make me want to go out on a spending spree for myself. Oh, I did toy with the idea of buying a new car when my old one played up in the bad weather, but I held off, thinking I'd research what the new model might be like.'

Bea persisted. 'You weren't short of money yourself?'

A bright, white smile. Too bright, too white? 'I have a private income from shares which my godmother left me, and my father gives me an allowance, too. I don't have to work, but our family has a bad case of the Protestant work ethic. Some people think we're boring because we don't go in for the high life; we look after the members of our family and our money. We don't gamble or drink or whore around. I've heard people call us miserly and strait-laced. Well, I suppose we are. It's in the genes, you see?'

She tried to make a joke of it, but the searching look she gave Chris spoke of her anxiety that Chris might judge her that way, too. Chris wasn't turned off by her candour. Rather the reverse, if Bea was any judge of the matter.

Reassured, Hermia continued, 'In our family, everyone works at something: charities, or community projects or arts foundations. We can afford to take on ill-paid jobs when we believe in the work that's being done. I took a degree in history and worked in social housing for a while. My father bought me a flat which I share with another girl, someone I was at school with. We get along fine. A couple of years ago I was headhunted to fund-raise for a children's charity. I did so, and I think I can honestly say I'm good at it. What did I need, more than I already had?'

But, thought Bea, you do like to shop for clothes in Milan,

and the smile you treated us to was a fraction too wide, too blindingly white. Have you told us the whole truth? And who is your dentist?'

Hermia picked up that Bea was not entirely convinced. 'Duncan said he was thinking of getting married and buying a house in the shires with his share, but I couldn't see myself setting up in a big house in the country with nothing to do but worry about cleaning and entertaining. I don't want to stop work. I'd hate to be idle.'

Chris put his hand over hers. 'You know I'm not interested in your money.'

'Oh yes, you are,' she said, better versed in the world than him. 'You want to make films, and you need a backer.'

A frown. 'I can make my own way. I want you, without strings.'

She gave him a long, intense look. 'You mean it now, but I'm older and wiser than you. Let's see how things work out, shall we?'

Bea tried another tack. 'So, which of the surviving members of the group is trying to bump you all off? What are their dreams for the future? Which one of you needs more than four million to carry them out?'

A shrug. 'Duncan doesn't need it. If this had never happened, I'd have expected him to marry and move out of London within the next five years, anyway. He has a good job, can afford to take on a big mortgage. He's well balanced, has chosen a girl from the same background as him, doesn't spend more than he earns. It's not Duncan.'

Oliver lifted a finger. 'What's more, it would be a bad move for anyone to knock him off, because he's the banker and presumably the only one who can access the money.'

Bea doodled on her pad. 'So who do you fancy as the murderer? Lord Fairley?'

Hermia's colour rose. 'Oh, it's not Jamie. I've known him for ever. His brain – such as it is – doesn't work that way.'

'Not clever enough?'

'He's quite clever in some ways, at getting on with people, and seeing how best to run his estate. He's a whizz at his job, getting his friends to lend out their houses for film and television programmes. He's kept the country house in good repair. But he's not . . . not financially *sharp*!'

Bea doodled some more. 'What would his dream be?'

'You'd have to ask him that.'

'You're supposed to be good friends. You must know what he wants out of life.'

'In general terms, yes. To end up no worse than he started. To hand on the estate in good nick.'

'Does he drink or gamble?'

'No, not really. Well, sometimes he drinks more than he should, but it's only to be sociable. He's very easy-going.'

'No signs of wear and tear in the finance department?'

'These are anxious times, of course. His estate produces enough to keep the house in good order, although farming doesn't pay much, nowadays and . . . No, he's fine. He lives in the top flat at the manor, lets out the rest. Drives a 4 x 4 in the country, naturally. Keeps a BMW for town. But he isn't a playboy, doesn't go clubbing, says he's past all that.'

'It was expected that you two would marry.'

A frown, a shake of the head. 'Our parents thought it, and we saw a lot of one another at one time, but there was never any spark.' Here she turned to look at Chris, and everyone else in the room felt the tension between them. Oh yes, there was a spark between Chris and Hermia. If they'd been plugged into the National Grid, they could have lit up the whole house.

Bea noted the effect they were having on one another and sighed. 'But Jamie is expected to marry and produce children?'

'That's so. We used to have a laugh, he and I, when some girl or other tried to get him interested in her. His father died last year, and he's been seeing a girl recently . . . She's very pretty, but I didn't think he was serious about her. But he popped the question yesterday. The idea that they might die soon has made both him and Duncan rush into action.'

'You said Duncan had chosen a suitable girl; what about Jamie?'

A shrug. 'As I said, she's a pretty little thing.' Hermia was neither pretty nor little. 'She's, well, a man's woman. I think that would be the right way to describe her. I'm sure she'll suit him very well.'

Bea made a note that Hermia didn't like Jamie's fiancée. Perhaps she wouldn't have liked anyone who married her childhood friend?

Oliver said, 'You're trying to tell us that Lord Fairley hasn't the brains to murder Tomi, Harry and Nick in the ways we know they were killed?'

'Jamie hasn't that kind of mind.' No hesitation. She smiled to herself. 'He's not a complicated sort of person. You'll see for yourself, won't you? I told him you'd want to meet him, and he says he'll be in later on this afternoon if you want to pop over.'

Bea put a query mark by Jamie. 'Next on the list is Gregor.'

She dropped her eyes. 'I don't know. He's tricky Dicky, wily as a fox. His father's Hungarian. He made a lot of money, though no one quite knows how. Gregor's handsome, charm incarnate, chucks money around, has a beautiful house, gave his ex-wife an adequate divorce settlement and is still friends with her. Everyone's good friends with Gregor; he won't let you be otherwise.'

'Does he dream of millions to come?'

Again she shut down on them. She shrugged. 'Possibly. He's got companies with offshore accounts, and they've got companies which have spawned yet more companies. He takes over this, sells that and buys Impressionist paintings. Some of his affairs are being investigated by the Fraud Squad, and yet he seems totally unconcerned, says they're not even warm and will give up soon. If this were a three-card trick, I'd say Gregor did it. But it's not a trick. It's deliberate murder. And somehow I can't see it.'

Oliver said, 'He's the one who could mop up a few extra million without feeling it?'

An indulgent smile. 'Oh yes. Diamonds for the latest piece of arm candy, a yacht in the Med, more visits to the bankers in Saudi Arabia. He has the ambition to buy a football club some day. But murder? I suppose I can see him arranging for someone to have an accident, but . . . No, I still don't see him knocking off old friends.'

'But you want it to be him. Why?'

She stared into the distance. 'It's like that old party game. If you have five people in a balloon and have to lose one of them so that the rest of you survive, then who do you throw out? You're right. My head says to vote for Gregor, even while my heart is saying he didn't do it. He's the only one who's refused to see you, by the way. Now, I really must go.'

She made as if to rise, but Bea stopped her. 'You've missed out Claudine.'

Hermia picked up her handbag. 'It's not her. She wouldn't have the time to think up such things. She's a practical, down-to-earth, deputy head of a secondary modern which always gets good Ofsted reports. Her long term, live-in relationship went sour last autumn, and she threw him out for getting drunk every night. She has someone else who seems a better match now, but I haven't met him. She said she'd be at home after school for a couple of hours if you wanted to drop by. Now, I really must go.'

This time she made it to her feet. She looked a question at Chris, who nodded. He said, 'I'm superglue, coming with you. I'm serious; I don't want your money.'

She flashed a smile at him, waved goodbye to Bea, ignored Oliver, and swept out.

Bea's phone rang, and she answered it.

'Your son,' said Miss Brook and put the call through.

Bea said, 'Max? I rang earlier, but Nicole—'

'It would be best if you didn't bother her for a while. I ought to have gone up north to the constituency last night, but decided to stay down overnight to look after her, so I'm in a hurry to get away now. Nicole's gone down with influenza, so we've got a nanny in to look after Pippin. Nicole needs bed rest and a quiet life. She asked me to phone you, to make it clear that she doesn't want or need visitors for the time being.'

Bea felt as if she'd been stabbed to the heart. She couldn't speak.

'You do understand, Mother, don't you?'

She cleared her throat. 'Max, I thought I was helping. What about the shopping and cleaning . . . ? Why won't you let me help?' She wanted to wail and cry, but knew that would only annoy him more.

'The nanny is properly trained and up to date with all the latest methods in child care. Her references are beyond reproach.'

'Is Pippin going to be all right?'

He barked, 'Of course he is.'

'How long do you think it will be before I can come over?'

He clicked off his phone. She put her receiver down. She

was going to cry. But no, not in front of Oliver, who must be going through his own version of hell at the way he'd been ignored by his best friend. Think about Oliver, and perhaps you won't cry.

Oliver was sitting in his chair, hadn't moved since Chris and Hermia walked past him and out of the room. His fingertips were together, one leg was casually draped over the other. His eyes were hooded.

Chris and Oliver had been friends at school. Chris had been the only one from Oliver's past to keep in touch with him when he was thrown out by his adopted family. When Maggie had brought Oliver back home with her and he'd started working for the agency, Chris had drifted along, too. It was Chris who had introduced Oliver to the Health Club, which had made so much difference to his physical well-being.

On the other hand, Oliver had always been the steadying influence on the mercurial Chris's life. They'd partied, and helped one another out in every way you could think of. Chris had had girlfriends, which Oliver hadn't; at least, not to Bea's knowledge. But Chris had never taken a girl seriously until now.

Five minutes ago Chris had walked past Oliver and out of the room without so much as a nod in his direction. Oliver must be feeling as if he'd been cut in two.

Bea got out a handkerchief, went to stand by the window, looking out. Blew her nose. How could Max have . . . ? He didn't realize, of course, how much he'd hurt his mother. Of course he didn't. And poor little Pippin . . .

Bea blew her nose again. Told herself to face up to it. Young people didn't want grannies telling them how to manage their lives.

Please, Lord, keep an eye on them? Let this nanny be a good thing. It really doesn't matter if they won't take advice from me, so long as they get good advice from someone, so long as Pippin thrives.

A rustle of cloth. Oliver came to stand beside her, also looking out on to the garden. 'The snow's all gone and the sun's come out.'

So they weren't going to talk about Chris and Hermia. Nor about Max and Pippin.

She nodded, sniffing. 'The leaves will soon be showing green. I really must try to get a walk in the park.'

'I'll come with you. That is, if Miss Brook doesn't catch us first and tell us we can't go out till we've eaten up all our greens.'

Bea managed to laugh. Used her handkerchief one last time. 'I suppose we ought to look at the junk room, see what needs saving and what we can throw away. Otherwise, Maggie will have the builders in before we can turn round.'

They almost tiptoed up the stairs to the first floor. Once there, they looked at one another and laughed. Bea said, 'I think I promised to ring a client back this morning. Do you think Miss Brook will haul me back down to deal with it?'

'I was going to have another look at Tomi's laptop.'

They climbed the stairs to the top landing. The door to the crowded box room stood open, and someone – Maggie? – had already pulled out some cartons to see what they contained. Bea inspected the first one. 'These were Hamilton's. Early seventy-eight vinyl records. Do we junk them?'

'I'll sell them on eBay for you, if you want to get rid of them. Some of them may be collectors' items. Do you think Hermia was being frank with us about her friends?'

'No, I don't think she was. Some things rang true; she likes and trusts Claudine. I think. When people look you in the eye like that and swear someone's squeaky clean, I start wondering what magic tricks they're up to. Did you think Hermia was sincere about Claudine?'

'It sounded to me as if Claudine's too much like Hermia for them to be close friends.'

'Maybe they are just that. Hermia doesn't approve of Lord Fairley's very new fiancée, does she?'

'There may be a touch of jealousy there. Even if she didn't want him herself, she might not be best pleased that he'd chosen someone else.'

Oliver had obviously decided not to speak of Chris. He pulled another box out. 'Railway lines?'

'Oh!' Bea smiled, remembering. 'That's Max's toy train set. There should be three boxes of it. He was mad keen on it for a couple of years and ran it all over the floor up here. I'll ask him what he wants done with it.'

'Next, two boxes of old paperbacks from the fifties, sixties, seventies. I wouldn't mind dipping into those some time.'

'Then you'll have to build yourself some shelves.' She fingered some, thinking back to the days when she was married to Piers, straight from school. Long before she met Hamilton. 'When we were young, we got planks of wood and some bricks from a builders' yard and made shelves that way for all our books . . . For everything, in fact. If you want to keep these books, we'd better get some shelving built into the new room for you.'

'What did you think of the banker, Duncan?'

'He's all right. Looks like a baby, but has a sharp mind. He seemed fond of Julian and genuinely distressed about Tomi. He wasn't really bothered about Harry and Nick, even though he was shocked by their deaths. He likes everything in its proper place, and this affair is upsetting to one of his temperament.'

'Old curtains.' Oliver opened another box. 'Any good? Oh, probably not.'

'Moths or mice?'

'Broken glass. Someone put some photographs on top of the curtains, and then someone else has put a box of books on top of them and smashed the glass.'

'Oh dear. That was probably me. Hamilton took down some old photos of his aunts – the ones who brought him up after his parents died – because the frame had come unglued. He intended to have them reframed, but never bothered.'

Oliver tipped the broken glass to one side, so that Bea could retrieve the photographs from what had once been a double frame. Two black and white pictures of women of a certain age, with kind but firm expressions. Old-fashioned clothes and hairstyles.

She said, 'These two sisters founded and ran the agency. They left it to Hamilton, who hadn't intended to take it on, but did. Then I came along, worked with him in it, and took it on when he died. I never knew them. A pity.'

Oliver looked over her shoulder. 'We could have the photos repaired and blown up. We could get them properly framed – I know someone who does that – and hang them downstairs in the agency rooms, together with a picture of you. Our clients would like the idea that the agency carries on through the years, guided by people of integrity. Maggie's picture will hang there one day, too. Maybe mine, as well?'

She was going to say his photo didn't belong there because he was going to make his name in the academic world, but stopped herself just in time. Oliver needed to belong somewhere, and he had, after all, done as much as anyone to get the agency back on its feet after Hamilton's death.

'Of course. And in due course of time, when you're hobnobbing with the great and good of this world, I'll ask Piers to paint you, and we'll put that picture up by Hamilton's in the sitting room.'

He coloured up, but said, 'Nonsense. You can't discriminate like that. What about Maggie? She'd have my guts for garters if I were painted and not her.'

She managed to laugh. 'Yes, of course. You're right. Can you get these photos done for me, please? And now –' she looked at her watch – 'we'd better catch something to eat, shove something in the oven for tonight's supper, and be on our way, if we're going to see Lord Fairley today.'

Friday afternoon

Claire put the baby down to sleep. His tummy was full. He'd burped up his wind. He squirmed, then relaxed. His hands opened, slowly, letting go of consciousness.

Claire tucked him in. She could hear Nicole whining and coughing in her bedroom. Nicole was going down with a nasty dose of flu, if Claire knew anything about it. Nicole really oughtn't to be looking after a baby when she was infectious, but Claire couldn't help because she was otherwise engaged this weekend, wasn't she?

THIRTEEN

Estate agents' eyes glisten when a Chelsea house – however small – comes on the market. Lord Fairley's house was early Victorian, and though not actually on the river, was a mere hundred yards away from it down a quiet street. Dark red brick, symmetrical large windows, three stories, idiosyncratic roofline. It was the kind of house Bea imagined Oscar Wilde might have lived in, or Macauley, or Dickens. It reminded her of carriages, ladies who wore crinolines, butlers in frock coats, nursery maids in caps, and parlour maids in black.

Bea heaved on the doorbell. It was one of those that you pulled rather than pressed. A satisfactory clamour arose inside the house.

A tall man opened the door; no butler in sight. Well, who could afford a butler nowadays? Or a parlour maid, come to think of it.

'Lord Fairley? I'm Bea Abbot, and this is my son Oliver. Hermia suggested we call.'

'Come in, come in.' The hall was too dark for them to see him properly, but he led the way to a room at the back of the house, which looked on to a small garden, bounded by ancient brick walls. The light was better here.

Jamie, Lord Fairley was well over six foot. Not athletic; no. String-bean thin, light-brown hair with a tendency to curl, puppy-dog brown eyes and a self-deprecating smile. Excellent clothes of the casual variety. A man who enjoyed life. He had none of Hermia's drive, but was probably a more relaxed companion. Less brains, but more good humour?

Immense charm. Bea thought that Chris had made her immune to a charming manner, but at first sight she liked Lord Fairley because he seemed to like her.

'Forgive the disarray. Bachelor quarters, you know.' Smiling, he gestured them to comfortable old armchairs, upholstered in leather which had not been treated with the proper care, and so were cracking here and there. The room had probably been furnished by his parents or grandparents, and not much changed since. The walls and ceiling had once been painted cream, but the paint had darkened with age; or possibly with nicotine from cigarette and cigar smoke? Lord Fairley's fingers were not stained with tobacco, so presumably he didn't indulge.

The pictures on the walls were Baxter prints – rather good ones at that – with a couple of framed silhouettes of Victorian ancestors on either side of the fireplace. The silver tray on the mahogany dresser could have done with a polish, and the windows needed cleaning.

Bea gained an impression of someone who liked to be comfortable, but wasn't going to polish silver or windows himself. Perhaps his fiancée would remedy this?

'You're here about Nick's death.' He shook his head to indicate how upset he was about it. 'Poor old Nick. I'll miss him. We played golf once a month, regular as clockwork.'

'It's not just Nick's death that's important. Harry's and Tomi's are too.'

He leaned forward in his chair, eager for them to share his viewpoint. 'Surely it's obvious Harry killed Tomi, and then killed himself? Nick, now. That was a bit of a jolt.' He stifled a yawn. 'Sorry. Late night. Celebrating.'

'Hermia told us you'd got engaged. Congratulations.'

He nodded, smiling, his eyes straying to the carriage clock on the mantelpiece, which would probably fetch a good price at auction, but which had stopped at noon. 'Mustn't be late. She's working, or I'd introduce you. I'm picking her up and taking her down to see Mother this weekend. You don't really think someone's bumping us off one by one, do you?'

Bea said, 'All three victims had barbiturates in their stomachs before they were killed. Doesn't that make you think?'

'Sleeping pills, you mean?' He rubbed his chin, and then the back of his neck. 'I've never had any truck with them. I hit the pillow and that's it. Out like a light.' He didn't appear to have anything to add to that, but waited to see what they had to say next.

Bea glanced at Oliver, who seemed not to want to help with the questioning.

'Lord Fairley, I wonder—'

'Jamie, please. When people say "Lord Fairley" I look round for my father. Dead now, of course.'

'Jamie, then. May I ask if the lottery money is going to make a big difference to you?'

A broad grin. 'Apart from nudging me into proposing to the sweetest little girl in the whole world, you mean? Well, now. Let me think. I won't have to work so hard, that's for sure. But more than that? Well, when I was younger I had the odd ambition, but life – as they say – puts paid to one's wilder dreams. I used to think how splendid it would be to rent a grouse moor for the shooting, or perhaps lay out a golf course on the far side of the estate. My father had plans to reinstate the lake in front of the house, which has got silted up over the years. I'm not sure I'd bother, though I'm looking forward to having some days out with the guns in the autumn.

'I expect my future wife will have her own ideas. I said to her, she can have a free hand at the Manor once my Mother's gone, but we'd better hold back till then. Mother has the whole of the ground floor at present, the first floor's let to a couple who work in the City, and I live in the attics. I don't know how Mother will take it if I ask her to leave. She can be a bit sharp, you know.'

'Isn't there a Dower House that your mother can retire to?'

'Yes, but it's let out at present. Bit of a bummer that. But then, with the windfall, I could afford to build Mother something in the village, or buy out one of the tenants.' He had a sunny disposition; smiling came easily to him. 'I'm not one for confrontation. Don't like the thought of giving Mother the push.'

'Getting back to Nick—'

He held up both his hands. 'Now, come on. Leave it to the professionals, that's what I say, and good luck to them. Poor old Nick. Married the wrong woman, you know.'

Bea tried another tack. 'What do you think of Hermia taking up with young Chris?'

An expression of puzzlement crossed his face. 'Who is this Chris, eh? Someone else was talking about him. He's trying to make pictures or something? A lad just out of college, wet behind the ears? What does she see in him, eh?

Except –' he gave a shout of laughter – 'does he want someone to mother him? She's good at that. Now don't get me wrong. I like Hermia. Known her since we first competed in pony gymkhanas aged five or six. Made of pure steel, all that family, know what I mean? She'll chew him up and spit him out and expect me to dance attendance on her again. Only next time I won't be available.'

He looked at his watch and gave a great sigh. 'Must keep an eye on the time. Promised to fetch Her Ladyship from work. So . . . ?' He got to his feet, and they did so, too.

'Thank you for seeing us,' said Bea.

'Not at all.' He bared his teeth in a happy smile and showed them out of the door.

Bea struggled to put her thoughts in order as they walked back to where she'd parked the car. 'He threw us out pretty promptly. Surely it's too early for a nanny to finish for the day? Oliver, what did you make of him?'

'Can he really be that insensitive? Has he been so protected, so cushioned by his background and wealth that he doesn't feel things as other people do?'

'Coddled first by his mother, and then by Hermia. I hope his fiancée knows what she's taking on.'

They reached the car. Oliver said, 'If he asked me to lend him some money, I'm not sure I would. May I drive?'

She tossed him the keys. 'Is the girl marrying him for his position in the world, or does she love him?'

'What's to love? A title, an obliging disposition and a lot of money,' said Oliver, cynical for a change.

'You can see why Hermia kept looking elsewhere. It must have been so unsatisfactory for her, always being the one to make whatever decisions were needed, and then having to carry them out. Or did she enjoy being in charge? Perhaps. Oh, I don't know. Are we going straight to Claudine's? She ought to be back from school by now.'

Oliver didn't reply, and Bea wondered if Lord Fairley's interpretation of Hermia's character was correct. If so, look out, Chris!

Friday late afternoon

Claudine lived in a street north of the Bayswater Road, where the terraced houses all looked the same. Red-brick, four steps up to the front door, eight steps down to the basement flat. These were larger and more expensive buildings than the house in which Tomi had lived, but half the size of the ones in which Duncan resided. The pavements were wide; there were trees in the street and Car Parking Zones everywhere.

'You stay with the car,' said Bea, getting out. 'We don't want to risk getting clobbered with a parking ticket. If you see any wardens, drive around the block. I shouldn't be long. I've got my mobile, so ring me if there's a problem.'

There were three bell pushes inside the porch. Bea rang and identified herself to the speakerphone, the catch on the door was lifted and a disembodied voice said Mrs Abbot should come up to the first floor.

A woman in her late twenties awaited Bea at the top of the stairs. She had a fall of long, straight, dark hair swept back from her face, was wearing jeans and a huge fluffy blue wool top over a T-shirt. She was well-groomed, spider thin, with understated make-up and an air of authority. She led Bea into a sitting room overlooking the road. Big sash windows; shiningly polished furniture, mostly modern. Instead of a picture, there was a red and cream carpet hanging on one wall above a low white-leather settee.

Claudine offered tea or coffee, which Bea declined.

Claudine looked at the clock on the mantelpiece – a square, silver-framed nineteen thirties affair, chunky but chic – and compared the time with her watch. 'I'm meeting my partner at the station to catch the Eurostar train soon. He had a meeting after school, so it's all a bit of a rush. We're going on to Brussels for the weekend.'

How wise of her to arrange to be out of London this weekend. Hermia had mentioned that Claudine had recently got herself a new partner. No commitment yet? There were no rings on her fingers.

'It's kind of you to see me.'

'Not at all.' Grimly. 'Hermia's made it clear we need to take extra precautions this weekend.'

'It's Gregor who's preventing you all from going to the police, isn't it?'

'There's a clause in the agreement. We can only break silence if everyone agrees. He did agree to let you do some poking about, but he won't agree to letting the police in. He says he can't take the threat to himself seriously, but if I know him he's employed a minder to watch his back.'

'How do you feel about all these deaths?'

'Julian's death was sad, but to be expected. Shirley, too; silly woman. Put her behind the wheel of a car and she lost all sense of danger. I liked Tomi. I said right from the start that I couldn't see her taking drugs, but when I heard that Harry had killed her and then killed himself, I thought that was it. It niggled me, but not enough to do anything about it. I've got a lot on at work – deputy head of a school, you know, doing well – but it's not the sort of job which leaves you time to think about anything much else.'

'What did you think about Harry killing himself that way?'

'I might have known he'd make a mess of it. Really, some men can't be trusted to tie their own shoelaces.'

'And Nick?'

'I hold no brief for Nick. He only acknowledged two sorts of women: those he could take to bed – whether he paid them or not – and those who scared him to death. I scare him to death. I mean, I did . . .' She winced. 'Sorry. Can't get used to the fact that he's dead. That they all are. It's –' a deep breath – 'yes, it's frightening.'

'You know they all had barbiturates in their system before they died?'

A long stare. 'You mean, they were drugged first and killed when they were helpless? That's horrible. No, I didn't know that.'

A change of tactic. 'What do you fancy doing with your windfall?'

'If I live till Monday, you mean? I plan to buy a small private school in an area where there are plenty of paying pupils, update the facilities, and run it myself.'

'Have you been making enquiries already?'

She reddened. 'That's no business of yours.'

'I was wondering if you'd shared the news with your partner.'

'That is *definitely* no business of yours.'

Which meant that she had? Bea wondered if any of the others – Jamie, for instance – had shared the news with his nearest and dearest. Under strict injunctions not to spread the news, of course. Hermia hadn't, probably. Harry and Nick? Nick might have done so. Tomi had dropped hints to her mother. Of course, they'd stood to lose the lot if word got out that they'd told anyone, but on the other hand, human nature wasn't easily bound by such promises.

A change of tactic. 'What do you think of the surviving members of the group? Duncan, for instance.'

A smile. 'Trustworthy. Good with money. We had a fling some years ago, but remain friends. He's the last person I can think of who'd want to kill us. I mean, for a start, he and Julian were very close. Duncan was devastated when he died.'

'Julian's death is outside our remit. Have you met the girl he wants to marry?'

'Yes, she's Julian's younger sister, so we've known her for ever. Nice girl. He'll be all right with her, provided they can keep the gambling brother at bay.'

'Hermia?'

A laugh, quickly fading away. 'I like Hermia. There's Jewish ancestry; some way back, I think. Some people say that's why she's supposed to be tight with her money, but all I can say is that whenever I've been strapped for cash to take the kids on outings, or if I hear of someone in need, she's always stumped up, on condition I keep quiet about it. We went on a wild trip rock-climbing in the Andes one summer holidays at a time when neither of us was particularly tied up with a man. She was great fun, though I wouldn't share a bedroom with her again; she snores.'

Bea smiled. 'I like Hermia too, but I am concerned that she's taken up with my son's young friend. Is she a man-eater, do you think?'

A more genuine laugh. 'I've heard something about that. Dick or Chris, or something? A brilliant young film director, is that right? Tomi used to go on about him. She liked him, said he was kindness itself, but eccentric. He sounds quite mad to me. He's not like any of Hermia's usual boyfriends. But, well, why not?'

'Why not, indeed? How about Jamie Fairley?'

An indulgent, slightly contemptuous smile. 'He's perfectly all right, but he'd have been more at home in the Middle Ages, if you see what I mean. Charging around in a full suit of armour, killing anyone who disagreed with him, and then apologizing for having knocked them off their horse. Not that I think . . . Sorry, I didn't mean that he'd have killed Tomi or Harry, and certainly not Nick. They played golf together a lot, you know. What I mean is—'

'I think I understand what you meant. He wouldn't have bothered to use sleeping pills to render his victims unconscious, but would have bashed them over the head with a blunt instrument straight away?'

'And then apologized.'

Bea laughed. 'All right. I get the picture. On the other hand, I'm not sure he's as clueless as he tries to make out, because he does seem to have his finances well under control.'

'He's hit on a job that he's perfectly fitted for. He's charming and exactly what businessmen think that a member of the aristocracy should be. I can quite see why Hermia couldn't bring herself to marry him, though. I hear he's got a new girl in tow.'

'What do you think of her?'

A frown. 'I may be prejudiced, but I wouldn't trust my partner alone in a room with her.'

'A predator?'

A shrug. 'She's pretty enough and seems very capable. Secondary modern education, then vocational training. Not university, though I'm not sure that matters nowadays. I expect we'll all get along fine, once we get used to one another.'

'And the last on the list; Gregor?'

A sigh. 'I like Gregor. He's fun. He wouldn't do any of *us* down, but I wouldn't trust him with a country cousin who had money to invest. If you see what I mean.'

'Gregor is the only one who has refused to see me. Do you think you could persuade him otherwise?'

'What would you hope to achieve by talking to him?' Claudine looked at the clock again and checked her watch. 'I'll have to throw you out, I'm afraid. I haven't finished packing yet.'

'I'll give you a lift to the station, if it will help.'

'Yes, it would. I was going to get a taxi. Can you hold on five minutes?' She disappeared into the back of the flat.

Bea went to the window and looked out. Yes, there was her car, with Oliver leaning against it, looking up to where she was standing. She waved to him, gestured five, and five again, with outspread fingers. He nodded. Fortunately there was no sign of a traffic warden.

Left alone, Bea prowled round the room. There was a drop-front bureau beside the fireplace. She eased the front open. Everything was neat and tidy. The bookcases showed a wide range of subject matter: evidence of an enquiring, intelligent mind. No romances.

On the mantelpiece there were silver frames displaying photographs of older people; professorial types? Upper middle-class? No photos of anyone Claudine's age. There was a scuffed leather briefcase on the floor by one of the easy chairs, together with a tottering pile of paperwork. Bea peeked; exam papers or children's homework. For him or her? Ah, something was marked 'Mr Snaith' or perhaps the word was 'Smith?' So the partner was probably another teacher. And if he was another teacher, might not Claudine have discussed her plan to buy an independent school with him?

Claudine reappeared, wearing a navy car coat and towing a small suitcase on wheels. Bea led the way to the car, and Oliver drove them to St Pancras station, where Claudine waved them goodbye, saying she'd try to contact Gregor by phone en route to see if he'd change his mind about meeting Bea. Then she was gone, and Oliver drove them home.

Bea said, 'I've got sensory overload.'

'TMI? Too much information?'

'I think we must get together with CJ and exchange notes. Try to work out what's important and what's not. Air our suspicions. See if they have any basis in fact. We don't need Chris or Hermia. They wouldn't be able to help at this stage.'

He nodded, but didn't comment. The rain had started again. Persistently, drenching everything.

Bea said, 'Do you think spring will ever come?'

Friday early evening

Claire fed the baby and walked around the flat, bringing up his wind. Nice baby. He was already looking more lively. How could you not love babies, even when – as with this one – they didn't love you?

Mrs was up and about, coughing, taking linctus, ought to be in bed with antibiotics. She said that her doctor had been so horrible to her about Baby, she couldn't bear to ask him for anything. In fact, she said she was going to change doctors just as soon as she was on her feet again.

Baby didn't show any sign of getting his mother's cold yet. Claire hoped he wouldn't, because he was rather fragile, definitely underweight.

As she nursed him, she listened to Mrs talking in her hoarse voice about herself, her important husband, and how much she disliked her mother-in-law, who'd been married twice and got rid of her first husband, who was now a world-famous portrait painter, and that served her right, because she now had to work for a living finding jobs for cleaners and cooks. She was the worst mother-in-law in the whole world. And so on. Mrs needed someone to talk to, and Claire was elected her confidante.

Which suited Claire. With the odd interjected query here and there, Claire was getting all the information she needed about the interfering Mrs Abbot, who ran an agency – not for nurses, as it happened – and had adopted two totally unsuitable people, who were probably hoping to cut Mr out of her will. The boy was very clever, no doubt, but of mixed race. 'Not that I'm racist, dear . . .'

As for the girl, she was a proper scarecrow, hair all stiff and gelled and usually some colour other than nature intended, and her skirts were up to here, my dear . . .

Claire put Baby down to sleep and covered him over. He fussed a bit, but not much. She looked at her watch. Her fiancée was collecting her soon and taking her down to meet his mother for the weekend, which meant Claire couldn't knock anyone else off their perch for a couple of days. A pity. She would have liked a try at Hermia, stuck-up creature! But time was against her. Or was it? If she could get back to London early enough on Sunday, then she might well chance one more throw of the dice.

Only three days to go. On Monday night they would all be celebrating. She told herself that what Jamie would get would be enough, even though . . . Well, if she still felt strongly about Hermia, there would be time enough in future to deal with her.

*And if Mrs Abbot senior started making trouble, then . . .
No, she wouldn't, couldn't harm Baby. Could she?*

*On her way out of the door, she checked that her little
brown bottle of All Ease was in her handbag. She never knew
when it might come in handy.*

FOURTEEN

Friday evening

CJ was free and arrived at the house just as Maggie was leaving for the evening. A date with a girlfriend, or with Zander? Maggie wasn't saying.

CJ was not in the habit of conducting affairs at kitchen tables. He handed Bea a bottle of something which looked expensive and turned into the sitting room.

Bea shut the door on the night. Another filthy night. It matched her mood.

CJ directed Oliver to draw the big dining table – so little used nowadays – further into the room, and seated himself in the carver's chair at the head. Oliver laid out his laptop and a batch of papers at one side, leaving Bea to uncork and serve the wine CJ had brought, before taking her place at the foot of the table.

Bea laid out the pads on which she'd been making notes; it seemed she'd used two, which was wasteful of resources, but she'd obviously picked up the wrong one at some point. She lifted her glass in a toast and called the meeting to order. 'We've all been working in different directions, and it's about time we tried to make sense of what we've got. CJ; can you tell us what's been happening with the police?'

'Nothing much. They've accepted the idea that Tomi was killed by Harry, who then killed himself, and that Nick got drunk and fell over the banisters. The Crown Prosecution Service is saying there's no evidence that anyone else is involved, so the police have dropped their investigation. Of course, they don't know about the money angle yet.'

Bea said, 'I don't understand what makes Gregor tick. Isn't he concerned about his old friends dropping dead?'

'I don't understand him, either. He says it won't hurt to wait till Tuesday before letting the police in on the secret. Duncan has been trying to get him to change his mind, without success. He has interests in half a dozen countries, and I suspect he's arguing with accountants somewhere – perhaps in Greece – about the amount he owes in tax and wants that affair concluded before his assets are considerably increased on Monday.'

Bea protested. 'That's not fair.'

'Duncan says that Gregor doesn't play by the same rules as the rest of us. Gregor acknowledges there is a problem if one of them is killing off the others, but he says they've only got to take some elementary precautions to keep themselves alive till Monday, when they collect what's due to them. He seems to enjoy walking tightropes without a safety net.'

Bea said, 'Precautions. Like advising Claudine to go off to Brussels for the weekend?'

'Sensible of her. The police confirm that the calls made from Tomi's mobile, saying she was going abroad for a few days, and later on the one from Harry's mobile telling the police where her body could be found, were all made from the Notting Hill area. Likewise the one from Tomi's phone asking Chris to collect her. Harry could indeed have made them.'

Oliver checked his data. 'They all live within a couple of miles of one another. Surely the police can get a better fix on them than that?'

'If they had reason to be interested, yes. At the moment, no.'

Bea nodded. 'All right. We understand the problem faced by the police, although frankly, confronted by three corpses which were all filled with barbiturates before death, you or I would want to shout "foul play". Oliver, you've got the results of the enquiries which Maggie and Zander have been making. Can we trace the drugs from them? In particular, the heroin which was used to help kill Tomi?'

Oliver shuffled paperwork. 'Maggie and Zander have added more information as it came in and cross-checked everywhere. The results are inconclusive. They've isolated the names of three people who have been reported as dealing in drugs. These three have been at parties attended by Tomi, Harry and Nick. It doesn't mean the others don't have access to drugs; just that we don't have an obvious connection. Anyway, if the others wanted to, I'm sure they could get drugs almost anywhere.'

CJ responded, 'Agreed. The three names are going to
the Drugs Squad, but without any evidence to link them to the
deaths, we're no further forward. I checked on the reported
deaths of the soldier Julian and the drunken driver Shirley
and found nothing untoward. Two bodies, correctly identified, both cremated.'

'Dead end,' sighed Bea. 'Oliver, do you have anything to
add from your studies of the contents of Tomi's laptop?'

'Not really. I'll have another session on it soon.'

'Moving on,' said Bea, getting into Chair mode. 'We've
all three been talking to the surviving members of the group,
except for Gregor. We've been bombarded with information,
with hints and suspicions and declarations of innocence, and
some of it is contradictory. A couple of times I've jumped
to conclusions about this person or that and been forced to
rethink. I've kept some notes of statements offered as fact,
but haven't had a chance to weigh one against the other. If
you've got the stomach for it, I'd like to run through what
we've heard from the beginning.'

She started with Chris's plea to help him find Tomi, and
finished up with a sore throat nearly an hour later.

'And that's it, so far. I don't know how you envisage the
murderer, but it seems to me that he or she must have access
to drugs – both heroin and sleeping pills – in considerable
quantities, and can get close to the victims without rousing
suspicion, which would indicate they move in the same social
circles. The use of barbiturates to render the victims unconscious before they are killed seems to indicate that there is,
perhaps, a physical in-balance; perhaps the murderer is smaller,
or shorter or weaker in some way? Next, they have transport,
or they wouldn't have been able to leave Tomi's body out at
Fulmer. That's as far as I've got. As to the people we've inter-
viewed, some of them I liked, some I trust. Not one of them
seems to me to match my profile of the murderer. Any ideas?'

Silence. 'Coffee,' said Oliver. 'Black.'

CJ lifted his empty glass. 'I'll join you.'

Neither of them made any move to make coffee for themselves, so Bea went out to the kitchen to brew up. Her mind
was buzzing with half-digested theories. She took two cups of
fierce black coffee back to the men, who accepted them with a
bare nod of thanks.

CJ performed five-finger exercises on the table. 'Bea, how about your impressions of them as people? Why do you trust some and not others?'

Bea shook her head. 'I don't think any of them told us the whole truth. I got the impression that they've all known one another for so long that they automatically put up barriers against outsiders.

'For instance, Duncan and Julian were fast friends from prep school. They all knew about and deplored Shirley's habit of drinking and driving. Claudine and Hermia get on so well that they've been on holiday together. Hermia and Jamie have been pushed together by their families since childhood and, though they don't want to marry, there's a strong bond of loyalty there. I can't see Jamie bestirring himself enough to murder anyone, but he frequently played golf with Nick. Nick pestered women even before his wife left him. Nick was not much liked, but they put up with him because they've all known one another for so long. He seems to have deteriorated since his marriage went sour. He went out with Claudine at one time, but he also made a pass at Tomi, who slapped his face.

'One of them – can't remember who – called Harry a cheapskate, and Hermia thought Tomi could have done better. The women both said how much they'd liked Tomi. They all admire Gregor and his ability to move money around, and none of them is willing to finger him to the police. They're ambivalent about Jamie's fiancée, but that might be because she isn't one of them.'

CJ said, 'Don't stop to think about it, but tell me, do you trust Claudine?'

No hesitation. 'Yes. If she didn't want to answer a question, she told me to mind my own business. She's too decisive, too busy to bother embroidering the truth.'

'Hermia?'

Remember that bright, white, eager-to-impress smile. 'Not entirely, no. There was something about the way she spoke of her career, her income . . . Did she protest too much that she didn't need the money?'

'Duncan?'

'At the time, yes. I thought he was whiter than white. Now, I don't know. The girl he wants to marry is Julian's sister, which means he's saddling himself with a gambler for a brother-in-law.'

CJ said, 'I've been making some enquiries. Duncan's firm is in the process of being taken over by a conglomerate, and the word is he's facing redundancy.'

Bea threw up her hands. 'He didn't say anything about that. He made out he was doing all right. I wonder if any of the others are in trouble, money wise. It would explain why they're all so cagey.'

'What did you think of Jamie?'

Bea looked across at Oliver. 'Oliver said he wouldn't trust him with a loan. I think he's had everything too easy, all his life. I think he's the kind who doesn't actually lie if he's in trouble, but somehow wriggles out of it. The others speak of him as if he were a slightly backward younger brother. Childhood links remain stronger than civic duty.'

CJ picked up his cup and took a sip of ultra-strong coffee. Tears sprang to his eyes, but he uttered no word of complaint. 'If the police start interviewing them, those childhood links will break down.'

'But not until Tuesday morning, by which time someone else may be dead.'

'Who do you reckon is next for the chop?' asked Oliver.

Bea said, 'How should I know? They're all taking Gregor's advice, I assume. Hermia has anchored Chris to her side. Jamie and Duncan have got themselves attached to women. Claudine has gone off to Brussels for the weekend; she has a new partner who . . .' Bea hesitated. 'Now there's something else that's been bothering me. Suppose the murderer isn't one of these five, but someone whom they've talked to?'

'What?' said CJ. 'They all swore themselves to secrecy.'

'Possibly some of them kept that vow, but we do know that some of them talked about it amongst themselves. For instance, Claudine mentioned her dream of buying a small independent school to me. She plans to run it herself, possibly with the aid of her new partner, who is also a teacher. I think that if I were in Claudine's shoes I might well have been tempted – in strictest confidence, of course – to confide in him.'

Oliver sipped his coffee with every evidence of satisfaction.

'Which makes Claudine's partner keen to knock out some of the others, in order to increase her share of the proceeds?'

There was a considering silence.

'Prove it,' said CJ, but he sounded half convinced.

'It's human nature,' said Bea. 'Keeping secrets is not easy; particularly ones which are going to bring you good fortune. For instance, Tomi's mother said she knew her daughter was due for a windfall. All right, I know her mother wasn't even in England at the time of Tomi's death – at least, I assume so – but she's not the only one who might have been given a hint that the future was going to be bright. Let's face it, if you were a man proposing to a girl, you'd probably give her a hint that you're going to be better off than she might have imagined.'

'You think Duncan might have talked to his girlfriend?'

'Dropped a hint, yes. The other possibility is that a partner or friend might have overheard one of the telephone conversations which Duncan and Hermia made to their friends, telling them of the big lottery win. Duncan said he'd made sure the people he phoned were alone, but all that means is that he asked them if they were alone, and they said, "Yes." That might not have been the exact truth.'

Oliver drank the rest of his coffee. 'Do you think there might have been a joint effort? One of the survivors, plus an accomplice?'

Silence.

CJ groaned. 'This widens the field so much, it's practically all horizon.' He pushed aside his coffee, almost untouched, and got up. 'I don't see that we can do anything more for the time being. Each one of the five has been warned of the danger. Monday sees the division of spoils, and after that we can hand the matter over to the police. And it's way past my bedtime.'

Oliver snapped shut his laptop, said, 'I'll see you out,' and left as well.

Bea, exhausted, stretched out on the settee, shucked off her shoes and put her feet up, only to start upright on hearing an altercation at the front door. Oliver put his head back into the room, but before he could speak a tall figure in black pushed past him. Piers, her first husband. In some kind of trouble?

'Sorry to barge in on you like this,' he said, shutting the door in Oliver's face.

'Trouble?' said Bea, imagining a thousand different tragedies affecting her family. She waited, sending up an arrow prayer. *Dear Lord, it's bad news, I'm sure of it. Give me strength, courage. And common sense.*

Piers paced the sitting room floor. He was almost, but not quite, wringing his hands, concentrating on some inner torment. 'Bea, what do you know about Pippin's new nanny?'

'Nothing, except that they've got one. Why?'

'I don't know. Maybe I'm imagining things. I'm sure I am. But you could check her out, couldn't you?'

'Calm down.' Her own pulse was racing. Piers wasn't one to get into a state for nothing. 'Start at the beginning.'

He made a big effort to calm himself, and sat down. 'I went round to Max's this afternoon. He'd gone off up north early, and Nicole was drooping around with some kind of fluey cold. She said you two had had a row and that he'd forbidden you the house for the time being. I told her that I thought that was rather harsh. I said she should look at it from your point of view, that you wanted desperately to help, but perhaps had not been altogether wise in the way you did it.'

'Ouch,' said Bea. 'Yes, I suppose I was tactless, but—'

'Being a portrait painter is sometimes like being a psycho-analyst. People talk freely while I'm working. I've heard often enough how bereft women feel when their sons get married and cut down on communication. You remember that old saying, "my son is my son till he gets him a wife, but my daughter's my daughter all of her life"? That happens all the time.'

'Yes,' said Bea, sighing. 'I've learned that the hard way. I must never ever offer advice, even when I see things going wrong.'

Piers wasn't listening to her. 'Pippin was awake and fussing, but not crying as he has been most of the times I'd dropped in. I asked if I could pick him up, and Nicole said we'd have to ask permission from Nurse, who had taken charge of him. So out popped this pretty little thing, and she said she'd heard all about me and knew I'd be careful. So I lifted him up and

walked around with him, and he looked up at me, and we
chatted away to one another. Well, I suppose I chatted, and he
listened. It was the first time he'd ever listened to me, and I
felt . . . honoured.

'I said it looked as if he were putting on weight at last, and
Nicole said that yes, he was, at long last, and it was all due
to Nurse. Nurse dimpled away at me and made sure I saw
the ring on the fourth finger of her left hand. Now I'm used
to women throwing themselves at me, hoping I'll fall at their
feet and ask them to sit for their portrait. She didn't do that,
but she . . . she was sizing me up, far more than was usual for
a casual encounter.

'I got quite a shock when I met her eyes, because the way
she was looking at me . . . I couldn't pin it down at first, but it
came to me later that inside that pretty little head lived
Tyrannosaurus Rex, and that she'd been sizing me up for the
kill.'

'Oh, really?' Bea was tired and wanted to go to bed.

He was stubborn. 'All right, I didn't take to her. It might
have been a trick of the light. A moment later she was all soft
and maternal. She took Pippin from me and cooed at him. He
stared back at her, but he didn't smile and for some reason I
felt extremely alarmed. You'll say I'm making this up, and I
can't prove anything. Afterwards, I couldn't get her out of
my mind. I went home and tried sketching her in charcoal
and she turned into a vulture.'

Bea pressed her fingers over her closed eyes. 'You know
I can't interfere.'

'I got her name. Claire Stourton. She came through a day
nannies agency. I thought you might check up on her.'

'I can't do that without giving a reason. You know perfectly
well that this spat with Nicole is all about control of Max and
Pippin.'

'Yes, I know that. Nicole's always been jealous of you, and
with reason. Max does pick them, doesn't he? Well, I've done
my bit. Warned you. I don't see what else I can do.'

'Keep dropping in on them, will you?'

'A spy in the camp?'

'Precisely.'

He left, and she dragged herself up to bed, praying on each

step. *Dear Lord, help. Dear Lord, what's going on here? Piers isn't usually fanciful. If there is something amiss here . . . Dear Lord, protect Pippin.*

Tomorrow she'd check on Clare Stourton.

Friday night

Claire sat up in bed. Jamie snored beside her, out to the world.

She was high on excitement. Five down, which meant they were going to be very rich indeed. Tomorrow might be difficult; meeting the mother-in-law-to-be was bound to be a strain. Claire planned to be as sweet as pie, and she knew that Jamie would see her through it. He knew how lucky he was to have her at his side.

A pity that the others had been warned they were in danger. Claire blamed the interfering Mrs Abbot for that. If it hadn't been for her, there might well have been another victim. Unless she could get back early on Sunday . . . but that didn't look possible at the moment.

Well, well. Monday night would see the clan gathered at Duncan's, when they'd toast their good fortune in champagne. Claire liked champagne. A pity she couldn't put one of her specials in Hermia's glass . . . but there, calm down, calm down. Perhaps she'd done enough and should draw a line under her little ventures.

They had enough to live happily ever after. All due to her.

Saturday morning

Bea woke to the sound of gentle rain falling outside, and to the feeling that the house felt warmer than it had been. Perhaps the temperature had risen. If so, *Thank You, Lord, and thank You for a good night's sleep. And please don't let me obsess about things I can't do anything about.*

She drew back the curtains. There was no frost on the garden, and the light was growing brighter and stronger every minute. As she watched, the rain ceased and the sun broke through the clouds. A good omen?

Maggie was on the phone all through breakfast, first chasing up a tiler who hadn't finished a job to her satisfaction, and then to Zander, arranging to meet him at the station for a day

trip to Brighton. Oliver brought a laptop to the breakfast table.
He ate and drank absent-mindedly, frowning away. Perhaps
he ought to have his eyesight tested?

When they'd finished eating, Bea shooed Maggie out,
cleared the table around Oliver, and went down to see what
if anything needed her attention in the agency.

Miss Brook was on duty and nothing needed Bea's attention that very minute, so she logged on to the Internet and
made a list of agencies which specialized in day nannies.
There were a considerable number. She told herself that Piers
had been overreacting yesterday, and that there couldn't
possibly be anything wrong with Max's new nanny. Still, it
didn't do any harm to check. If she could find out where
Claire lived, she could call on her, see if she really was a
snake in the grass.

She struck lucky at the third agency. Yes, they had a Claire
Stourton on their books, and did Mrs Abbot wish to book her
for her new baby? Ah, wait a minute, Claire was with a Mrs
Abbot at the moment. Was there something wrong? Claire
came most highly recommended.

'No, everything's fine,' said Bea, improvising. 'She's with
my daughter-in-law, in fact, but there was some talk of my
paying part of the agency bill. My son wants to do everything himself, of course, but—'

'Ah, yes. The Member of Parliament. Of course, we are
accustomed to providing nannies for the very best houses.'

'Indeed. But I was wondering . . . I'm not sure how to put
it . . . I don't wish to upset him, but I was thinking I might
perhaps be able to show my appreciation of Claire's efforts,
or even defray some of the expense, without him being aware
of it?'

'I'm afraid we don't have any facility for splitting the bill.
You must make such arrangements direct with your son.'

'Of course, I will do that. Perhaps I might be able to deliver
Claire some flowers or chocolates or something? Just a small
token of my regard.'

'Which I am sure will be much appreciated. She is not
working this weekend, but will be back on duty on Monday
morning. Oh, I see she's taking some time off on Monday, a
personal matter. She'll be back on duty on Tuesday morning
and you can catch her then.'

'Thank you very much. You've been most kind.'

Mm. That didn't get Bea any further, did it?

She looked at the emails in her in-box and was about to tackle them when somebody thundered down the stairs and threw open the door into her office. Chris, of course. With Hermia in tow. Hermia was laughing, Chris was not.

'Mrs Abbot, I've had the most wonderful idea. Oh, are you working? Am I interrupting something important?'

'What could be more important than attending to you, Chris?'

Hermia continued to smile. 'Well, I do think it is a good idea, actually. Can you take a break, Mrs Abbot? Where's Oliver? We need him, too.'

Bea took a deep breath, prepared to blast the pair of them out of her office, and hesitated. With a jolt she realized that whatever else the pair of them had been up to, they'd not wasted any time getting to know one another better. They were radiant. Of course, Chris was often radiant with ideas, but this was different. He was growing up fast. Even his voice seemed to have deepened.

As for Hermia, her hair had a softer line to it, her cheeks were flushed with excitement, and she was looking up at Chris; with amusement, yes. But amusement mixed with admiration.

'You see,' said Chris, turning Bea's computer screen away from her so that she couldn't work at it, 'I had an idea. This is Saturday, right? And the rain's stopped. You know how you wheedled the truth out of Brian when we brought him in, how you got him to say exactly what happened the last time I saw Tomi, right? I said to Hermia that you'd almost hypnotized him. Now, if what he said was true, and he turned so that the sun wasn't in his eyes when Tomi left us, then it follows that I must have turned, too, to face him. So the sun would have been in my eyes. Or was it? I've thought and thought, and Hermia's tried prodding my memory, but I can't remember exactly what happened next.'

He took a deep breath. 'So I thought that if we went out there now and Oliver pretended to be Brian, and Hermia pretended to be Tomi, and you were there to ask the right questions, then perhaps it would come back to me. Right?'

Hermia was still smiling. 'We do realize you must be very

busy, Mrs Abbot, but if you could take half an hour off? It's only just down the road.'

'Why not get Brian back to help you out?'

Chris shook his head. 'I tried that. He's off to the races, doesn't want to be held up, thinks we're mad—'

'Which we probably are,' said Hermia. 'But it's worth a try, isn't it, Mrs Abbot?'

'Yes, it is. You collect Oliver – who's somewhere around – I'll tell Miss Brook I'm off for an hour, and I'll meet you upstairs.'

FIFTEEN

Saturday morning

The library was only a hop, skip and a jump away. Even though it was not on a bus route, it was almost as busy as the High Street. The rain had stopped, and the icy wind had dropped. The pavements gleamed wet, but were rapidly drying. Were those buds on the trees really trying to open? Was spring on its way at last?

Chris led them to a spot outside the entrance to the library. 'I was standing here, with my arms full of books. We'd just come out of the library and were facing one another. Tomi was here, on my right, nearest the library. Hermia; would you stand here? We were talking – arguing, actually – about a Joseph Wright of Derby picture we'd both seen, which has wonderful shadows in it. She thought the shadows were too heavy to be convincing, and I said they conveyed more that way. Brian came up the hill towards us. He called my name. I turned round to see who was calling and so did Tomi. Facing into the sun.'

Chris and Hermia both turned to look down the hill. Oliver stepped up close to them. The sun obliged by shining all around them.

'Wait a minute,' said Bea. 'Brian said he'd have liked you to introduce him to Tomi, but you didn't, did you?'

'He's a bit of a lech. I didn't want to inflict him on her.'

'All right, so you stood there, talking. Tomi was on the inside; you were on the outside, nearest the traffic. You were looking partly down the street and partly back to the library. Tomi could see past you, down and across the street. Is that right?'

'Correct.'

'Then you got caught up in admiration of the sunglasses that Brian was wearing, so I suppose you turned more towards him and away from Tomi?'

Chris said, 'The sun was in my eyes, and I had to screw

them up to see him. He had on these superb, aviator style glasses. I really must find out where he got them.'

'Meanwhile Tomi tried to put two of your library books into her big green bag. And failed. Will you mime that, Hermia?'

Hermia did so.

'Now,' said Bea. 'Chris is concentrating on Brian and his sunglasses. What is Tomi feeling or doing?'

Hermia nodded. 'She's bored because he's stopped talking to her, and she can see he's not going to introduce her to the newcomer. She's decided that he's not her type, anyway. She's thinking about the party that evening. She'd been going to buy something new for it, hadn't she? She was probably on the fidget, wondering if she'd have time to go shopping then and there. She's starting to look around her, thinking how best to get away.'

'Chris, of course, is perfectly oblivious,' suggested Bea.

Chris blushed. 'Yes. Well. I'm talking to Brian, and the sun's in my eyes. I'm not looking at Tomi. Then she says she's seen someone, and the next thing I know, she's gone.'

'Down the hill?'

'No.'

'Up the hill?'

'No. Brian said he thought she'd gone across the street, and . . .' Chris froze. He shot a quick glance across the road and frowned. 'She said she was off, had seen someone. She moved behind me and stepped out into the road. I said, "Take care," or something like that, and I think I caught a glimpse of her weaving through the traffic.'

He pressed both hands to his eyes. Took his hands away from his eyes and turned to look across the street. 'There was a mini parked on the other side of the road. Tomi was heading for it.'

'Colour?'

'White.' He sounded uncertain. 'Could it be? I don't know anyone who owns a white mini.'

Hermia gasped. The whites of her eyes showed.

Chris put his arm around her. 'Are you all right? What's the matter?'

Hermia said, 'Cramp. Silly me. Ow! I'll be all right in a minute.' She hobbled around, grimacing.

Bea and Oliver exchanged looks. Bea said, 'Hermia; you know someone who owns a white mini, don't you?'

'I suppose everyone does. There are plenty of them about. Ow!' She rubbed her calf.

There weren't plenty of them about, no. They were pretty rare, in fact. Bea ran through in her mind what cars the group owned. Julian; no. Shirley; no. Both were dead before Tomi was killed.

Duncan wouldn't run a mini. No way.

Claudine didn't have a car, did she? She was going to get a taxi to the station.

Hermia had a stylish sports car.

Harry; Nick? No way. Both would have driven big cars.

Jamie? A 4 x 4 and a BMW.

Gregor; don't make me laugh!

So the mini didn't belong to any of the Famous Five, *but Hermia knew of one, and wasn't telling!*

Why? There could be only one reason. She was protecting someone.

Someone who was not one of the Five, but who might be linked with them?

Which meant one of the girlfriends. Duncan's or Jamie's?

Or did the Mini, perhaps, belong to Claudine's partner? No. It wasn't a car which a man would choose to drive nowadays. In the old days, perhaps, but not now. Nowadays it was a car for youth, or for a woman. But perhaps Bea was wrong about that, as she'd been wrong about so many things recently.

Chris had got Hermia around her shoulders, making her walk up and down. He kept saying, 'Press the ball of your foot down, hard.'

Hermia gradually straightened up, but her colour was still bad. She tried to laugh, to pretend that nothing was wrong.

Oliver wasn't fooled. Neither was Bea.

Always ask the easy question first. 'Hermia, what's the name of Duncan's girlfriend?'

'Mandy.'

'What's Jamie's fiancée called?'

Hermia looked straight into Bea's eyes. 'I can't think. Something quite ordinary.'

A lie. 'How about . . . Claire?'

Hermia turned into Chris's shoulder and began to cry.

Bea had half expected and half dreaded that it might be Claire. Hermia's reaction confirmed it. A murderess was in charge of little Pippin! Bea felt herself sag at the knees.

Chris was bewildered. 'What's going on?'

Oliver took control. 'Taxi!' He waved a passing cab to their side and piled them all in.

Back home, they took refuge in the kitchen. Oliver – who had always said he hadn't the brains to work the coffee machine, and so left all that sort of domestic work to the women – produced cups of strong black reviver all round.

Hermia began to cry, complaining that her leg was still hurting her. She said she really must go home and take some painkillers, and that she had a thousand things to do. When she got up to leave, Bea told her to sit down, and for a wonder Hermia did as she was told.

'What *is* going on?' asked Chris. Yet his light, bright eyes were now on Bea, now on Oliver, and then fixed on Hermia. Was he beginning to suspect his goddess had feet of clay?

Bea tried to pull her socks up. Metaphorically. Every now and then she felt a shudder run through her. She put her hand out to the telephone and withdrew it. Nicole wouldn't listen if Bea rang to say she'd employed a murderess, would he? How had Claire got into that household, anyway? Surely Pippin was safe? Who would kill an innocent baby?

Answer: anyone who would go round knocking off their fiancée's friends like that might be capable of anything.

Oliver said, 'Drink up.' They obeyed. Bea made a face and reached for milk and sugar. The others took it black.

'Now, Mrs Abbot,' said Oliver, taking the easy question first. 'How do you know the name of Claire, and why did the mention of her name nearly cause you to pass out on us?'

Bea took a deep breath. 'A girl called Claire Stourton has got a position as day nanny to my grandson. My first husband, Piers, visited them and was so distressed by what he saw of her that he asked me to check her out. I don't *know* any more than that about her. You can say I'm going way over the top, imagining things, but it frightens me to think that someone unsuitable might be able to hurt Pippin. I'm trying to be sensible about it, but I can't. If there's a link between this girl and the lottery deaths, then . . . I'm not going to have hysterics, but I do think we should know.'

Oliver asked the second, difficult question. 'Hermia, I think you must tell us what you know about this girl Claire. Is it the same one?'

Hermia looked at her watch and tried to get off her stool. 'It's getting awfully late and—'

Chris pushed her back down on to her seat. 'If you want us to help—'

Hermia shook back her hair. 'Please, Chris. Leave it. I need to go home. You promised to look after me, so I'm asking—' She tried to smile. 'No, I'm not going to beg. But if you could just trust me over this one thing . . . ?'

Bea watched with interest. This was make or break time for Chris. If he took Hermia at her word, they could never be equal partners in the game of life.

Bea could see him wavering. He wanted to trust Hermia, but he'd grown up just enough to have doubts. Would he sit on those doubts? He might. He could decide to trust her no matter what, and that would set the tone for any future disagreements. She would always say, 'Trust me!' and he would always do so.

He wasn't giving in that easily, though. He looked at Bea, who returned his gaze with one of deep anxiety. He turned to Oliver, his oldest and best friend, who was also looking anxious.

Finally he faced Hermia. 'I can see you know something, something important, that you don't want to talk about. We've only just met, and there's stuff about you that I don't know yet, and that's OK. We've time to find out these things. What I do know is that you have lots of good friends, and you've always stuck by them. I love that about you. But if one of your friends committed a murder, would you go along with it?'

Hermia did her best to smile. 'No, of course not. None of them have, I assure you. Now, if you don't want to come home with me, I'll—'

Oliver interrupted. 'And if the friend of a friend was about to commit a murder?'

'I'd . . . I'd want to warn my friend.'

Oliver moved in for the kill. 'That's what you're going home to do now, isn't it? To ring Jamie and warn him about Claire?'

'This is ridiculous!' She was fighting back. 'He wouldn't. She wouldn't. I hardly know her. We've only met a couple of times, at parties and such. She's devoted to him.'

'Devoted enough to commit murder for him?'

'No!' The word rang out, with conviction. Then more softly, she said, 'I don't know. I can't judge. It's true that I've never felt easy in my mind about . . . Oh, this is mad . . . She couldn't, could she? Yet I have seen her switch off a smile in a nanosecond. Which doesn't mean anything. I'm prejudiced because she has this squeaky little voice which drives me insane, but as I said to Claudine, that's no reason to think she'd make Jamie a bad wife. Although, honestly, we never thought he'd go so far as to propose to her, however good she was in bed.'

Bea took a turn. 'But that's exactly what he's done, isn't it?'

Hermia turned to face Bea, woman to woman, begging for understanding. 'He needs to get married sometime, and why not now? Especially now? All this bother has concentrated his mind, that's all. He's proposed to the nearest available female, and she's said yes. That's all there is to it.'

'Do you think she's sincere when she plays lovey-dovey with him?'

'I'm not in her confidence. I don't know her well enough to judge.'

'But,' said Bea, 'you do intend to ring Lord Fairley and warn him when you get home?'

'I might. Yes. Only, I've just remembered, Jamie's taking Claire home to meet his mother today. So your precious grandson is no longer at risk; if he ever was, which I doubt. Claire loves babies. I've heard her say so several times, and I believe her.'

Well, that was a relief. Of sorts. It didn't mean she hadn't murdered several adults, though. Bea said, 'You've admitted she's not in love with him, so—'

'I didn't say that.'

'Why is she marrying him?'

'Why not? He has a title, he's very presentable and easy-going, has a house in Chelsea and an estate in the Home Counties. What's to dislike?'

Oliver said, 'But you do intend to warn him, don't you?'

She looked at him, and then looked at Chris. 'Yes, I do. What you're saying is absolutely ridiculous, but it would set my mind at rest if I could talk to him about it. Only, how I'm going to find the right words to say, I don't know. It's not exactly easy to tell a man that his fiancée is suspected of having knocked off your old friends.'

'Do you, personally, think she's innocent?'

Hermia spread her hands. 'Have you the slightest proof she's involved? What weight should be put on the fact that Chris might or might not have seen Tomi aiming in the general direction of a white Mini when he last saw her? You didn't see who was in the car, did you, Chris?'

He shook his head.

'Well, then.'

Oliver shook his head at her. 'You still intend ringing Jamie about this, don't you?'

'I . . . No, I don't think I am. Now, if you don't mind, I've got lots to do today. Chris, are you coming or not?'

Chris stood up. 'I'm coming because I've promised to keep you safe, and that's just what I plan to do.'

'But you don't approve of my refusal to ring Jamie?'

He smiled down at her. 'If I were in your place, I think I'd ring him. But you are you, and you're not me, and you must do as you think best. If it turns out that you made a mistake, then you'll accept that you did so and learn to live with it. People who never make mistakes, never get anything done. I love you, warts and all.'

She managed a giggle. 'Silly. I haven't got any warts.'

He produced his most charming grin. 'Maybe I have, though. Will you still love me when you find them out?'

She put her hand on his shoulder. 'Yes.'

Only after the front door had banged behind them did Bea close her eyes and relax. Oliver busied himself putting the dirty cups into the dishwasher.

Silence. Bea murmured, mostly to herself, 'We've done our best. We've seen them all and pointed out the dangers. If they only take care this weekend, they'll last through till Monday and get their money. I don't suppose she'll kill any more of them after that, because the money wouldn't go back into the kitty, but to their nearest and dearest.'

'True,' said Oliver, also speaking softly.

'I can stop worrying about Claire being in charge of Pippin, because she's not supposed to be on duty again till Tuesday, by which time the police will have been informed of what she's been going on and of our suspicions. We really have nothing to worry about now, have we?'

'I'm going to have one last look at the contents of that computer of Tomi's. I'm only about halfway through the deleted emails.'

'Shall we have some scrambled eggs on toast for lunch? I think I've a pot of home-made soup in the freezer.'

'Carbohydrates are always good when you're worried.'

Oliver brought his laptop into the kitchen and booted it up while Bea made lunch. Winston the cat arrived from the Great Outdoors and begged till Bea attended to his wants. Oliver fed himself one-handed, concentrating on his laptop. Bea stared out of the window and told herself not to worry. Worry didn't get you anywhere.

How could she mend fences with Max and Nicole? If she sent them flowers, Nicole would have all the bother of arranging them. If she sent a hamper of food, someone would have all the trouble of unpacking it.

The front doorbell rang, and they both jumped. It rang again before Bea could get there.

Mr Impatience stood there: a fine leather coat thrown across his shoulders, and a big smile lighting up his face.

'I'm Gregor,' he said, stepping inside without waiting to be invited. 'What a beautiful house, and you must be the famous Mrs Abbot?'

He was in his late twenties, of no more than medium height, but confident with the charisma that is the birthright of some Middle Europeans. He was dark of hair, swarthy of skin, with lively bright brown eyes that took in everything and laughed at everyone. Bea wouldn't have been surprised if he'd insisted on kissing her hand, but he didn't go as far as that.

'Won't you come in?' she said, which was absurd, because he was already in.

'Thank you.' Gregor gave her to understand, without saying a word, that he admired her in every possible way, and especially as a woman. Although, of course, he would never dream of overstepping the mark and making a pass at her . . . unless she were to invite it.

Flattered, bemused, and rather inclined to laugh, Bea led the way to the sitting room, expecting him to pay her some compliment about her decor, too. But no. He was far too clever for that. Instead he went directly to Hamilton's portrait on the wall and admired that.

'Forgive me,' he said, charm incarnate, 'I've heard so much about this portrait from Hermia, who knows a good thing when she sees it. Your husband was a man you could trust, I think. Painted by someone with a touch of genius; someone he himself trusted?'

The twist he gave this observation made her pause. Gregor was obviously charming; yes. But he also had a bright-eyed intelligence, which was as rare as hens' teeth. Would Oliver be like this in fifteen years' time? Ah, but Oliver lacked this man's light touch and his belief that life was an amusing game. On the other hand, Gregor might lack Oliver's integrity.

Oliver had entered the room behind them, and at once Gregor swung round to greet him. 'Ah. The Vunderkid. But no; that is to belittle you.' Gregor was perfectly capable of pronouncing his 'w's, but he'd put the word 'Vunderkid' in inverted commas when he said it. Being amusing. Now the artless smile disappeared, and he looked hard at Oliver, as hard as Oliver was looking at him. Bea had the impression that Gregor could read Oliver's history from the moment of his birth. Perhaps he could. What did Oliver see in his turn?

'Yes, of course. I understand,' Gregor said, softly. 'You have been given great gifts, my friend, but the greatest of these is your lodestar.'

Colour rose in Oliver's cheeks. 'Yes. Without Mrs Abbot, I am nothing.'

Gregor's eyebrows twisted. He threw off his coat, which landed in a perfect arc over the nearest chair, and seated himself. 'Now, you will be wondering why I am here. Claudine has been phoning me night and day. She makes me feel as if I am back in the headmaster's study, threatened with expulsion because I've been running a book on the house cricket competition. No doubt she is right to scold me, but being scolded by Claudine is not conducive to a healthy self-respect. So you see me here, penitent and ready to help you in whatever way I can.'

Gregor was going to cooperate? Good.

Bea laughed, offered coffee – which was refused – and sat down herself. Oliver found a chair nearby.

Gregor had a heavy gold bracelet on one wrist and a Patek watch on the other. His clothes were excellent. He'd probably parked a sports car outside, and it might even have CD plates on it, to avoid parking tickets.

He smiled, and the room lit up around him. Life was bright and joyful; life was amusing, and in his presence they felt the same way.

Bea struggled to remember what she'd been told about him. Married and divorced. Live-in girlfriends. Financial chicanery, being investigated by the police? She would have taken her oath that he'd be found guiltless, whatever he'd actually done. And he'd probably done plenty in his time.

Bea smiled because he was smiling. 'So what did Claudine say to make you come to me?'

He leaned forward, clasping both hands – a signet ring on his left hand – around his knees. 'She says you believe we are all in danger, that one of us is killing off the others. I don't agree. I have known my friends for so many years, too many years to count –' and here he waved his hands dismissively – 'and I don't believe it. Not one of them would think of killing in the way described.'

'They've all been in touch with you?'

'Of course. I am, how you say, the wise man, the one they bring all their little troubles to. They are like children to me, you understand?'

'Yes,' said Oliver.

Bea nodded. Gregor might not be as old as his friends in years, but in many ways he was as ancient as the hills.

Gregor said, 'So, I understand you have made yourselves responsible for investigating the case of dear little Tomi, and I am here to give you the benefit of my experience. Where would you like me to start?'

Bea said, 'You've all been ringing one another every day since Tomi's body was found, haven't you? But you're the one who didn't want outsiders involved, though you did eventually agree that Duncan could put CJ and myself in the picture?'

'That is correct. At first I thought . . . poof! Little Tomi dying in a ditch? What a tragedy. But I had many other matters to occupy my mind, as you may have heard. Yet I was sad to hear she had died. She had a certain *je ne sais quoi*, an integrity which was unusual. I took her to a Fine Arts gallery once; an experiment, you understand. It did not answer. She had no appreciation of modern art.'

Oliver was indignant. 'The world is the poorer for her passing.'

'A trite remark, my friend, though no doubt accurate . . . if you believe in man-made justice.'

'Don't you?'

A wave of the hand. 'There can be a distance between man-made and natural justice, don't you think? I acknowledge that my comment might have seemed crude. Even untimely. I will admit that she had an aura of goodness. Will that do?'

Oliver half smiled and nodded. Bea wondered if these two might, at some future time, become friends; friends who could argue about everything, agree on nothing, but still respect one another's point of view.

'So,' said Gregor. 'Tomi died. I was abroad, but their phone calls chased me all over Europe. Harry the Hard Done By —'

'What?' Oliver grinned.

'Afraid so. Never satisfied, always complaining, and whatever it is that's gone wrong, it's not his fault. Even Tomi got tired of listening to him at times. It was typical of him to wail that she'd stood him up when she went missing. I hear that your little film-maker got into a fight with Harry about her. Did he really give Harry a black eye? I wish I'd been there to see it.'

'Chris did hit him, but not very hard. Incidentally, Harry was much bigger than Chris.'

'He's a young cock sparrow, I'm told.' The idea amused him. 'It was like Hermia to pick Harry up and say, "There, there, Mummy's here." If foolish. I believe she'd had another of her spats with Jamie at the time, which I suppose explains it.'

'Did she often have spats with Jamie?'

'Mm, now and then. She's no fool. If she'd married him, she'd have been the man of the house, always having to rescue him when he got into trouble . . . and be bored to tears within the month. So – tell me about your young cock sparrow.'

Saturday noon

Claire had left her mobile telephone number with Nicole in case of emergencies. She rarely worked weekends, and this Saturday it was out of the question for her to do so, since she was being introduced to Jamie's mother.

Jamie's mother was a frigid monster, not unlike – Claire imagined – the appalling Mrs Abbot. The meeting had not gone well, though the two women had been polite to one another. Claire had been shown round the quarters which Jamie occupied on the top floor of his beautiful but slightly bedraggled stately home and had enthused about it. Of course. Jamie had been pleased with her. Everything was going according to plan.

Nevertheless when Nicole rang, Claire was not unhappy to hear that she was desperate for her to return, if only for an hour or two, over the weekend. And, though Nicole understood Claire had something booked for Monday morning, perhaps she could fit in a couple of hours on Monday afternoon as well?

The red tide of excitement rose in her, and she began to make plans. Why not return to London early? It would give her one last opportunity to knock out another claimant to the Jackpot. Hermia, of course, was first on the list.

SIXTEEN

Saturday noon

Bea was amused. Instead of answering questions, Gregor was asking them. So he wanted to know all about Chris, did he? 'Well, what have you heard?'

He rolled his eyes. 'Which version would you like? Harry said he was an insolent yob, wet behind the ears. Tomi said he was sexy in a Bohemian sort of way, although not exactly her type, and that he had a father who was something of an *éminence grise*. She believed he was a budding genius, who'd dropped out of university to make films. Hermia said he was single minded, a good friend, had integrity and a lot of charm. I understand he's appointed himself acting minder to Hermia.'

'Does that surprise you?'

A quick frown. He hooked one knee over the other and spread his hands.

Bea concluded, 'You care about Hermia.'

A shrug. 'Of course. We are very old friends. All of us. That is the problem, isn't it? Those of us who are left, we must look out for one another.'

'Did you like Nick?'

'Hah. An idiot. When he was young, he was taken in by a girl older than himself, who said he'd made her pregnant. He married her, was loyal to her. She lost the baby at four months and the doctors said she couldn't have any more. She left him to pursue a much older, richer man, and he took to chasing love wherever he could find it. I felt rather sorry for him, actually, having had much the same thing happen to me.'

'We heard you'd been divorced.'

A twist of the mouth. 'She was beautiful, young and said she loved me to distraction.' He kissed his fingertips. 'She also loved racing cars and racing car drivers. I believe she's happily living with one now. We had no children, fortunately.'

'You play the field, as Nick did?'

'Not as Nick did. Certainly not. I am far more discrimin-
ating, and I don't pay for it, except occasionally with the
sparkle of diamonds.'

Oliver stirred. 'You say you went out with Tomi once, and
that Nick tried it on with her, too. She wasn't promiscuous.'
He made it a statement, but Bea heard the note of doubt.

Gregor hastened to reassure him. 'No, of course not. She
was a beautiful girl, intelligent and gracious. She had the
glamour of having starred in a small art film that had won a
prestigious prize. It was no wonder that the men she met
wished to improve their acquaintance with her. My reading
of the situation was that she was flattered to be singled out
by older man with money to spend, that she liked being taken
to good restaurants and being introduced to a different lifestyle.
From my own observation, she was fond of Harry, but didn't
take him seriously. She would have drifted on to a better
prospect in time, no doubt.'

Bea did some swift mental arithmetic. 'Jamie.'

'A busy lad, our Jamie; what with Hermia on one side,
Tomi for special occasions, and his pretty little chick for
everything else.'

'What do you know of his girlfriends?'

'His fiancée?' A shrug. 'A particularly nasty small child.
Hermia?' He waved his hands around. 'Delightful girl. Intelligent,
hard-working; what's not to like?'

'Were you never inclined to push your luck with her?'

'Hermia loves me dearly as a friend and companion, but
she's formed the opinion – I'm sure I don't know why – that
I have a frivolous side to my nature. Perhaps she is right. I
find it hard to live up to her high standards. Besides which,
she's taller than I am when she wears heels. No, no. We are
good friends, that is all.' He looked up at the clock on the
mantelpiece and checked its accuracy with his watch. 'Now,
if you will permit me, I really must take my leave. I have
some important calls to make. Do, please, feel free to contact
me at any time.'

He got to his feet, as did Bea and Oliver. Bea said, 'I suspect
that you personally will be hard hit if you don't get that money
on Monday?'

'True, dear lady. As will some of the others. We're all
greedy little tykes at heart, don't you think? I've asked Duncan

to arrange for the money to be transferred electronically to our individual accounts on Monday afternoon, which he assures me he will do. Oh, and by the way, we shall be holding a little party at Duncan's on Monday at eight to celebrate. Hermia suggests her young cockerel makes a DVD to record the moment when we all turn from pumpkins into fairy-tale princes and princesses. Would you both care to join us? Hermia's little boy can bring his camera, young Oliver here can manage the lighting equipment – as I gather he has done in the past – and perhaps you, dear lady, will take charge of the recording machine?'

He swung his superb coat on to his shoulders and made his way to the door. 'Don't bother to see me out, and oh – before I forget – I've advised everyone concerned to drink nothing but bottled water till Monday night when we break out the champagne. Perhaps you might wish to do the same? I should hate anything to happen to either of you – or to the young cock – before then. He's been sent back home for the weekend, by the way. Hermia is going with a party of friends to the theatre tonight. Very wise of her. She'll be safer there than in the company of a randy young college dropout.'

Bea felt herself smile, because Gregor was smiling, too.

'I'll see you out,' said Oliver, also smiling.

'No need,' said Gregor, but Oliver insisted. When Oliver came back into the room, he'd lost his smile.

So had Bea. 'Did he have a chauffeur-driven car outside?'

'A minicab was parked on the other side of the road, waiting for him.' Oliver rubbed his chin. 'Now, what was all that about, apart from the obvious?'

'He wanted to make sure we weren't going to the police before Tuesday. He seemed to speak freely and to give us a great deal of information, but most of it we knew already. He didn't want to talk about Jamie and his new fiancée, and he didn't mention Duncan's girlfriend. Quite deliberately, I think. I'm not sure why. He's a very clever young man. What did you make of him?'

'I liked him. I don't trust him, though. I can see why everyone else wants him to be the murderer, although they know very well that he isn't. It's just not his style.'

That chimed with Bea's view, too. 'An interesting remark

about Claire Stourton. He called her "a particularly nasty small child".'

Oliver was fretting. 'He made out that Tomi was promiscuous. She wasn't.'

Bea shook her head, which he could take any way he wished. The girl had gone out with Harry and Gregor and had rebuffed Nick. Had she gone out with Jamie, too? It sounded like it. She hadn't gone out with Duncan, because he'd got his own girl on tap. Or had he?

It was a grim and dismal afternoon. The rain hadn't let up. Bea turned up the central heating and switched on the big side lamps. Drifting past the mantelpiece, she picked up and dusted the silver photograph frame showing her smiling family: Pippin in Nicole's arms, with Max standing behind them.

She was not going to cry. No.

'I'll tell you one thing he got right,' said Oliver, 'and that's you. I didn't feel able to tell you this before, but I was terribly homesick when I first went to uni. I understood how it was that Chris dropped out. I'd sit and imagine you here in this room with the lights on as it got dark. Sometimes you were playing patience at the table by the window and looking up at the portrait of Mr Abbot. I'd make believe that you were thinking of me at that moment and wondering how I was getting on. I'd get my mobile phone out a dozen times a night and wonder if I dared ring you. Then I'd say to myself that it was time to grow up, that you didn't want me bothering you all the time. Now you can have a good laugh.'

Sentimental, or what? He'd seen her grieving over Max and Pippin, and had made his confession to make her feel better. It had worked. She did feel better.

In the normal way of things, he was going to grow away from her very soon and start thinking more about a new girl-friend than about Bea. He might even try to find his birth mother and father, and transfer his love to them. But, for now, she was his lodestar. So be it.

At this very moment, it was up to her to reassure him. 'My dear boy, you've no idea how many evenings Maggie and I have sat on after supper, wondering what you were doing and what friends you were making. We'd try to work out what nights you saw certain friends or went to jazz or whatever.

Maggie even ticked off the days before you were due to return on the calendar in her room.'

He grinned. 'I made that bad an impression, did I?'

'Oh, you.' She pretended to chase him from the room with a cushion. He went, laughing.

It was a Saturday afternoon, and the agency office was closed for the weekend. It was raining so she couldn't go out for a walk. Where was Maggie? Out with Zander? Well, that was a good thing, wasn't it?

She was restless. She'd done what she could to bring Tomi's murderer to justice. On Tuesday morning the police would be told the motive behind the killings – if that was what they were. From then on, the matter would be in the hands of the professionals. She had done her bit.

What more could she do, apart from mope around the house worrying about Pippin and Max? If she hadn't an efficient cleaning team, she could have done some house-work. If she knew how many people would be in for supper, she'd have baked a cake. Well, she could still prepare a nice supper.

But before that, she'd order a bouquet of flowers and a hamper of delicacies to be sent to Max and Nicole. She went down into her office and booted up her computer. Rain – or was it sleet – pounded against the window. Ugh. Nasty.

She sent the order through, and then decided that, weekend or no, this was a nice quiet time in which to catch up on work. No phone calls to interrupt. No callers.

By order. Now, she really could do with a good session on the account books . . .

Her concentration was usually good. After a while she lost track of time.

Someone knocked on her door and came in. Oliver, with a frown on his face. 'Can you spare a minute? I've been going back over Tomi's emails. I went over them earlier and didn't notice anything out of the ordinary; nothing to make me think she was other than I'd thought her. Knowing a bit more about what men she'd been seeing, I went back to read through everything again.'

'And you found – what?' What did she remember about this? Not much, and that was the truth.

'It's a something and a nothing. To start with, there's hardly anything personal in Harry's emails. I've double checked to make sure. When Tomi first got the computer, she used it to email her parents and a good friend back in Nigeria, and they replied, usually once a week. It's trivial stuff mostly: a tiff she'd had with someone in the supermarket who jumped the queue – which she said was most un-British – and she complained about how cold the flat was. She wrote that she was getting on nicely at work and was tempted to buy a rather expensive pair of shoes. All safe subjects.'

'Did she mention Harry?'

'She explained that Harry had given her the computer, that he was very nice and was taking her to all sorts of places she wouldn't have known about by herself. She added that she wasn't taking him seriously. From her emails and their replies, you can see that her parents were concerned that she might get involved with someone unsuitable, so her replies were fairly guarded.'

'She didn't mention anything about meeting Zander at a church event?'

'No, she didn't mention that. Her parents were worried about the film Chris had made with her, believing that "exposing" herself to the riff-raff like that would harm her reputation and make her unfit for a suitable marriage. She tried to reassure them by saying that Chris was like a brother and took the greatest care of her. She didn't mention that anyone else had asked her out. I double and treble checked. I put in the names of everyone else in that group and not one came out, except Hermia, and that was only because she'd given Tomi a lift one night – which again, we knew about already. She told her parents about Hermia, and said she was very nice. Tomi used the word "nice" a lot.'

Bea sighed. 'Hermia crops up everywhere. There was a link there; they both read their bibles. Apart from that, did Tomi say that they socialized much? I wouldn't have thought they did.'

'There was only that one mention. Tomi reported going to parties, to a concert, a gallery, but she hardly ever mentioned who she had gone with. We know she went to an art gallery with Gregor, but she doesn't mention his name. To read her emails, you'd think she never went anywhere except with Harry.'

'Which we know is not true. A pity she didn't mention more names. What about the friend she sent emails to? Was she more open there? I seem to remember something . . . No, it's gone.'

'No names, no pack drill. But there was one entry which I thought might be significant. Tomi wrote that she'd been taken to a rather posh "do" at a big hotel. It was a first for her, and she'd been worried that she wouldn't know how to behave and that her dress wouldn't be good enough. Afterwards she wrote that her escort had been a perfect gentleman and hadn't tried anything on. She added that she didn't want her friend to get any ideas about this man, because it had just been a one off, and anything more would have been impossible. She didn't say why she thought the relationship wouldn't work.'

Bea thought about that. 'I remember that. It must have been either Duncan or Jamie. Which? Hang on, didn't Hermia say something about . . . ? Ah, I remember now. Hermia said Jamie had taken Tomi to a dance at the Dorchester and everyone had liked her. Gregor said something about Jamie keeping her for "best", too.'

'They seemed to have shuffled the girls around like crazy. Claudine, Tomi and Hermia went out with everyone in the group at one time or another.' He disapproved.

Bea sighed, rubbed her eyes. 'We've done what we can until Tuesday morning. I'm going to cook an elaborate supper, and then – if you've nothing better on – I suggest we go to the pictures and see something mind-bendingly awful to take our minds off the problem.'

'Do you fancy a horror film?'

'Most certainly not. Nor anything with people getting blown up, or killing one another, or living in squalor, or pushing drugs.'

'No reality check, then?'

'None,' she said, with fervour. 'Nothing depressing, by order.'

'Shall I see if I can get tickets for a musical in the West End?'

'Bless you, my child. The very thing. But remember – nobody is to die at the end.'

Soon enough he'd be acquiring a girl friend of his own and

wouldn't think anything of her being left alone on a Saturday night. It wouldn't be long before he found the company of an eighteen year old girl more attractive than that of a woman old enough to be his grandmother.

The weekend

The time passed, somehow. Bea enjoyed the musical, and almost managed not to fret while she was in the theatre. At bedtime she looked for Winston the cat, who often chose to spend his nights on her bed. She could have done with his comforting presence, but that night of all nights he chose to sleep on top of a cupboard in the kitchen and refused to be coaxed down.

She slept badly and spent a considerable amount of time on her make-up next morning. She swept her fringe sideways across her forehead and decided she needed a trim and a manicure while she was at it. She was due at the salon soon, wasn't she? Perhaps she'd look for a new pair of boots while she was at it, to cheer herself up. Something like the Italian ones that Hermia had been wearing. There she went again. Fretting.

She went to church and tried to concentrate.

Dear Lord above. You know I'm a complete idiot at times. Forgive me. I know I ought to be thinking only about You, and instead . . . Well, You know the way my mind works at times. I am trying, honestly I am, but my thoughts keep drifting away.

All I can be sure about is asking You for protection for all those I love and care for. You know the list. I don't need to spell it out for You.

I remember someone telling me – was it my dear Hamilton? Probably – that You liked to be asked to attend to our problems. I expect that from Your point of view, this stupid muddle that I've made of my relationship with Max and Nicole is small beer. I suppose. I really am grateful that You've brought Oliver and Maggie into my life, and I do thank You for them. I really do. Praise be, and all that.

But . . . Well, You know what I'm worrying about, don't You? And yes, I do realize I haven't been listening to the service at all, which only goes to show that I have the attention span of a fruit fly. I'd really better get out and about, go for a long walk or something. So, forgive me. And thanks. And . . . keep an eye on me, will you?

Monday morning

'The great day dawns,' said Oliver, rubbing his hands as he arrived for breakfast.

'What "great day"?' asked Maggie. She was in one of her ebullient moods. Today she was wearing scarlet and Lincoln green; a colour combination to frighten the horses, but which seemed to give her the courage to tackle her work schedule on a dull Monday morning.

'Ouch,' said Oliver. 'Forgot you didn't know. It's the Day of Judgement. The case we've been working on finishes today, and we can tell you all about it tomorrow. Hopefully.'

Maggie crunched toast, offering Bea another cuppa. 'Why can't you tell me now?'

Bea sighed. 'I wish we could. It'll all be over by midnight. Until then, we're sworn to secrecy. The Black Dog is sitting firmly on my shoulders today. Don't you ever get a feeling that something nasty is about to happen?'

Oliver reached for the last slice of toast. 'It doesn't interfere with my appetite.' The front doorbell pealed and they all froze, knowing the voice of doom when they heard it.

Oliver said, 'No one else could have been killed overnight. Could they?'

'Which one?'

'What?' said Maggie.

On her way to the front door, Bea went through the list in her head: Duncan, Gregor, Jamie. Hermia and Claudine. She told herself she was being ridiculous, that it was probably Miss Brook at the door, having forgotten her key to the agency rooms below. And knew it wasn't.

It wasn't.

It was Chris and Hermia, holding up a distraught-looking Claudine between them. Hermia didn't look happy, either. At least the girls were still alive, though neither looked as tidy as usual. They were both wearing heavy jackets over thick jumpers and jeans, and brogues.

Chris hadn't shaved that morning and was also wearing the kind of clothes you pull on in a hurry: jeans and a T-shirt under a lumber jacket. He, however, looked very much alive; excited, even. He also looked thinner about the face.

Hermia put her arm on Chris's, to signal that she was going to take the lead. Bea reflected that if Hermia had been in an earthquake, she'd have been the first to keep her head, to start restoring order and repelling looters . . . with a gun, if necessary. Could Hermia shoot? Well, if not, she'd soon learn how. 'Mrs Abbot, I realize it's rather early, but we're seeking sanctuary. May we come in?'

Bea ushered them in.

Chris said, 'We've had a bit of an upset and need carbohydrates. Can you run to sugary tea and biscuits?'

'If you're busy, we could make tea for ourselves.' Hermia tried to sound light-hearted and failed. Perhaps her self-control was not as iron as it had appeared to be?

Chris and Hermia practically carried Claudine into the kitchen and sat her down on a stool. The deputy head looked very far from her usual competent self – and why wasn't she at school today? Her hair was all over the place, her nose was shiny and her eyebrows barely in existence. She had no handbag with her. 'Mrs Abbot, we're so sorry to barge in on you like this,' she said, in a voice which went high and low and cracked. 'So sorry . . .'

Her mouth went out of shape, and she turned her back on them all, giving way to tears. Hermia put her arms round Claudine and said, 'There, there.'

Maggie and Oliver stared at Claudine, then switched their eyes to Chris.

Chris said, 'We spent the night at the hospital. We can't go back to Claudine's or Hermia's. I said you'd be able to cope if anyone could, Mrs Abbot.'

Bea reached for the kettle. 'Maggie; do you have to be off somewhere, or can you stay for a few minutes? I promise to fill you in later, but this is an emergency. Can you take the girls up to your bathroom and see that they have everything they need before you leave?'

Maggie nodded. That was one thing about Maggie; in a difficult situation, she could be trusted to take a hint. She looked at the enormous watch on her wrist. 'I could cancel this morning's jobs, but it would only make for more difficulties later on. I'll take the girls upstairs and then be off.'

Bea continued, 'Chris; do you want the bathroom, too? You know where the one is on the first floor, don't you? Oliver; will you tell Miss Brook we're held up for a while, but will try to get down later?'

Maggie guided Hermia and Claudine up the stairs. Chris went off after them, to peel off on the first floor. Oliver, narrow-eyed, watched them go before disappearing down the stairs to the agency rooms.

Bea rested her forearms against the cupboard door and laid her forehead on them. *Dear Lord, it's happened. Whatever it is. Help, please.*

She foraged in biscuit tins, sliced bread and laid it out ready to be toasted. Found clean mugs and plates, put them on the table. Added the box of paper tissues.

Chris appeared first, smiling with relief. 'Thanks, Mrs A. I knew I could count on you.'

Oliver reappeared, moving silently around, helping Bea to lay out a suitable repast. Maggie thundered down the stairs, put her head round the door to say she was off now, and banged the front door on her way out.

Tentatively, slowly, the two girls descended the stairs and made their way to the kitchen. Claudine looked neater, but there were dark smudges under her eyes and her mouth was held in tight lines. Maggie must have found her a clean comb, for her hair was once more smooth and tucked behind her ears. Both girls had tidied themselves up, though neither was wearing tights or socks under their jeans.

Hermia made her way to Chris's side and took a stool beside him. Claudine perched on the stool she'd been given before. Oliver reappeared, on silent feet, and took his stool into a corner, out of the way.

Winston the cat plopped in through the flap on the kitchen door, yawned, and paced the room, sniffing at each pair of trousered legs till he came to Chris's, whereupon he raised his enormous yellow eyes and one paw, in his usual begging position. Chris, of course, was a sucker for it. He picked Winston up to give him a cuddle while Bea took orders; buttered toast, tea and coffee.

'Eat first,' she said. All three nodded.

Claudine said she couldn't eat anything, but eventually managed one corner of a piece of toast. And then a whole slice.

Hermia determinedly chomped through everything in front of her. Bea could read Hermia's mind: eat while the going's good, because you need it, and you don't know where your next meal is coming from.

Bea was beginning to admire Hermia, though she wasn't sure that she trusted her.

Chris pushed his third cup of tea away. 'Explanations are due. Right? Claudine?'

SEVENTEEN

Monday morning

Claudine had a little colour in her face now. She looked at the clock on the wall, then checked her watch. 'I should have been at school an hour ago. I'm never late. I ought to ring them, but I haven't got my mobile.'

Bea pushed the landline phone towards her. 'Be my guest.'

Claudine took a deep breath and made the call. 'Is that . . . ? Yes, Claudine here. I'm afraid I won't be in today. There was a . . . an incident last night. Alan ate or drank something which made him ill. He's in hospital now, so he won't be in, either. They say he's going to be all right, but I'm . . . Well, you can understand I'm very anxious. I'll probably be able to get him home later. If you could make my excuses, rearrange my schedule . . . I'll ring you as soon as I know anything more.'

She tried to put the phone back on its rest, and managed it at the second try. 'It was meant for me, of course.'

Hermia muttered, 'From the beginning, Claudine.'

'Yes, of course.' She pressed her fingers to her forehead. 'We had a good time in Brussels, returned on Eurostar, dead on time. On the way back I took a phone call from Gregor, who said he'd been to see you. He suggested I drank only bottled water for the time being. We took a taxi from the station. While Alan paid the taxi, I went ahead and opened up. There was a bottle of flavoured mineral water outside our front door. I thought it must be from Gregor. I picked it up and took it in, but I wasn't thirsty because we'd had sandwiches and a mineral water on the train.

'Travelling tires me out. Alan loves it. I wanted to go to bed straight away and he wanted to stay up and talk. We had a bit of a spat.' She closed her eyes and shuddered. 'I keep thinking, if only . . . But he's going to be all right, they say.'

Hermia pressed Claudine's hand and she continued. 'Alan said he'd stay up to mark some papers. I said I'd get up early and do mine. He's a night owl, I'm an early bird. We're really not compatible. Anyway, I went to bed. Actually, I slammed the door on him and stomped off. It was only about half past nine, but I was tired. I had a long hot bath, went to bed and fell asleep.

'I woke up about half past twelve and went to the bathroom. He hadn't come to bed and the light was still on in the living room. I went in, thinking he'd fallen asleep over his papers, and he had. At least, that's what I thought at first. So I shook him, and he just flopped back. He was snoring. He doesn't usually, you know.

'Then I saw the bottle of water was almost half empty. I'd had a cheese sandwich on the train, but he'd had ham and I suppose that had made him thirsty. I suddenly thought that maybe that bottle of water hadn't been put there by Gregor. I dialled nine nine nine, and they said to get Alan on his feet and walk him around till the medics got there, though there might be a delay because there'd been a multi-car smash nearby and the roads were blocked. I tried to get him on his feet, but couldn't because he's much bigger than me, so I rang Hermia. I knew she'd help, no matter what time it was.'

Here she turned Hermia's hand within hers and gave her a ghost of a smile.

'Hermia came, and we walked him up and down between us. When the medics arrived they tried to wake him and couldn't, so they took him off to pump out his stomach and I threw on some clothes and Hermia took me to the hospital and we waited and waited. We talked about how I'd found the bottle and that it might have been intended for me and not for Alan. It was about four o'clock by then. Hermia rang Gregor on her mobile, and he said he hadn't delivered any bottled water to me, nor to anyone else.'

Hermia took up the story. 'So I rang my flatmate, got her out of bed, asked if she'd found any bottled water lurking outside our front door, and she had. She'd got back home before me last night, you see. Knowing no better, she'd picked it up and popped it in the fridge. I told her some joker had been leaving doctored drinks around and that Alan had drunk some and was terribly ill, so would she put it on one side till I could get home and explain. She was going to ring the police, but I said I'd do it.'

Claudine said, 'We knew that if we told the police before we got our money, we'd lose it. I said I didn't care, and Hermia said she didn't care, either. We agreed that if Alan didn't come round soon, we'd tell. Only, he did come round. The relief! I cried and cried. Couldn't stop crying. It was only then I realized I'd forgotten my handbag with my keys and hankies and everything, and the doctors had been asking if we knew what Alan had taken, and of course we didn't know, except that it was probably something in the bottled water that had appeared just like magic on my doorstep.

'So we thought we didn't need to tell the police, but would wait till Tuesday – tomorrow – when we'd all agreed we'd have to tell, anyway. Only then the doctor came out to talk to us, and he said . . . he said . . .'

She gulped, and Hermia carried on.

'The doctor said that they'd pumped out Alan's stomach, that he was conscious, but hadn't a clue what it was that had sent him to sleep. The doctor said they really ought to know, because different poisons needed different treatment. I thought it would only have been barbiturates because that what was used before, so he ought to be all right—'

Claudine shook her head. 'But I was terrified. I said we had to get one of those doctored bottles to the hospital, fast. That's when Hermia thought of Chris and rang him.'

Chris put the cat down on to the floor and took up the tale. 'I found a taxi and met them at the hospital. Hermia made the hospital staff get Alan's keys out of his trousers, so I took them and drove her car to Claudine's flat and let myself in. I got some rubber gloves from the kitchen and found a paper bag and put the bottle in it. I looked for Claudine's handbag, but couldn't find it.'

Typical, thought Bea, that Chris hadn't been able to find it.

'Then I went back to the hospital to deliver the bottle and see what else I could do to help. Claudine was allowed in to see Alan for five minutes. The doctor said they'd keep him under observation for a few hours and, if all went well, we could fetch him early this afternoon. But Claudine was afraid to go back to her flat by herself.'

'That bottled water was meant for me. Whoever it is that's doing this knows where I live.'

'Whoever it is,' said Hermia, 'knows where all of us live. We didn't know what to do or where to go. Then Chris suggested that you, Mrs Abbot, might let us stay here till this evening. Tomorrow we can go to the police.'

Bea said, 'Did you warn the others?'

'Gregor knows, yes. I also rang Duncan and told him, but he hasn't had a suspect bottle delivered to him. Jamie's phone was switched off, but I left a message. I don't think – I hope – they're not being targeted, too.'

Claudine reached for another tissue and blew her nose. 'The awful thing is, it's made me realize I don't love Alan as I should. I feel wretched that he's been poisoned instead of me, but I'm not agonizing over him. I know I ought to be, but I'm not. That makes me feel guilty, too.'

Really? She'd been giving a good imitation of a woman deeply in love.

'Cheer up,' said Chris, patting her arm. 'It could have been a lot worse. You said he was a heavy sleeper. Suppose it had been you who'd drunk the stuff, and he hadn't woken in the night. You'd be dead by now, I suppose.'

Claudine gave a muffled shriek, but Hermia threw back her head and laughed.

'You are awful, Chris.'

'No, what's awful,' said Chris, 'is that the nurse I gave the bottle to lifted it out of the paper bag with ungloved hands, shoving her dainty mitts all over it and destroying any fingerprints.'

Hermia wasn't having that. 'The person who's doing this is far too clever to leave fingerprints.'

Bea stirred herself. 'You know who's doing this, don't you, Hermia?'

Hermia gave her a bland look. 'Haven't a clue.'

'Oh yes, you have. You've all discussed it ad infinitum. You all know who it is, and none of you will tell because you don't want your fellow conspirator to lose his share of the jackpot.'

Hermia shook her head. 'It doesn't matter now that Alan's recovering. On Tuesday we'll tell all. Until then, we keep shtum.'

Claudine pushed her hair behind her ears. 'Mrs Abbot, do you think we could stay here till it's time to go to Duncan's?'

Hermia shook her head. 'I'm not going to a champagne rave-up in these clothes, my dear. Either we risk going back to my place to change, or we go shopping for something decent to wear.'

'We have to collect Alan from the hospital this afternoon.'

'I gave them my mobile number, so he can contact us when he's ready to leave.'

Chris started putting the dirty plates in the dishwasher. 'I can fetch him in a taxi and bring him here, if you like. Is he invited to the party? I know I am. I'll have to go back home, anyway, to fetch my equipment.' He arched his back, yawning hugely.

Claudine's eyes had sunk into her head. She, too, yawned, jaw-breakingly, covering her mouth with one hand. Hermia looked at Claudine and Chris with a degree of disillusion. Hermia could probably keep going all day, if she put her mind to it. Bea could see her computing the odds and guessed what she'd say next.

'Mrs Abbot.' A nice smile. 'Do you have a settee on which Claudine could crash out for a while? Chris can go home for a couple of hours, but perhaps I can help you with some filing or cleaning or something?'

Bea allowed herself to entertain the idea of Miss Brook permitting Hermia to work in her domain and wondered who would come out top dog. Miss Brook had the advantage of age and experience; Hermia, on the other hand, was a human bulldozer. It might have been fun to let it happen, but no; unkind to animals.

'Better still,' said Bea, 'Claudine will undress and take a shower and go to sleep in our spare bedroom. Hermia, you will doss down on the settee next door with one of our spare duvets. If you'll leave your mobile phone with me, I promise to wake you if it rings. That should give you both a couple of hours' sleep before it's time to fetch Alan from the hospital and get into your glad rags. Chris; you're to go home and do the same thing. Right?'

'You're very kind, Mrs Abbot,' said Hermia, and they could all hear she was trying to mean it.

'Mrs A, you're brilliant,' said Chris, yawning again. 'I'd better take a taxi home, because Hermia will need her car later.'

Oliver emerged from his quiet corner to ask a question of Bea without words. On receiving a nod he said, 'I'll run you home, Chris.'

Hermia frowned. 'Yes, I suppose that's best. But Chris; not a word to your father, understand?'

At which point Claudine almost fell off her stool. She jerked herself upright and tried to laugh. 'Did I fall asleep?'

Bea tossed her car keys to Oliver and took Claudine's arm to lead her out of the kitchen. 'Let me see you safely upstairs.' She led the girl to the spare room, drew the blinds down, found fresh towels, and showed her the bathroom next door. 'Do you need anything else?'

'No, thank you. I'm asleep on my feet.' She sank on to the bed and chucked off her shoes.

Bea left her to it and went to rummage for a spare duvet and pillow. She heard the front door open and shut as Chris and Oliver left the house.

She found Hermia sitting at the bottom of the stairs, staring wide-eyed into space. Her face had lost all its colour. She began to weep, silently at first, and then with great gasping sobs. Now that the need for action had passed, Hermia was suffering a reaction.

Bea steered the girl into the sitting room, lowered the blinds at the windows and arranged pillow and duvet on the settee. She made Hermia sit down, slipped off her shoes and helped her to struggle out of her jeans.

As Bea covered the girl with the duvet, Hermia's hand shot out to grasp Bea's wrist. 'I didn't think there'd be any more attempts on our lives, I really didn't. You think we're just being greedy, but you don't know, you can't know. Duncan's being made redundant and daren't tell Mandy because he thinks she wouldn't marry him if she knew how skint he was, and Jamie's deep in debt though he puts a good face on it. As for Gregor, I daren't think what's going to happen to him if he can't square the tax man. I gambled there wouldn't be any more murders, and I was wrong, wasn't I?'

The truth at last. 'If there's any blame going, then CJ and I are also to blame because we both agreed to keep quiet. We didn't know how badly off you all were, but—'

'Claudine's fine. Or she was till she discovered Alan isn't the love of her life.'

'She discussed her plan to buy a school with him, of course?'

'She says not.'

'The others talked, though?'

'Gregor? Don't be daft. Of course not. I don't think Duncan did, either. He was scared of what Mandy would say. She's Julian's sister, you see, and they've had more than enough of gambling in that family.'

Yes, it made sense that Duncan would be wary of discussing it with Mandy.

'You've told your father?'

Hermia settled herself more comfortably. 'I recorded a message and left it on the hall table to be given to him tomorrow. If I die he'll see I'm avenged.'

Was she lying? Did it matter? 'Let me have your mobile phone. I'll wake you as soon as the hospital rings.'

Hermia shook her head. 'Chris told me all about you and your detective work. You'd check to see who else I've been ringing on my phone, and it's none of your business.'

'I wouldn't know how.' But Bea grinned, because she knew someone who might just know how to trace calls, or to get them traced. Which reminded her that she hadn't heard Oliver come back in yet.

She left the darkened room and stood in the hallway, thinking hard. What if she was wrong and it wasn't Claire who was the murderer after all? Could it be Gregor? No. He might well ruin someone financially – yes, Bea could see him doing that – but to slip barbiturates into someone's drink? No.

Duncan. CJ and Hermia had confirmed that he did indeed have a motive, for if he really was being made redundant, then he needed that cash more than ever. Bea tried to imagine Duncan killing someone. Would he use barbiturates? Bea shook her head. No.

Mandy, now. Hermia believed the girl didn't know about the lottery money, and she'd given a good enough reason why. But that was only Hermia's reading of the situation and might not be correct. If Mandy had known about the lottery money, would she really have recoiled in horror? It didn't sound at all likely. Who rejects so many millions on a point of principle?

On the other hand, would Mandy have wanted to improve her fiancé's chances of a bigger share of the pool by killing off his friends? Not enough information. What sort of girl was she? Well, perhaps she'd be at the party tonight.

Jamie. Difficult to read. Smoo–oth, boyish and charming on the surface. What went on underneath? Laziness? Inertia? Hermia said he was deep in debt. But how would he kill, if driven to it? Not with poison.

Which left Jamie's new girlfriend Claire Stourton, who may or may not have owned a white Mini, to which Tomi may or may not have been lured on the day of her death. A girl who had been described in venomous terms by Gregor, and who might well have felt her position threatened vis-à-vis Jamie if he'd started to ask Tomi out. If – and it was a big 'if' – Jamie had talked to Claire, had told her about his debts and said that the lottery money would take care of everything, then Claire would have a motive to see if his share could be increased. Claire, who had been put in charge of Bea's little grandson . . .

At which thought Bea ground her teeth. Too many 'ifs'.

Oliver returned from his errand and tossed the car keys on to the hall table. He used his softest voice. 'Safely delivered.'

Bea nodded and replied as quietly. 'Safely put to bed.' She led the way to the kitchen. 'Can you count the number of lies we've been told over this past week? The truth's only just beginning to come out now. Hermia says the men all need money, but didn't mention herself.'

Oliver checked that the door to the hall was closed. 'Chris just told me that Hermia beggared herself to lend Jamie the money to redo the ancestral leaden roof. If he receives his share this afternoon, he'll repay her. If he doesn't, and she misses out on her share of the jackpot, she'll have to sell the shares which give her a comfortable income and compete in the job market to earn her living. He swore me to secrecy, but you've choked it out of me, right?'

'So she has a motive, after all, and an even bigger reason to defend Jamie. No wonder she wants us to hold off till tomorrow.'

'How do you read him? Could he have done the murders?'

'I wouldn't have thought they were his style, but if he got Claire to do the dirty work then yes.' Bea sighed. 'I'm told that British justice ensures no one may gain from a crime they've committed. If he's convicted, what will happen to his share?'

'You're getting ahead of yourself, but it's an intriguing thought. Does his share go back into the kitty or does the Crown take it, or what? Presumably he'd get what was due to him after Julian and Shirley died. If the police stick to the theory that Harry killed Tomi and then killed himself, then he'd get a larger share—'

'And if, as seems likely, the coroner brings in a verdict of accidental death for Nick, then he'd get his share of Nick's as well. So unless they can prove something – and I don't at the moment see how they can – he could get away with it.'

'There's the attempt to kill Claudine, which has left Alan in hospital.'

'I agree with Hermia; there won't be any prints on the bottle. Chris says the doctor got to him in time.'

'It's all most unsatisfactory,' said Bea. 'Can you see a loophole, Oliver?'

'No. It's all circumstantial. Tomi goes to a party in the flat above hers, is spotted by Harry and introduced to his circle. She accepts invitations from Gregor and Jamie; rebuffs Nick. Then she's killed. Harry is blamed for it. Harry kills himself. Nick, shocked at the tragedies which have befallen his friends, gets sozzled and falls to his death. Alan picks up a bottle of doctored water, which anyone at all might have left outside his door, and drinks from it. Where's the evidence that we can take to the police? There isn't any. There's been no phone call from the hospital yet?'

They both listened out for a phone ringing. Nothing. Bea looked at the clock. Maggie wasn't back yet; it would soon be time for lunch. A few hours after that, they must dress for the party that evening. She looked at her calendar. Heavens, she was due to have her hair cut that afternoon. Well, that was good in one way, because it certainly needed attention, and she could have a manicure at the same time – with luck. But she'd wanted to have one last go at Tomi's emails. How long did she have?

Another thing. 'Oliver, do you want to buy yourself an evening rig-out? I'm sure you'll need one at university some time, won't you?'

He grinned. 'We're just hired help tonight. Like waiters. Suppose you dress up, though? Be magnificence personified. Bring out the bling. Be the Grand Inquisitor. They're expecting to make a short film recording the occasion, so with Chris behind the camera and me on sound, you can ask slanted questions which may bring out slightly different versions of the truth. Being on camera often hypnotizes people into tongue-tied silence, but in this case the champagne will be flowing and the relief they all must feel that they've survived and won themselves a crashingly good windfall may loosen their tongues.'

Monday afternoon

Claire sat on Jamie's bed. She tipped more champagne into his glass and leaned over to nuzzle his neck. She was a trifle anxious. By now they should have heard of another conveni-ent death, but no; it seemed not. Ah well, she'd done her best, hadn't she?

She kissed the base of his throat. Butterfly kisses all the way up to his mouth. He smiled, but there were lines of strain around his eyes and mouth.

'Third time lucky,' he said and set her aside to access his bank account . . . again. 'It's in. Thank God.' He closed his eyes, relaxing against the pillows. 'The future's bright. At last.'

She slid down beside him. 'Can't we skip that dreary party tonight?'

'I wouldn't miss it for the world. Duncan's champagne's always good, and Hermia says they're going to video the occasion. It's going to be quite a party. They've brought in some detective or other to keep us safe. An oddity, Mrs Abbot. I met her the other day. She was asking questions, don't suppose she got anywhere. She's going to be there, too.'

She froze, then relaxed. The friends had all got their money and wouldn't want to make trouble now, would they? They might suspect, but that was a different matter, and while she held Jamie in thrall she was quite safe.

As for evidence . . . there was none. Claire put a hand to her mouth. The four mobile phones and Tomi's diary! What a fool she'd been not to ditch them ages ago. She daren't drop them all together into the nearest rubbish bin, which might raise suspicion. They would have to be disposed of one by one, in different places. Tomorrow, first thing. And what about the little brown bottle of sleepy juice? There was just one more adult dose left. Could she put it in the garbage here? No, it might be traced back to her.

She'd promised to go to work this afternoon, so why not drop it in the garbage at the Abbot's flat? No one would ever look there for it, and it would be amusing to think of evidence being thrown out by that woman's own family.

Jamie sighed. 'Anyway, we have to go to the party so that I can give Hermia a cheque.'

'What for?'

He yawned. 'A loan she made me when the bill came in for repairing the roof back home. The money's come through just in time. Now I can pay off all my debts.'

'Debts?' Her voice was hard. 'How much do you owe?'

'Just over a million and a half to Hermia, and another million or so to various tradesmen.'

She went rigid with fury. Had she worked so hard, done so much for him, only to find he'd frittered away over two million pounds? And to Hermia, of all people, the only one of the group who looked as if Claire were a turd on the pavement.

Well, watch out, Hermia, for I'm still a force to be reckoned with, and one day soon I'll find a way to wipe that smug smile off your face. Perhaps even tonight . . .

She looked at the clock and bounced out of bed. She was going to be late to the Abbot's. The baby needed her. She paused, adjusting her bra. Of course, if that interfering mother-in-law were going to cause trouble for Claire, there might be something Claire could do about it. She could always leave a little sleepy juice in one of the baby's bottles for his overnight feed, couldn't she? No one would be surprised if he died, because he really was a puny little thing. And it would be a pity to waste the last dose.

EIGHTEEN

Bea and Oliver settled down to work in the kitchen so that they could hear if Hermia's mobile rang. They both jumped when their own landline sounded off, but it was only Maggie, spitting feathers because the decorator hadn't done the job to her exacting standards. She said that unless she was needed urgently, she was going to stand over him till he got it right.

Within minutes of her ringing off, Hermia's phone rang. Oliver got off his stool and ran into the hall, only to meet Hermia staggering blearily out of the sitting room, her mobile clamped to her ear. She screwed up her eyes as she listened to what was being hoarsely shouted at her – and shout was definitely the word.

She said, 'All right, all right. I'll get there as soon as I can. Sorry. I'm glad you're feeling better—'

This set whoever it was off again. Bea rolled her eyes at Oliver and put the kettle on.

Finally Hermia made it to a stool and sat down, shutting off her mobile. 'That was Alan. He's discharged himself, says he's perfectly all right except for a sore throat and wants to get back into the flat, only he can't because we've stolen his key, so he's taken refuge in the pub on the corner of the road. I said we'd get over there as quickly as we could. He doesn't want to stay at the flat any more. He seems to think Claudine dosed the bottle of water with something nasty on purpose. I can't think why she should, but that's what he says. He wants to collect his things and take them over to his brother's in Peckham. He says Claudine needn't try to talk him round, though I don't think she'll even try, do you?'

Claudine walked in, holding on to the door, yawning. She reached a stool and collapsed on to it. 'Was that Alan?'

Hermia repeated the gist of the conversation she'd just had. Claudine shook her head. 'He'll be hell to work with for the rest of the term, won't he? I'm glad he's all right, of course. But it's an ill wind . . . I'll be glad to get him out of the flat.'

'Coffee or tea?' said Bea.

Hermia wanted coffee. Claudine said, 'Green tea if you have it.'

'I wonder,' said Claudine, who'd got the fidgets. 'Do you think we could borrow someone's computer to—'

'See if the money's in?' Hermia flushed. 'I'm so stupid. I'm always slow when I first wake up.'

Oliver said, 'Use my laptop,' and pushed it across to her.

The girls laughed, though there was no reason to do so. Nerves, of course.

'Silly us,' said Hermia, her eyes brighter than usual. 'Of course it's there. It's just that it's been so long waiting.'

Hermia accessed her account, her colour high. She closed her eyes and breathed deeply. 'It's there.'

She turned the laptop over to Claudine, who fumbled the job. Tears stood out on her lower eyelids. Finally she got through. 'Yes, it's there!'

A moment's silence and the two girls got their arms around one another and started jumping up and down. 'We're rich!'

'I never really believed it would happen!'

'Oh, thank the Lord!'

Indeed.

Both girls began to cry. Hermia embraced Oliver, because he happened to be standing next to her. Claudine punched the air, gave Hermia a high five.

Hermia grabbed her mobile phone again and ran out of the room, talking into it. Claudine sought for and found the box of tissues, using them one after the other.

Relief. Between gulping sobs, she said, 'Thank God I never told Alan the whole thing, or he'd have been hanging around my neck, wanting his share. All I said was that I was expecting a few thousands by way of inheritance from an ancient aunt and, with that and a bank loan, I was proposing to buy into an independent school. He said he might have some savings to put in, but I won't need him now, will I? He can't come back to me on that, can he?'

No, probably not.

Hermia ran back into the room, her cheeks still brilliant with colour. 'Gregor says he's got his. But, since so many of us have died, we're scrubbing the celebratory meal at the restaurant. It would be too ghoulish thinking that that's where so and so was sitting last year. Anyway, we're all too excited to sit and wait for food in a restaurant. So Duncan's organizing the champagne, and we're all to dress up and take a partner – that's if we want to – and meet at his place at eight. Then Chris will make a video recording the occasion, and we can go on to eat somewhere after that, either as a group or with a friend or whatever. Gregor wants Chris to get to Duncan's in about an hour, to start setting up. I'd better tell him.'

Off she ran again.

Claudine finally pushed the box of tissues away. Her eyes showed her brain was engaged in calculation. 'I don't need a man, do I?' The question was rhetorical. 'I always thought I'd get married, but I never wanted children of my own, and I certainly don't want men making up to me for what I've got.'

Bea said, 'Best not tell anyone, then.'

Claudine sniffed. 'I can keep a still tongue in my head.' She probably could, too. She added, 'More than some can.'

'Who do you think has shared the secret? Gregor?'

Claudine almost laughed. 'Of course not. Nor Duncan; what with worrying about his job and not being sure that Mandy loves him for himself, he's fit to be tied. He says he's going to propose to her tonight before he tells her about the lottery money, otherwise he'll never know for sure whether she really loves him for himself or not. I couldn't be doing with that.'

'Understood. Do you think Hermia told anyone, apart from her father?'

'She says she didn't tell even him, and I believe her. She says most of the men she knows have one eye on her father's money, anyway, and she wasn't about to weight the odds even more.'

'That's why she kept going back to Jamie? Because he had something other than money to offer her? Didn't she fancy being Lady Fairley?'

A shrug. 'The title didn't weigh with her. He's a childhood friend. They could be comfortable going around with one another, because they knew neither was going to get serious.'

'Except that things changed when Tomi arrived. Or did they change before that, when Claire arrived?'

Claudine drew back. 'I liked Tomi. She meant no harm. I was really sorry to hear that Harry killed her.'

Mm. Yes. Well, maybe.

Hermia burst back into the kitchen. 'Chris says he's all hyped up and ready to go.' She laughed out loud. 'Chris is a doll, isn't he, Claudine?'

'Watch it! Dolls can be played with and put back in the toy cupboard; men can't.' Claudine got off her stool, looking at the clock. 'I think I ought to get going. I need to clear Alan out of the place and get ready for the party.'

Hermia looked at her watch. 'I must be on my way, too. Thank you so much, Mrs Abbot. You've been just great. I don't know what we'd have done without you.'

Nice manners.

Claudine tried to tidy her hair. 'I must look a mess. Mrs Abbot, can I get a taxi at the end of the road?'

Oliver helped her into her jacket. 'I'll see you out, help you to get one.'

Hermia waltzed around the kitchen, punching numbers into her mobile. 'I could have danced all night . . . Is that you, Jamie? You've heard? Yes, I'm on my way home now. You heard we're meeting at Duncan's first . . . ?' Her voice died away as she followed Oliver and Claudine out of the house.

Bea reached for her own phone. Was the danger really over? Her head said that it must be over, because any more killings wouldn't increase the size of anyone's share. Tomorrow they were all free to talk to the police, but – Bea sighed – even if the police were told everything, would they decide to follow up on cases which they'd already closed? The odds were against a prosecution, even if the remaining five friends did go to the police. If only they could produce even one piece of evidence.

Whenever Bea thought about Tomi, she felt anger surge through her. To let her death go unavenged was all wrong. Apart from that, the killer had got away with murder three times, so what was to stop him or her at three?

She considered that it might be a good idea to take a precaution or two. She made some phone calls and started to clear the kitchen, only to be interrupted by her landline ringing.

This time it was Chris, with instructions for her and for Oliver. 'There's some kind of confrontation planned for the party.

Hermia plans to announce that she's going to the police, in order to see what happens. That's really why she wants me to film the event, to capture people's reactions. I'm afraid this might put her in danger, but she says nothing could possibly happen to her in the group. Can you dress all in black, Mrs A, and keep to the shadows? Watch out that no one tries to slip her a lethal dose of something?'

'Will do.'

'The thing is, I'm not sure Hermia's got the killer instinct, so she may need some help. Oliver says you know one or two things they don't. Perhaps you could put a couple of tough questions if she fails to get through?'

'I suppose so.'

'And, well, I may try to rig up something to record . . . I'll have to give it some thought.'

He rang off. Bea put the phone down and wondered exactly who was pulling the strings tonight. Was it Chris? Unlikely.

One name pushed itself forward. Gregor. The more she thought about it, the more Bea suspected that he was the master puppeteer behind the group. Hermia might well have suggested that she tell the group about going to the police and that Chris make a video of the event, but only Gregor could have persuaded everyone to cooperate. Tricky, slicky Dicky. Untrustworthy with money, but the linchpin of the group. Remember he'd said they all took their troubles to him? She'd bet he knew the precise degrees of debt which each person owed. He must know – or suspect – who was responsible for the killings. Would he really be keen to bring the police in on the matter? Y–yes, provided he could keep in the background himself. Let someone else play the Grand Inquisitor; hence the invitation to Bea.

Yet, as Bea went off to the beauty salon, she realized that she felt comfortable about leaving the conduct of the evening in Gregor's hands. Tricky he might be, but she had a feeling that under all that persiflage, he cared about right and wrong. She put in some praying to cover all the bases.

Monday evening

Bea surveyed herself in the full-length mirror. Hair, make-up, nails; all in order. She'd had a shower and had even had time to check on something that had been niggling at her on the laptop containing Tomi's files. She twisted sideways to make sure her long black silk tube of a dress clung where it should and hung straight where it shouldn't. She usually wore a padded gold lame jacket lined in black over it, but had turned it inside out so that only the piping shimmered in the light.

She saluted herself in the mirror. 'Here comes the judge.'

She made one more phone call, checked that her small black evening bag held everything she needed, and left for the party.

As the clock on Duncan's mantelpiece struck eight, Bea retired to a dark corner while Oliver, also dressed in black, prepared to play the part of butler.

Bea was interested to see that Chris, who also dressed in black and with a hood over his bright hair, lost all his boyishness when behind the camera. Most of the side lamps in the room had been turned off, while two powerful lamps had been rigged up to cast light over a brocaded settee, placed centre stage, so to speak. A boom hanging over the settee from a tripod held one microphone, while Oliver had concealed another under a small table nearby.

As Oliver ushered in the first guests, Duncan put down his glass of whisky and moved forward to greet them. Duncan was wearing full evening rig, as was Gregor, who had a raven-haired beauty on his arm. Bea thought the girl must be a model, so tall and thin was she. She was wearing a wisp of a dress that left her arms bare and showed off some extravagant jewellery, with a multicoloured glittering evening bag slung on a chain from one shoulder. Her IQ was probably not as high as her heels.

Miaow. Bea told herself not to judge the book by its cover.

Gregor shielded his eyes for a moment against the powerful lights, and then dismissed them from his mind. He was always on stage, anyway.

'Congratulations all round!' Gregor hugged Duncan, who hugged him back, though with slightly less exuberance. Gregor introduced his companion by the name of Marigold.

The girl said, 'Pleased to meetya.'

Perhaps, thought Bea, these were the only words the girl might utter the whole evening. Was she really chewing gum? Unbelievable!

Another ring at the door. Gregor accepted drinks from Duncan and turned to greet Claudine, who was looking as cool and soignée as if sleepless nights had never existed. Her fall of straight dark hair was held back by a high Spanish-style comb; she carried a tiny gold evening bag to match her high heeled shoes. She was swathed in folds of dark green taffeta, which clung to her excellent figure and allowed her to look down her nose at Marigold's conspicuous lack of boobs. The women checked out each other's long, elegant legs and decided, without words, that honours were even.

Then in bustled Hermia, laughing and crying, kissing everyone in sight on both cheeks and giving Gregor a third for luck. She was wearing a glittering silver sheath dress which left her beautiful shoulders bare and showed off a prettily curved figure. Her dress screamed 'Paris', as did her silver clutch purse. She might lack Marigold's slenderness and Claudine's sophistication, but her warmth made her the focus of the room. She blew a kiss at Chris with a mischievous expression, but he refused to take his eye off the camera to socialize, even for her.

Close on Hermia's heels came a long pale streak of a girl, who looked as if she were not quite sure she wanted to take part in a rave-up, but Mummy had always told her to smile and tuck her tummy in when wearing a new dress, and so she did. Pale blue wasn't a good colour for her, and she probably looked at her best in riding kit. Landed gentry? This must be Mandy. Yes, she walked past everyone, smiling and nodding, but not kissing, to end up beside Duncan, who was dispensing drinks. A lively babble of voices showed the party was off to a good start.

Last came Jamie with the prettiest of little blondes on his arm.

The temperature in the room dropped five degrees and the room went quiet.

Jamie was also in evening dress. Claire was in white satin, trimmed with fluffy feathers, and carrying a huge designer handbag. Was the dress home-made? Was the length wrong? Something about her outfit wasn't quite right. All the women in the party knew it immediately.

After a moment's hesitation Hermia put the smile back on her face and went to kiss Jamie; just once, on one cheek.

She held out both her hands to Claire and said, 'Lovely to see you again, Claire.'

Jamie had his arm around Claire. 'Congratulations are in order for more than the money. Show them, Claire!'

Claire held up her left hand, on which flashed a diamond ring.

Jamie was pleased with himself and Claire. 'We bought the ring this morning.'

Hermia's smile looked rigid. 'Why, Jamie! How wonderful! When's the wedding to be?'

The others crowded around making the right noises, but not much kissing went on. Bea, watching from the back of the room, saw Gregor exchange a wide-eyed look of dismay with Hermia. It seemed that neither liked this engagement much.

'Come and sit down.' Duncan ushered the happy pair to the settee.

'A drink first,' said Jamie, high on excitement.

Claire was smiling, too. Sleek and satisfied. Like a cat. Look what I've caught!

'A toast, a toast!' cried Gregor. 'Come, let's all gather round the settee so that we can register the moment on film. Claudine, are you with us? Jamie and Claire should sit in the front; no, I insist. I'll stand here with my arms round the two best looking girls; Hermia, Claudine – and Marigold, where have you got to, girl?'

Marigold obediently went to his side. Yes, she was definitely chewing gum.

From nowhere Oliver appeared with a small camera. Kneeling before them, he snapped away. Flash, Flash! He hadn't got in Chris's way at all, but the flashing of his camera distracted everyone nicely. Soon perhaps they'd forget all about Chris, which would help them to relax and perhaps speak more openly.

Gregor raised his glass. 'Everyone got a drink? Then here's to us and to Lady Luck! Don't spend it all at once!'

Oliver moved closer. 'Say "champagne" everyone!"'

They all chorused, 'Champagne!' and laughed loudly. Yet there was a new constraint in the room.

Bea thought, They all know. Every single one of them knows; or suspects, more likely. Except, perhaps, the fond husband-to-be?

Gregor was Master of Ceremonies, of course. 'Now, my darlings, for posterity. Let's take it in turns to say what this moment means to you.'

Jamie stood, saying he wasn't going in front of the camera till he'd drunk a good deal more than he'd taken on board yet.

'Duncan! Duncan!' Hermia started the chant.

Duncan grabbed Mandy and took her to the settee. Mandy blushed and looked embarrassed. She was drinking tonic water, not champagne. She looked around at the group, trying to smile, aware she was the newcomer and perhaps feeling confused and somewhat out of her depth. Ignorant of the reason for the celebration?

Oliver said, 'Look at Duncan, please!'

Like the well-brought up little girl that she was, Mandy looked at Duncan, and as she did so, her expression eased. Bea thought, She loves Duncan. Good.

There was a sheen of sweat on Duncan's forehead. He took Mandy's hand in his. 'Mandy, you know I've been working up to a proposal for weeks.'

She glanced around at the others, her colour coming and going. 'Yes, but Duncan; in front of everyone?'

'You did say you didn't care about my being made redundant?'

She had a reassuring smile. 'You'll find something else. You always said you'd like to try starting up an Internet company. We can sell this flat, which would give us enough capital to move out of London, and I can commute to my job. We'll manage. Did you need to have all your friends around you before you got up enough courage to ask me to marry you?'

He'd forgotten the camera, and his friends. 'I wanted you to be sure of what you were doing. So yes, I am asking you to marry me.'

'The answer is 'yes', of course.' She leaned towards him, expecting a kiss, but he took both her hands in his, and raised them, holding her off. Meanwhile his friends began to thump on the floor and shout, 'Yes!' and, 'Go for it!'

Duncan looked around. 'Please; let me finish. Mandy, would you still marry me if I came into a great deal of money?'

She was puzzled, not sure whether to smile or not. 'That would be very nice, but it's not necessary.'

'The thing is, we played the lottery —'

She drew back a little, frowning. 'Oh, no! Not you! You know my brother—'

'It wasn't like that. I don't gamble. I never would. It was a joke, to cheer Harry up. We won rather a lot. Enough to give us a country house and enable us to start a family, if you like.'

Her colour rose. She withdrew her hands from his and stood up. 'You mean, all that about us having to be poor . . . You were testing me, to see what I'd say?' Angry tears stood out on her cheeks, and she rushed out of the circle of light.

'I'm an idiot.' He went after her. 'Forgive me. I do love you, but I couldn't see how to break the news to you without—'

He tried to put his arms around her. She resisted. The sound of a slap startled everyone. Heads jerked round to where Mandy stood, hand still raised in the air. Duncan looked shocked. Had she really clobbered him? Wow!

Gregor was equal to the occasion. 'Kiss her, you fool!'

Everyone else began to stamp on the floor. 'Kiss her! Kiss her! Kiss her!'

Duncan kissed her. She squirmed a bit and then gave in. But it wasn't till after she'd put her arms around his neck that everyone relaxed. Bea noticed that Chris had not moved, but was still filming the group around the settee. Following Gregor's orders?

'Ahh,' said Gregor.

'That brought tears to my eyes,' said Hermia.

'Excuse us for a moment,' said Duncan, pulling Mandy after him out of the room. The girl was half smiling and half crying, but not unwilling to go with him.

'Splendid!' said Gregor, holding out his empty glass. 'Will someone kindly refill . . . ? Ah, thank you, Claudine. Everyone, here's to us!'

Cheers all round. Big smiles. Gregor spread himself on the settee, arms stretched out, smiling up at the camera. 'So now it's my turn in the confessional. Well, folks! You probably guessed I was in big trouble with the tax man. I argued one way, he argued another, and when it came to court, the judgement went against me – with costs! But that's life, isn't it? I had budgeted for losing, but I must admit that I hadn't set aside enough to satisfy the vultures completely, and the prospect of spending some time in prison has been haunting my dreams. So here's to the smile on the face of the tiger, and solvency plus. And there's more.'

Here he took a gulp of champagne. 'Some of you may have doubted that I'd surmount all my troubles and come out on top, so I'm here to confirm that I haven't lost my Midas touch. Far from it. It's business as usual for yours truly. Moreover, one of my other business concerns has come up trumps, and very soon now I'll be looking round for a nifty little yacht to buy. This time next year we'll hold an anniversary party on it, somewhere in the Mediterranean.'

Catcalls, cheers and whistles. Flash!

Bea noticed that Duncan had come back into the room, his arm around Mandy – who wasn't resisting his attentions any more.

Gregor stood to take a bow. More catcalls and whistles. More laughter. Gregor led Claudine to the settee and settled her there. Claudine was flushed with champagne and triumph. She looked fantastic. Flash! went Oliver's little camera, and Claudine didn't even wince.

Claudine's glass was refilled, and she raised it to her friends. 'Yes, I'm deliriously happy, but I'm also thinking of those who aren't here tonight and should have been.' Tears began to slide out of her eyes. 'Six months ago, ten of us met here to celebrate a birthday, and then we lost two of our oldest friends in quick succession.'

Gregor raised his glass. 'To Julian and Shirley. Our reckless, wonderful, never-to-be-forgotten friends. Let's drink to them.'

Claudine used her forefinger to wipe tears from her cheeks. 'And then Tomi. I really liked Tomi. She had such style! And she brought so much common sense to our group. Common sense is so rare, don't you think?'

Claudine was misty-eyed and beginning to lose precision of speech.

Gregor nodded. 'Here's to Tomi. A tragedy.'

Claudine swept her arm around. 'As for Harry, if he killed her, let him drown in hell. And stupid Nick, falling down the stairs. What a waste! I've known them for ever, and yet I don't miss either of them that much. Isn't that awful?'

Gregor had the bottle ready to refill her glass. 'But for you, the future's bright.'

'Yes, it is. No men. Men aren't worth it. I don't care who hears me say that. Give me the money, and I'll run a school you'll all be proud to send your children to. I'm all right, Jack; and I'm glad Alan's gone.'

Flash! went Oliver's camera.

'Sure you're glad,' said Gregor, helping her to stand and stagger over to an armchair. He removed the empty glass from her hand and settled a cushion at her back. 'Now it's Hermia's turn.'

Hermia was sober enough. She seated herself, smiling, sipping at her glass, which was still nearly full. Duncan stopped kissing Mandy long enough to go round replenishing the glasses of the rest of his guests, and then returned to Mandy's side. Marigold – where was she? – hovered on the outskirts of the group, looking glamorous and clueless.

Hermia raised her glass to her friends – and not to the camera. 'I joined in our lottery bid because everyone else did, and not because winning anything would mean much to me. I've always had a cushion of money to guard me from reality. Now I'm asking myself what I'd have been like if I'd had to struggle to earn my own living.

'When one of my friends needed a large sum of money I took out a loan for him, putting up my family shares as collateral. I knew it was risky, because a voice at the back of my head told me he might not be able to repay and, sure enough, if it hadn't been for the lottery win he wouldn't have been able to do so, and I'd have had to find out what it's like to work for a living.

'Only, after Tomi died, and then Harry, I began to worry. Weren't their deaths a little too timely? Might one of us really be trying to improve the odds? If so, if we really had a murderer in our midst, then what should I do about it? Go to the police, obviously. But if I did that, I'd lose my share of the lottery money. And, if the police weren't interested in Tomi and Harry's deaths, then there was no need for me to worry, was there? So I sat on my conscience.

'Then came Nick's death. The rewards for keeping quiet multiplied, but so did the fear. I talked to each of you in turn and saw the same question and the same fear in everyone's eyes.

If we talked to the police, we'd lose the lot, and we all had rather a lot to lose. I agreed to keep silent, to wait till after the pay-out, and I have done so. But tomorrow I go to the police. I have no proof of my suspicions. I don't know whether they'll believe me or not, but that's what I have to do.'

NINETEEN

Monday evening

Claudine stretched herself out in her chair, eyes closed. 'We've been over and over this, Hermia. If there were the slightest smidgeon of evidence, I'd agree to take it to the police, but as things stand, I can't see the point of doing so. Nothing would come of it, the plods would be all over us, it would get into the papers, and we wouldn't be able to lead a normal life for months. There'll be no more deaths. So, I vote to leave it be.'

'Amen to that,' said Gregor. 'I can't say I'd be willing to have them buzzing round me.'

Duncan had his arm firmly around Mandy. 'I vote we leave things as they are, too. What do you say, Jamie?'

'Oh, leave it be,' said Jamie, lazily. 'We're all against you, Hermia. And if none of us back you up, what chance do you have of convincing the police to act?'

'Maybe none, but that's what I'm going to do. In the meantime, Jamie; have you a cheque for me?'

'Naturally. Of course.' He drained his glass, impeded by Claire, who had hooked herself on to his arm. 'Where's my cheque book?' He patted his pockets.

Claire pouted. 'You left it on the dressing table, my sweet.'

His eyes narrowed. 'Did I? Oh, I suppose I must have done. Hermia, I'll let you have a cheque tomorrow, right?'

Hermia had lost her smile. 'Jamie, I've known you since you were five years old. You've always brought your troubles to me, expecting me to rescue you, and I always have until now. I've known you "forget" your chequebook before, which is why I reminded you this afternoon that I wanted the money tonight.'

'I didn't mean to forget. Honest. I really thought I'd put it in my pocket.'

Hermia shook her head. 'Are you hoping I'll meet with a convenient accident, so you don't have to repay me?'

He flushed. 'No, Hermia. You can't believe that!' He risked a glance down at Claire, still hooked on to his arm. 'Did you take it out of my pocket, my love?'

She pouted. 'I thought it spoiled the line of your jacket. So sorry. I didn't realize it was important.'

Gregor tugged on his ear. 'Jamie, how about we borrow Duncan's laptop and you transfer the money to Hermia's account here and now? After all, this is the night when we finish with the old and start anew. And don't say you've forgotten your access codes, Jamie, because nobody will believe you.'

A titter of amusement.

Jamie laid on the charm. 'I know I'm a bit of an idiot, but don't you think that's a trifle unkind? Of course I want to repay Hermia. She saved my life with that loan.'

Hermia said, 'Jamie, of course I trust you. I'll help you by putting in my own bank details if you promise not to peep. As Gregor says, let's do it, and then we can all relax.'

Jamie gave in with a good grace. 'I try never to mix business and pleasure, but it will be a pleasure to clear my name. No one gets to call me a skinflint, right?' He unhooked himself from Claire and went to the bureau, where Duncan was booting up his laptop. Claire followed, frowning. Had she really removed his chequebook, or not? Mm. Probably. On balance. Yes.

Hermia waited for Jamie to access his account and then took over, shielding the details from Claire, who was standing very close behind. Too close? Yes. Close enough to see Hermia's password. Hermia gave Claire a look, and she moved away.

Claudine was almost horizontal in her chair, having kicked off her high heeled shoes. Her speech was beginning to slur. 'Good old Jamie. Running true to form as usual. The thing is, Jamie, that we all know you too well. I'm amazed that you've actually cut the umbilical cord to Hermia by getting engaged to Claire, but now you have, be warned; you're on your own now.' She waved her empty glass around. 'Is there any champagne left?'

Click, click went the keys of the laptop.

Duncan popped open another bottle. 'Who'd like a top-up?'

In a low voice, but clearly heard by everyone, Mandy asked, 'Are we nearly done yet? I'm starving.'

Jamie closed the laptop. 'Done. With interest.'

'I didn't ask for interest,' said Hermia.

'Nevertheless, I owe it to you; clean slate and all that. Phew! What a relief, eh? So where are we planning to eat?'

There was a general movement of personnel, a gathering up of handbags and girlfriends.

And that, thought Bea, was as far as the group were going to take it. Only Gregor had the killer instinct to take the matter any further, and he lacked some of the information that had drifted Bea's way over the past week or so.

Time for her to act. With an arrow prayer for God to guide her aright, she stood up and stepped forward into the circle of light around the settee.

Several people did a double take. 'Who's . . . ? Oh.'

'I didn't see her sitting in the corner. Why . . . ?'

'To refresh your memories, I'm Bea Abbot, investigating the untimely death of your friend Tomi. I have found a witness who says that, about noon on the day of Tomi's death, she was last seen getting into Claire's white mini opposite the library in Kensington. Claire, where did you take Tomi after that?'

'What?' Claire, sitting by herself on the settee, looked all around her, smiling, but also shocked. 'Who says? It's a lie.'

Chris didn't move or speak. Just as well, as strictly speaking he couldn't identify Claire as the driver of the mini, nor could he be sure that Tomi had actually got into the car.

Claudine struggled to sit upright. 'Come to think of it . . . Did I dream it, or did Tomi say she was going shopping that day? She wanted a new top for the party that evening, and she wanted to look around for another evening dress. I remember she said something . . . Now, what was it? Hermia; didn't you tell her about a boutique? Claire; was that where you took her?'

'Don't be silly. It wasn't me. I wasn't anywhere near Kensington that day. Someone is mistaken if they say that I was.'

Jamie looked puzzled. Claire patted the settee at her side, but he ignored her.

Bea went on. 'I'm sure the police will be able to find out

if Tomi was ever in Claire's car. Fingerprints and so on. I'll ask you again, Claire. Did you or did you not give Tomi a lift that day?'

Claire pulled a face. Shrugged. 'I suppose.'

'You'd phoned her earlier, when she was in the pub, to arrange when and where to pick her up?'

Another shrug. 'I may have done.'

'I've been reading Tomi's emails. She was being invited to all sorts of places and was worried that she hadn't the wardrobe to fit. She didn't earn enough to buy designer clothes. She told a friend that she'd heard of a boutique for once-worn dresses. Which one of you told her about it?'

Hermia was frowning. 'Well, I did, if it's the same one. It's in Cookham, not far out of town. I offered to take her, but I had something else on that weekend and couldn't make it.'

'So she got into the car with Claire and was never seen alive again. Did you offer to take her out to Cookham, Claire? Let me remind you that she was found in a country lane in that direction.'

A shrug. 'No, of course not. I knew of a little boutique behind Oxford Street and offered to drop her off there.'

'Oxford Street on a Saturday morning? That was brave of you. Only buses and taxis are allowed.'

'I went round the back streets, but I couldn't park there, of course, so I let her out at the corner of Wigmore Street and went on home. I don't know what she did after that.'

'What was the name of the boutique?'

Another shrug. 'I'm not sure. Plum or Purple or something? I've only used it once or twice.'

'You could take us there, couldn't you?'

'I suppose so.'

'Good. The police will be interested to hear that, and no doubt they will want to interview the staff to see if they remember Tomi. She was a very striking looking girl, wasn't she? They'll be bound to remember her.'

Claire looked at her watch. 'As someone said a while ago, where are we eating tonight?'

'One moment. Claire; when did you meet Jamie?'

'Oh, I don't remember. Months and months ago.' Wide eyed, she blew a kiss to her fiancé. 'About a year ago, isn't it, sweetheart?'

'Not quite.' He'd lost his smile and didn't return the kiss.

Duncan frowned. 'Wait a minute. It was Nick who brought you along to one of our parties, can't remember which one. In the autumn? Can anyone else remember?'

Hermia picked that one up. 'My birthday and Tomi's were very close. We had a joint celebration to which Nick brought Claire. It was in the last week of September. No, the first week in October.'

Bea said, 'That would be after you'd all heard about your lottery win. You had a good party?'

'Yes, but we were all a bit subdued. Shirley had got herself killed earlier that week. We all drank too much. The shock, you know. Nick passed out in the loo. Who took Claire home? Was it you, Duncan?'

Duncan shook his head. 'No. Jamie and I put Nick in a taxi and gave the driver his address. Jamie wasn't feeling too good, but he offered to take Claire on home in another taxi.'

'Phoo! Jamie was almost as drunk as Nick, crying into his whisky,' said Claudine from the depths of her chair. 'First Julian, then Shirley. He couldn't make out whether he was more glad to have a bigger share of the cash, or more sorry to lose old friends.'

'So Claire went home with Jamie,' said Bea, 'and between his grief and the drink, he told her about the lottery money.'

'No, no,' said Jamie. He was smiling, but uneasy, gulping champagne. 'Of course not. I didn't, did I, Claire?'

Hermia gave him an old-fashioned look. 'You never could keep a still tongue in your head when you've had too much to drink.'

Claire's colour had risen. 'He never said anything.'

Gregor said, 'Wait a minute. Claire; Jamie told me afterwards that you stayed the night with him.'

Claire gave a light laugh. 'What if I did? Someone had to look after him, and anyway, he was the perfect gentleman.'

'Most ungallant of me. Sorry.' Jamie grimaced. 'Too drunk to remember.'

'I believe,' said Bea, 'that Claire found out, either on that night or soon after, that Jamie was coming into money, and that through the deaths of two of his friends the amount had been greatly increased. She wanted some of that money. She also fancied a title. How could she get it? The easiest way was to get Jamie to fall in love with her. He looked easy, but Jamie was no pushover. He'd had girls throw themselves at him for years, without causing a ripple in his mind. For years he'd had a platonic relationship with Hermia, who gave him her company when required. He knew that some day soon he ought to think about marriage and siring an heir, but thus far he hadn't done anything about it. So there was little Claire, billing and cooing at him. Sweetly pretty, but no money and no background. A splendid companion for the odd tumble in bed, but was that enough? Well, there was no need for him to commit himself yet, was there?

'And then there was Tomi. Tomi was beautiful, inside and out. The group had accepted her into their midst. She also owned a share in the lottery money. Harry had given Tomi his old laptop and, before the batteries died, she was in the habit of emailing her parents and friends with news of what she'd been doing. She told them about Harry, who had introduced her to some new friends, and she told them about being taken to a big society event, at which I believe she acquitted herself well. Isn't that so, Hermia?'

'Why, yes; Jamie brought her to a ball at the Dorchester. She was lovely. Everyone liked her. I thought Jamie could do a lot worse than marry her. She was still going out occasionally with Harry, but she wasn't serious about him, or anyone. I urged Jamie to win her, if he could.'

Bea focused on Jamie. 'Were you still seeing Claire while you went out with Tomi?'

He fingered his chin. 'There was no harm in it, was there? Claire and I had an understanding.'

'You mean, sex. You weren't going to take her to these big society functions though, were you? You'd taken Tomi once, she'd fitted right in, so you intended to take her again. You told Claire so, didn't you?'

'Well, in a roundabout way, I suppose; yes. But—'

'What did you think when Tomi disappeared?'

He grimaced. 'I was annoyed. I'd already bought the tickets for the dance when Harry told us she'd gone off to France with a new man. What was I supposed to think? If she could be that fickle, why should I bother my head about her?'

'So you took Claire to the dance instead?'

'Why not?'

'When it came out that Tomi had died, what did you think?'

'I was sorry.' He moved his shoulders restlessly. 'She was a bit of all right.'

'Your finances improved with her death, and of course you had Claire to fall back on.'

He flushed. 'You're making me out to be one self-centred hombre.'

'You were looking out for number one.'

'I was shocked by Tomi's death. And then to find out that Harry had done her in, well, it took a bit of getting used to. As for Nick –' he shook his head – 'he played a good game of golf, and I'll miss him something chronic. So many deaths! It was hard to carry on, day by day. I tell you, I was on the verge of taking a long holiday away from England, away from it all . . . except, of course, that the finances wouldn't allow it. Replacing the roof of the old place nearly ruined me, and if it hadn't been for Hermia, I'd have been deep in the doodahs.'

'And there was Claire, ready to sympathize and to give you what you needed.'

'Just so.' He took another gulp of champagne and looked at his watch. 'Shouldn't we be going?'

'*Everything* that you needed? How soon did you notice that being with her meant you got richer, and richer, and richer?'

'That's . . . offensive.' He laughed, as if at a joke, and yet there was something akin to panic in his eyes. He knew what Bea was getting at. 'Oh, come on. You don't really mean—'

'How soon did you promise her marriage?'

'I . . . You are making out that I—?'

'At some point you worked it out, didn't you? I expect you found it gratifying that someone would want to kill in order to improve your finances.'

'No, no. Ridiculous. Oh, come on! This isn't funny!' Faked laughter. He glanced around at the others, looking for support.

'You protest too much. Your friends all say you have a fatalistic, lazy streak in you. You probably didn't want to examine your suspicions too closely, but on one level you knew perfectly well what was happening. So long as you didn't challenge Claire about what she was doing, you could rationalize the situation. You regretted Tomi's death, but you didn't take it to heart, any more than you grieved for Harry. You're only sorry

Nick died because he used to play golf with you. It probably amused you to think that such a large fortune was going to come your way without your having to lift a finger to help. So, you let it all happen. And since you wanted to marry and have children some day, why not reward Claire for all her efforts on your behalf? Why not promote her from arm candy to wife?'

A frown. A shake of the head. 'That's more than offensive. That's libellous.'

'Your only worry then was, how to stop her killing you after you were married. How are you going to manage that, by the way?'

'I don't believe this! Claire; tell her . . . Hermia; this is ridiculous!'

Hermia took a gulp of champagne. 'He'll get his solicitor to draft out a new will saying that if he died in unexplained circumstances, everything – and I mean everything, the houses, the estate, everything – would go to a distant cousin who bears his name. He'd leave Claire with a pittance.'

Bea said, 'Is that what you're planning, Jamie?'

He shrugged. 'When a man in my position marries, he has to think of the future of the estate, so he usually makes that sort of will, yes. Claire, tell them they've got it all wrong.'

Hermia put the boot in. 'But just in case, Jamie; don't you think you'd better reconsider your engagement, at least for the time being?'

Jamie was in the habit of looking to Hermia for advice. Could he see that she was offering him a way out of his entanglement, a way that would leave him in sole possession of his new wealth?

'I suppose . . . It sounds callous, but it might be best, yes. Claire, don't look like that. I mean, I know it's stupid, but perhaps we'd better be cautious, just till this is sorted out.'

Claire shrank back, her mouth distorting. 'You bastard!'

'Now, come on, Claire. Fair's fair. If you really did go off with Tomi that day . . . I mean, if you can prove that you haven't done anything, then of course . . . You know I'm desperately fond of you, but perhaps it would be best to do what Hermia says.' He let himself down on to the settee, staring at the carpet. Taking another gulp of his drink.

Bea wondered how much of this was acting. Jamie was too

self-absorbed to feel great distress when his friends had died. He'd been having fun; he'd heard nothing, seen nothing and said nothing. He'd got his money and couldn't be charged with anything but stupidity. Or could he?

Claire began to weep. 'You said you loved me!'

He shook his head. 'I'll get over it, I expect. Make a clean break. Keep the ring. I don't want it back. If you've left anything at my place, I'll see it's sent on to you.'

'But only this afternoon . . .!'

He looked uncomfortable. 'Well, I didn't know then what I know now. I believed in you, Claire. I'm in shock.'

Tears of rage stood out on Claire's cheeks. 'If you throw me off, I'll . . . I'll tell them you forced me to kill them, that it was all your idea, not mine! I'll tell them how brutal you've been to me!' She pinched her arms and slapped her face, raising livid pink marks on her pale skin. 'They'll believe me. If I lose, then so will you!'

He gaped at her, out of his depth. He looked around at his friends, seeking support. 'I didn't do anything, I swear it.' Silence. 'Hermia, you believe me, don't you? Gregor?'

Claire laughed, a hard sound. 'You see? They know you always come out smelling of lilies. They don't believe in your protestations of innocence.'

'Yes, but I—'

She flushed a pretty pink in triumph. 'It was he who killed Tomi, of course. I gave the girl a lift to his house and left her there. I haven't the slightest idea what he did with her after that, and when I asked him later what had happened to her, he hit me. After that he went after Harry and then Nick, and . . .' Here she managed a sob. 'He told me that if I ever said anything to anyone, he'd kill me, too.'

'You . . .!' Jamie was appalled. 'You lie!'

'You taught me well.' She shouldered her large handbag. 'So, shall we go home and forget what's been said here tonight? I'm willing to let bygones be bygones, if you are. Nobody is going to go to the police, are they? For dear Jamie's sake. He'll marry me as planned, and we'll live together happily ever after. Agreed?' The injuries she'd inflicted on herself were setting into bruises. She was the very picture of innocence and distress.

No one moved.

Claire laughed. 'So. Come along my darling. Beddy byes for little boys. And Mumsy-wumsy Claire will give him an extra special cuddle tonight, won't she?'

She held out her hand to Jamie, and with horror Bea saw that he was in two minds about accepting it. If he went home with her, he was damned. And he was damned if he didn't.

Time to act. *Lord, You know everything, including what makes for high fashion and what ruins the look of a good outfit. This is all about fashion, isn't it? Tomi wrote in her emails that she wasn't sure her old red dress would do for another society 'do', but a friend had suggested where she might buy a good dress from a specialist boutique. Hermia was busy that last day. But Claire . . . Oh yes, Claire could have offered to take Tomi out to Cookham, and on that cold day she'd have offered Tomi a drink from a flask, and when she was dead, she tipped her out of the car into some bushes at the side of the road. So, help me now to sort this out.*

As Claire leaned towards Jamie, so Bea reached out to pluck the handbag from off Claire's shoulder. Huge designer bags were all the fashion for daytime, but at night evening bags were supposed to be tiny. Like the other women, Claire was wearing a short evening dress, but they were all carrying small purses, which had made Claire's large bag look incongruous.

'What?' Claire made a grab for the bag, but she was too late.

Upending it, Bea let a scatter of items fall on the settee.

Hermia started forward. 'Why, isn't that Tomi's pink mobile phone! See? I gave her a sparkly star tag to put on her phone for her birthday, and she gave me one. Whose are those others?'

Duncan leaned over. 'Hello! That looks rather like my old phone. I had one just like it, anyway. Lost it months ago.'

'That diary,' said Claudine. 'Didn't Tomi have one with a poppy on the cover? I remember comparing mine with hers, which is similar.'

'Don't touch! There may be fingerprints!' Hermia turned on Claire. 'Why are you carrying five mobile phones around with you? And whose are they? One will be yours, and another's will be Duncan's – which explains why I didn't get an answer when I phoned him at his old number. Did you use the phone Duncan lost when you arranged to pick up Tomi on the last day or her life, or did you use your own? Either way, there'll be a record of your phone call on one of these phones.'

'What nonsense!'

'Then there's Tomi's, the one with the sparkly tag. Was that the one you used to tell people she'd gone off of her own accord, and then to lure Chris out to where you'd left her body?'

'How dare you!'

'The third and fourth, were they Harry's and Nick's? You used Harry's to alert the police as to where to find Tomi, didn't you? You took the phones after you killed their owners, because if the police got hold of them, they could trace the calls you'd made earlier, arranging to meet your victims. You took Tomi's diary too, in case she'd made a note that she was due to meet you that day.'

A deep flush. A lie was being thought up. 'One of the phones is mine, yes. Jamie gave me the others to carry for him.'

Jamie drew back. 'What? Claire, why on earth should I—?'

A toss of her head. 'Because putting them in your pockets would spoil the line of your jacket.'

Claudine swivelled round in her chair. In a conversational tone she said, 'Tomi was last seen getting into your car, the autopsy proves she was not sexually assaulted and the motive was not robbery. But she did stand in your way too, Claire. You have her mobile and her diary. Proof at last!'

'I suppose she dropped them when she got out of my car. I found them later.'

'Wait a minute,' said Hermia. 'If Claire is right, then Jamie's fingerprints should be on that mobile. Is that right, Claire?'

'He . . . he stood over me till I texted the messages for him.'

'Never!' said Jamie, spilling his drink in horror.

'That would take a stretch of the imagination,' said Hermia. 'However, moving on to Harry's death. Jamie was out of town that afternoon, and I can prove it because we were working on a charity event together. Where were you, Claire? Harry had a visitor that day, who took great care to wipe all finger-prints off the place before they left. Mrs Abbot is right; the police can trace calls made from mobiles nowadays. Jamie couldn't have stolen Harry's phone that day, but you could. Which one of these is Harry's, Claire?'

Claire gaped, and then dived for the phones. One of them was going to betray her. Only she knew which.

Before she could lay her hands on them there was a fast blur of movement and Claire was knocked to the floor, arms flailing, and came to rest with a pair of long, elegant legs scissoring her neck.

Marigold. Whom everyone had forgotten.

Gregor lifted his glass. 'She's a black belt in some weird form of judo. I thought it might come in handy.'

TWENTY

Monday evening

C laire screamed. 'Help! Jamie, tell her to let me go!'
  'Let her up,' said Bea, 'but don't let her anywhere near the contents of her bag.'

Marigold leapt to her feet, caught Claire by her waist, dumped her on the low table in front of the settee, and stood over her.

Jamie wiped the back of his hand across his mouth. Was he going to be sick? 'I can't believe this is happening.'

Bea said, 'Now for the clincher. I was concerned when I heard Claire had taken on the post of nanny to my grandson, so I asked two friends to go over there early this evening, to see if everything was all right. I was afraid that Claire might have heard I was investigating Tomi's death and want to get back at me through my grandson, perhaps by tampering with his feeds.

'I was right to fear the worst. I rang my friends just before I left to come here and they said they'd tasted the baby formula which Claire had prepared and thought it was suspect, so they've replaced it with some they'd bought on the way over. In the garbage they found an empty bottle which had once contained sleeping pills. The label on the bottle had been made out to a woman whose name they didn't know, but my son recognized it as being the name of Claire's last employer. One of my friends – my assistant Maggie – is sleeping there overnight to make sure the baby's all right. My other friend – who happens to be the baby's grandfather – is keeping the bottle and the formula Claire made up, to be tested for fingerprints.'

Claire laughed. 'You won't find any fingerprints.'

'How do you know that?' asked Bea. 'Unless, of course, you were responsible for seeing that there weren't any.'

Silence.

The red tide engulfed Claire. She opened her mouth wide

and screamed. And went on screaming till Marigold poked her in the back. She stopped, breathing hard. Her eyes were wild, but she controlled herself.

Jamie said, 'You mean she tried to kill a baby, too? She's a monster!'

Bea said, 'Some of you may know a Mr Cambridge, who is well acquainted with police procedures and who already knows the background to this case. At his suggestion, a hidden microphone has picked up everything that's been said here tonight and it's been recorded on tape in the next room . . . which is where he's been sitting all this time. May I ask him to join us?'

Gregor pulled a face. 'He'll bring in the police, of course. But yes, I don't see any alternative.'

Hermia nodded.

Duncan sighed. 'I'm sorry about all this, Mandy. Would you like to leave before the police come?'

Mandy proved her worth. 'Certainly not. I'm sticking with you. If we're not going to go out for food, shall I see if I can rustle up some coffee and sandwiches?'

Claudine stood, unsteadily. She held an empty glass in one hand and one of her high heeled shoes in the other. 'Anticlimax. Chris, do we need the camera and sound recording any longer?'

Chris lifted his hands from the camera, and Oliver came forward to disconnect the overhead microphone.

Claire tried to stand, but Marigold – who must be made of iron – put her hands on Claire's shoulders and held her down.

Claudine lost her balance and stumbled, raking down Claire's cheek with the spiky heel of her shoe.

Claire screamed. Blood seeped from the cut. Everyone froze.

Claudine said, 'Oops! So sorry! What a horrible accident!'

'Yes,' said Hermia, in a strangled voice. 'An accident.'

Jamie collapsed into a chair and put his head in his hands.

Claire screamed, both hands to her face. 'Help me!'

Bea felt numb. No one could have anticipated that Claudine would administer her own concept of justice. Claire might easily have lost an eye, though she hadn't. She was going to need stitches, though. Perhaps a police surgeon would see to that? Possibly a rather cack-handed police surgeon who might not do a terribly good job of patching Claire up? Claire's pretty face might well be marred for good, which served her right. Bea was ashamed of herself for thinking that, but not deeply ashamed, though she supposed she ought to be.

Hermia dithered, and then clicked her tongue against her cheek. 'Mandy, do you think we could find a plaster for Claire's cheek? We don't want blood on the carpet, do we?'

'Claire,' said Gregor. 'Compared to the friends we've all lost, don't you think you've got off lightly?'

Claire was beside herself. Foul language ripped from her pretty little mouth. 'I'll sue you all, see if I don't.'

A new voice broke in. 'I saw it all. An accident, surely.' The door to the next room stood open, and there stood CJ. How long had he been there? He said, 'Good evening. I think I know everyone here . . . except, perhaps, Miss Mandy?'

Bea sank back into the shadows. She guessed that from now on Hermia would do the explaining, Mandy would provide sustenance, Jamie would follow someone else's lead, and the others would keep their mouths firmly shut.

'What's going to happen to me?' asked Claire, once more the pathetic little child.

Nobody replied.

Tuesday morning

Bea and Oliver got home in time for breakfast. She was wiped out with tiredness, too weary to eat. She drank two cups of tea and stumbled up to bed, leaving Oliver – who was hideously bright and cheerful even after a night without sleep – to deal with floods, hurricanes, tsunamis, epidemics, and the morning's post.

Thank You, Lord. Praise be. I'm so tired I can hardly think, but I do thank You. I'm not sure You think we all acted as You would have done. I'm not sure how guilty Jamie really was. But You know, and I trust You to be judge and jury in this case.

Thank You for keeping Pippin alive and well. As for Claudine; I know I ought to be horrified, but I'm not sorry she did that to Claire. Yes, I know it was awful, but . . . Well, I'll try to be sorry about it. Tomorrow.

I'm glad Duncan and his girl got together. And Gregor, what a joker. The joker in the pack. The trump card.

Claire's face when Marigold got her in that amazing head
lock . . .
Thank You for Piers, and Maggie. Oliver and Chris. For justice.
Will Hermia and Chris ever . . . who knows? Perhaps.
And my little Pippin . . .

Bea slept and dreamed she was nursing Pippin. She picked
him up out of his cot and cradled him against herself. She
could feel his little heart beating against her breast.
Praise the Lord.
She smiled in her sleep. Tomorrow she'd make it up with
Max and Nicole. She'd apologize profusely and swear never
to criticize their domestic arrangements again. She'd find
them another day nanny; someone older and not as pretty as
Claire. Pippin would put on weight and become a happy little
bunny . . . and all would be well.

A week later

Bea returned from her twice weekly visit to see her grandson
to find a bouquet of flowers on her desk. This was no cut-
price bunch plucked from a pail in a convenience store. This
was something a florist had lovingly put together from exotic
flowers, encased in protective sheets of plastic and supplied
with water so that it could stand on its own without the
necessity of having to put it in a vase. It would have been
expensively paid for by credit card.
Ah. Chris?
'May we come in?'
Yes, Chris. And behind him was Hermia. Both were smiling.
Chris seemed to have filled out since she last saw him. He'd
had his hair cut shorter; most becoming. Hermia had let hers
grow longer. Were they emphasizing his masculinity and her
femininity? Hermia looked nervous, or perhaps . . . shy? Could
Hermia ever be shy?
'Ta-ra,' said Chris. He held out an envelope made from top
quality paper. 'With thanks, from Hermia and Gregor, Duncan
and Claudine. Jamie's contribution is still to come.'
'What?' Bea laughed, because he was laughing. She opened
the envelope and four cheques fell out, each one for a very
significant amount. 'But—'

'I know, I know,' said Hermia. 'There was no contract, and you didn't ask for any money, but without you we'd never have been able to solve the mystery. We'd have gone on wondering and worrying and feeling guilty about it. The police couldn't or wouldn't act until you found the evidence to send Claire to jail, and Jamie would probably have married the girl. He says he's lost his chequebook, but I'll screw the money for you out of him somehow. We agreed that Chris should deliver the money, since he started this whole thing off.'

Chris was grinning. 'We heard you were planning a loft conversion for Oliver and Maggie, and thought it might come in useful.'

'Yes, but this is too much!'

Chris's smile disappeared. 'What price do you put on avenging Tomi? Not to mention the others who have died? How many other people would Claire have gone on to kill, if you hadn't stopped her?'

Bea looked out of the window as a scatter of raindrops hit the glass. The sycamore tree was greening over at the bottom of the garden, and the bright polyanthus and wallflowers in the big pots were a delight to the eye. No such delights where Claire had gone. There was some talk of her being unfit to plead. She'd be locked away for years, whatever happened.

Hermia produced another envelope. 'Duncan and Mandy asked me to bring you an invitation to their wedding next month. He's selling his flat, and they're moving out into the country. He'll invest his money wisely and hopes to keep it a secret from his gambling brother-in-law to be.'

'And here's another invitation,' said Chris, flourishing it, 'for my long-deferred birthday celebration. CJ is arranging for six of us – that's you and him, Hermia and me, Oliver and Maggie – to have lunch in Paris via Eurostar next Friday. Do say you'll come.'

'What a lovely idea. I'd be delighted.'

'There's more good news,' said Hermia, incandescent with pride in Chris. 'My father has had long talks with Chris and seen what he's done so far. He thinks Chris has great potential—'

'Though I've a lot to learn, I know. Anyway, he's on the board of a number of charities, and he wants me to make some short films for publicity purposes about the work they're doing.

Such films are usually dead boring, and it will up to me to make them interesting. Meanwhile, Gregor has found me a replacement for Tomi. She's not at all like Tomi in some ways, but the camera loves her. And you won't believe this, but Hermia's changing jobs—'

'I want to get more hands-on experience, working with the homeless—'

'And Claudine says, "Hello," and to tell you that she's back with Alan, who's fully recovered his health. She wants you to know she's kept her mouth shut. She says you'll understand.'

Bea nodded. For all Claudine's protestations that she was better off without Alan, she'd been distraught when she'd thought he might die. 'And Jamie?'

Hermia sighed. 'The police are still considering whether or not to charge him as an accessory, but with the money he's got he can afford a good solicitor, and we've all sworn he's a stupid fool, but no murderer.'

Chris grinned. 'He tried to appeal to Hermia to go back to him, but she said, "Oh, grow up, Jamie!" so that's that. I expect he'll soon find someone else to mother him, and that's all right so long as it's not my girl.'

'Will Claire press charges against Claudine?'

A shrug. 'We're all agreed it was an accident.'

'So all ends well and Tomi is avenged?'

'It's never over "till the fat lady sings". There'll be a trial, and we'll have to give evidence unless Claire is found unfit to plead. But yes, in a way it's over.'

Once they'd gone, Bea sat down to consider the four cheques laid out before her. She had an impulse to tear them up, but desisted. If Jamie had sent her a cheque, she probably would have torn it up, but the others' hands were clean. Weren't they?

True, they hadn't known precisely what had been going on, but Bea thought they'd probably all had their suspicions – some more so and some less. Could they be expunging their guilt by giving away some of their money?

What do You think, Lord?

Judge not, lest ye be judged.

Well, that could work either way, I suppose.

She wondered about buying herself some boots like Hermia's. But no; she'd have to go to Milan to buy anything as good-looking.

Well, she could, couldn't she? She hadn't had a holiday for ever, so why not fly off to Milan, spend some money, and return with a new wardrobe?

Hm. She'd think about it. She put the cheques in her drawer, and turned to answer the ringing of the telephone. Business as usual. *Praise the Lord*.